HIGH TEA AND MISDEMEANORS

Titles by Laura Childs

Tea Shop Mysteries

DEATH BY DARJEELING
GUNPOWDER GREEN
SHADES OF EARL GREY
THE ENGLISH BREAKFAST MURDER
THE JASMINE MOON MURDER
CHAMOMILE MOURNING
BLOOD ORANGE BREWING
DRAGONWELL DEAD
THE SILVER NEEDLE MURDER
OOLONG DEAD
THE TEABERRY STRANGLER
SCONES & BONES
AGONY OF THE LEAVES
SWEET TEA REVENGE
STEEPED IN EVIL
MING TEA MURDER
DEVONSHIRE SCREAM
PEKOE MOST POISON
PLUM TEA CRAZY
BROKEN BONE CHINA
LAVENDER BLUE MURDER
HAUNTED HIBISCUS
TWISTED TEA CHRISTMAS
A DARK AND STORMY TEA
LEMON CURD KILLER
HONEY DROP DEAD
MURDER IN THE TEA LEAVES
PEACH TEA SMASH
HIGH TEA AND MISDEMEANORS

New Orleans Scrapbooking Mysteries

KEEPSAKE CRIMES
PHOTO FINISHED
BOUND FOR MURDER
MOTIF FOR MURDER
FRILL KILL
DEATH SWATCH
TRAGIC MAGIC
FIBER & BRIMSTONE
SKELETON LETTERS
POSTCARDS FROM THE DEAD
GILT TRIP
GOSSAMER GHOST
PARCHMENT AND OLD LACE
CREPE FACTOR
GLITTER BOMB
MUMBO GUMBO MURDER

Cackleberry Club Mysteries

EGGS IN PURGATORY
EGGS BENEDICT ARNOLD
BEDEVILED EGGS
STAKE & EGGS
EGGS IN A CASKET
SCORCHED EGGS
EGG DROP DEAD
EGGS ON ICE
EGG SHOOTERS

Anthologies

DEATH BY DESIGN
TEA FOR THREE

Afton Tangler Thrillers writing as Gerry Schmitt

LITTLE GIRL GONE
SHADOW GIRL

High Tea and Misdemeanors

Tea Shop Mystery #29

Laura Childs

BERKLEY PRIME CRIME
New York

BERKLEY PRIME CRIME
Published by Berkley
An imprint of Penguin Random House LLC
1745 Broadway, New York, NY 10019
penguinrandomhouse.com

Library of Congress Cataloging-in-Publication Data

Names: Childs, Laura, author.
Title: High tea and misdemeanors / Laura Childs.
Description: New York: Berkley Prime Crime, 2025. |
Series: Tea Shop Mystery #29
Identifiers: LCCN 2024036750 (print) | LCCN 2024036751 (ebook) |
ISBN 9780593815441 (hardcover) | ISBN 9780593815458 (ebook)
Subjects: LCGFT: Detective and mystery fiction. | Novels.
Classification: LCC PS3603.H56 H54 2025 (print) | LCC PS3603.H56 (ebook) |
DDC 813/.6—dc23/eng/20240823
LC record available at https://lccn.loc.gov/2024036750
LC ebook record available at https://lccn.loc.gov/2024036751

Printed in the United States of America
1st Printing

The authorized representative in the EU for product safety and compliance is
Penguin Random House Ireland, Morrison Chambers, 32 Nassau Street,
Dublin D02 YH68, Ireland, https://eu-contact.penguin.ie.

High Tea and Misdemeanors

1

The killer in the camo shirt, black tactical pants, and blade sunglasses crept ever so carefully between rows of orange chrysanthemums and Chinese silver grass. All around, late summer flowers and native grasses blazed crimson and gold while fuzzy yellow bees bumbled from blossom to stem. The killer didn't pay much attention to this bucolic autumnal display but was strictly focused on the mission at hand. Slowly, pressing forward, the killer crawled on hands and knees, eyes finally locked on the back wall of the greenhouse that was now a tantalizing fifteen feet away. Then, head lifted like a wolf sniffing the wind, the killer scuttled the remaining distance through late-blooming dahlias, hunched over and moving fast. Collapsing in the loamy soil, shoulders and back pressed hard against the greenhouse, the killer enjoyed a moment of blessed relaxation. *Almost there.*

Breathing back to normal now, the killer peered carefully around the side of the greenhouse. There were six cars and a Jeep, all unoccupied and parked a good fifty yards away, clustered near a series of small white cottages. Looking right, the killer saw the wedding arch, resplendent with curling ivy and woven with white pampas grass, sunflowers, and red bittersweet. Four dozen white folding chairs were set up neatly in front of it. No invited guests had arrived yet, probably wouldn't for an hour or so. So all was good.

Now for the tricky part. Standing upright, the killer dodged around the greenhouse and sprinted the length of it, pant legs brushing tall stalks of foxtail grass as club moss squished underfoot. Spinning around the front of the building, the killer grabbed the door, yanked it open, and darted inside. Just for a second, the killer had caught a glimpse of one person, an older man, silver-haired and wearing a tweed jacket. But, luckily, the man hadn't glanced this way.

Standing inside the greenhouse, heart thump-thumping, the killer felt a swell of anticipation. Hundreds of lush green plants and ferns along with six dozen cymbidium orchids had been draped from the ceiling like some fantastical verdant hanging garden. Below the flora and fauna, a long dining table was set with white linen, crystal goblets, fancy china, and silver flatware. Everything perfect for the wedding reception.

The killer's mouth pulled into a sneer. Like *that* was going to happen.

Five seconds later, this most dangerous uninvited guest climbed onto a chair swagged in white tulle and hopped aboard the long table, footprints making muddy imprints on the Belgian linen. Grabbing a wrench from a hip pocket, the killer reached up and carefully loosened four bolts in the mechanism that controlled the greenhouse's overhead windows. Then, tromping down the middle of the table, kicking a teacup out of the way and feeling a perverse pleasure in doing so, the killer reached the second mechanism. Twist, twist, and then that was done, too. What was the old saying? Righty tighty, lefty loosey? Well, the hinges were loose all right. Loose as a goose that was about to get its neck wrung. Now to set the mechanism on a hair trigger . . .

And there it was. All the anger and planning and revenge fantasies had been distilled down to this. To the bride and groom rushing through the doorway, flushed with excitement on their wedding day, only to find . . . well, their world would come crashing down on them soon enough.

In the gingerbread cottage that served as the event center kitchen for Foxtail Flower Farm, it was an entirely different story. Tea maven Theodosia Browning, who'd been tapped to cater high tea at Bettina and Jamie's wedding reception, was busy stacking rainbow-hued French macarons on a silver four-tiered tray. Drayton Conneley, her tea sommelier at the Indigo Tea Shop, was double-checking his stash of Harney & Sons Wedding Tea as well as his proprietary Happily Ever After Tea, a blend of jasmine, lemongrass, and rose petals.

And then there was Delaine Dish, the bride's high-strung aunt, wearing a pink Chanel suit and four-inch stilettos, running around like a chicken with its head chopped off.

"It's Bettina's wedding," Theodosia said with a wry smile. "But you're the one with pre-wedding jitters."

"Because everything has to be *perfect*!" Delaine cried.

"Henry James once said, 'Excellence does not require perfection,'" Drayton said in measured tones. Delaine's hysteria and theatrics were starting to annoy him.

"Well, Henry James isn't invited to this wedding, so I'm going to keep working my eyeballs off," Delaine said. She frowned, looked around, and muttered, "Where did I put the bouquets and boutonnieres?"

"The cooler in your car?" Theodosia said.

"Right," Delaine said as she rushed out the door.

"She's driving me berserk," Drayton said once Delaine had gone.

"Have faith, it will all be over soon," Theodosia told him. She was in a playful mood this morning because she was looking forward to the fantasy and romance of this autumn outdoor wedding. She and Drayton had driven out early with baskets of scones, freshly made tea sandwiches, and sliced cheeses. The crab claw and shrimp platters would be arriving shortly—along with a minister, a bartender, and four waitpersons.

Wiping her hands on her apron, Theodosia touched a hand to one of her sapphire blue earrings, which matched her eyes to perfection. As luck (and genetics) would have it, Theodosia had been born with vivid blue eyes, masses of auburn hair, a fair English complexion, and a wit and sense of humor that were undoubtedly inherited from Irish ancestors on her mother's side. She was clever, accomplished, and, as owner of the Indigo Tea Shop on Charleston's famed Church Street, an entrepreneur in her own right.

Drayton was sixty-something, cultured, droll in his manner of speech, and always impeccably dressed. He'd lived in China, worked at the tea auctions in Amsterdam, and once taught courses at the Culinary Institute of Charleston. Now he was a professional tea sommelier and a proper fixture at the Indigo Tea Shop.

"Do you think . . . ," Drayton began, then was interrupted by a clatter at the front door. Delaine, her heel caught in the doormat, struggled as she balanced an armload of flowers.

"I've got to keep these cool for another forty minutes," Delaine announced as she finally pulled herself free and lurched in.

"Lots of room in the cooler," Drayton said. He reached out and opened the door for her.

"Thank you, thank you," said an agitated Delaine. She stuffed the flowers into the cooler, stepped back, and touched a shaking hand to her heart.

"Take a breath and try to relax," Theodosia urged. "Everything's practically done, and your guests should be arriving soon. Don't burn yourself out when you've got a beautiful day ahead of you."

"I don't want any screwups," Delaine said. "Which is one of the reasons I've strictly forbidden *anyone* from entering that greenhouse. After all our hard work, I want the flowers and decor to be a fabulous surprise for Bettina and Jamie."

As Theodosia fixed a bow on her basket of scones, she happened to glance out the window. "Then somebody better remind Celeste there's no peeking allowed, because I see her tiptoeing toward the greenhouse."

"Celeste? Bettina's maid of honor?" Delaine screeched. "That little snoop. I was afraid something like this would . . ." Her words trailed off in an angry mumble as she burst out the door again. She saw Jamie Wilkes, the groom, lounging in front of a live oak, smoking Lord knows what with his best man, Reggie. "Jamie!" Delaine shouted. "Don't let Celeste go snooping in that greenhouse!" She pointed and gestured frantically as a small blond figure in a gauzy cream-colored dress headed straight for the door.

Jamie, his lanky figure turned out in a black Zegna suit, lifted a hand to Delaine and jogged over to try and intercept the ever-curious Celeste.

Delaine, who was still watching the goings-on like a hawk, said, "He's not going to catch that little ninny."

"What can it hurt if she looks inside?" Drayton offered. "It's not that big a deal since . . ."

His words were interrupted by a strange metallic ratcheting sound that clattered and clashed, then rose in pitch as if steel wheels were grinding hard against rusty rails. Seconds later there was a cataclysmic crash and the thunder of falling glass.

"No," Delaine said, frozen in place like a statue, a look of disbelief on her face.

Drayton's head shot up. "What just happened?"

"Don't know," Theodosia said. "It sounded like metal and glass and . . . oh dear Lord . . . did something happen to the greenhouse?"

Theodosia pushed her way past a stunned Delaine, leaped down two steps, and flew across the grassy yard to the greenhouse. Or what was left of it. Because it looked as if the entire front wall had collapsed and an enormous slice of the glass roof had imploded.

"No, no, no!" Theodosia shouted as, without hesitation, she waded into an enormous pile of plants, ferns, orchids, metal struts, and shattered glass to try and rescue Jamie and Celeste. Part of the dining table had also upended and collapsed on top of them, so Theodosia prayed that it had shielded them from falling glass. Grabbing two linen napkins, Theodosia wrapped them around her hands for protection and started digging through the debris. She grabbed a bundle of orchids and tossed them aside, kicked away a pile of ferns, and uncovered the lower half of a twitching and moaning Jamie.

Okay, here's Jamie. Gotta get him out, then find Celeste.

Theodosia grabbed a corner of the table and tried to lift it. No way, it was an impossible task. As she started digging again, she was suddenly aware that Drayton was right beside her.

"Grab Jamie's legs and try to pull him out from under,"

Theodosia said. Water poured down from overhead hoses that had pulled loose, turning everything into a soggy mess.

Drayton bent forward and grabbed two black loafers. But as hard as he tugged, Jamie wouldn't come free.

"Help me," Drayton said.

Theodosia grabbed one leg while Drayton took the other, and together they pulled, straining like a team of workhorses but finally making progress. Moments later, they'd freed a battered and bleeding Jamie from the wreckage.

"Now we've got to find Celeste!" Theodosia cried.

Which was easier said than done. Theodosia had to get down on her hands and knees, crawl under the collapsed table, and feel around in the muck. After pushing aside broken teacups and waterlogged flowers, she finally located a thin bare ankle.

"Got her, I think," Theodosia said. "But I have to work carefully. There's so much glass on top of her." *And blood . . . so much blood.*

Grim-faced and determined, she and Drayton gently scooped and shoved and pulled and tugged until Celeste was dragged free from the wreckage. But unlike Jamie, Celeste was glassy-eyed and unmoving, with a jagged chunk of glass protruding from her neck.

She looks as if she's been drugged, Theodosia thought. *Or . . . is she dead?*

She couldn't dwell on that now. Time was of the essence, and they needed to get help.

"Did you find them?" Delaine shrieked. "Are they okay?" She'd been joined by Haley Parker, Theodosia's chef and baker, Bettina and Jamie, the bride and groom, and Martha and Zach Hempel, owners of Foxtail Flower Farm.

"Stay back!" Theodosia ordered everyone in no uncertain

terms. She didn't want any freak-outs. Cooler heads had to prevail and render aid to these two people who'd been practically buried alive.

"Drayton, call 911," Theodosia yelped. "Get an ambulance out here. Get *two* ambulances." In the back of her mind she worried that Jamie needed an ambulance while Celeste might not.

Drayton grabbed the phone from a stunned Delaine's hand and immediately punched in 911.

Theodosia took a moment to glance up at the greenhouse, where gears and chains and motors dangled freely. And the one thought that ran through her mind like chase lights on a theater marquee was, *This was no accident, this was intentional. Someone tampered with those gears.*

Dipping a hand into her apron pocket, Theodosia pulled out her phone and started dialing as well.

"Who are *you* calling?" Drayton asked. He was already on the line and talking to the dispatch operator.

"I'm calling Riley." Riley, Pete Riley, was Theodosia's significant other and a detective D-2 in the Charleston Police Department.

Back in Charleston, Riley's phone rang once, twice, then he picked up with a lazy "Hello there."

"You have to get out here!" Theodosia cried, fear and urgency coloring her voice. "Like, right now!"

"Sweetheart, I don't even have my tux on yet," Riley said.

"Forget the tux!" Theodosia snapped. "There's been a murder."

2

Sheriff Joe Ambourn and his two deputies were the first to arrive, followed by two ambulances that came screaming in. The EMTs tumbled out and, with barely a wasted motion, were down on their hands and knees, pulling equipment from their medical packs. Two of them started working on Jamie; two went to the aid of Celeste. Because Jamie appeared to be semiconscious and was mumbling responses, Theodosia hurried over to where Celeste, pale and still, was being tended to.

"Priority one," the first EMT said to his partner. Theodosia figured *priority one* must be code for a big bad problem as both EMTs worked feverishly on Celeste. They bagged her and started chest compressions, worked on her for a good ten minutes, but Celeste didn't seem to be responding to anything they did. In fact, her lips were beginning to turn blue.

Drayton walked up behind a stunned Theodosia and said, "How is she doing?"

"Not good," Theodosia said. Her own heart was thudding

with worry, working overtime, and she wished she could magically imbue Celeste with some of her own precious energy.

Drayton took Theodosia's arm and gently pulled her away. "Let them work on her while we check on Jamie," he said. Drayton was managing to stay calm and unflappable even in the midst of a crisis.

They found Jamie lying flat on a gurney and in the process of being loaded into the back of one of the ambulances. Theodosia knew Jamie was alive, and maybe even kicking, by the sounds of his groans and hoarse mumbles.

"Jamie!" Theodosia called out. "Hang in there."

Jamie lifted his head momentarily, moaned, "Uhh," and then disappeared into the ambulance.

"How is he really?" Theodosia asked the EMT who'd loaded him.

"His breath sounds are decent, and his heart is strong," said the EMT, a young man whose name tag read S. GRIFFIN. "But his nose is broken, he's sustained some serious cuts and abrasions, one very bad cut on his right hand, and there are possible skull and rib fractures. So the ER docs have to take a careful look at him." Then the EMT vaulted into the ambulance, pulled the door closed, and they sped off, siren wailing, lights flashing.

"This is so awful," Drayton said. "How can something like this happen?"

"Maybe it didn't *just* happen," Theodosia said.

Drayton turned his head sharply to stare at her. "Hmm?"

"This greenhouse tumbling down all by itself . . . seems very improbable to me."

In the minutes since the collapse, the crowd around the greenhouse had grown considerably larger. Besides Sheriff

Ambourn and his two deputies, there was a field investigator from the local ME's office, Martha and Zach Hempel, one TV news van, the minister, two additional caterers, and various and assorted wedding guests. The guests had arrived for the festivities but were promptly shocked into silence when they found out what had happened and now wore appropriately stunned expressions on their faces.

And a partridge in a pear tree, Theodosia thought to herself. As well as a horse-drawn carriage, meant for the bride and groom's send-off. She watched as the bewildered-looking driver, at seeing something amiss, suddenly reined in his big chestnut horse.

Worming her way through the crowd, Theodosia was shocked to see grim faces on the two EMTs who continued to labor over Celeste.

"Anything at all?" Theodosia said in a loud whisper. "Is she breathing? Is her heart still beating?"

Neither of the EMTs answered, but one of them managed an awkward grimace.

It was a nonanswer nobody wanted to hear. Sobs broke out as more guests arrived, and some began filming the chaos on their cell phones. Delaine was still running around, screaming like a tornado warning siren. And Martha Hempel had collapsed into tears.

When Theodosia finally saw Riley jump out of his blue BMW, she pushed her way through the crowd, now almost a swarm, and threw herself into his arms. "You came," she said. It was almost a sob.

"Of course." Riley was in control emotionally but looked tense. "Are *you* okay?"

"I am now," Theodosia said. Pete Riley was, as always, an

oasis of calm, even in a maelstrom of shock and uncertainty. As Theodosia pressed herself against him, she could feel his Glock 22 in its shoulder harness, and it made her feel . . . safe.

Pete Riley whispered to Theodosia as he kissed the top of her head. He was used to dealing with tragedy, adept at investigating homicides and serious crimes. At age thirty-seven, he was one of the up-and-coming detectives on Charleston's police force, a tall, intense man with an aristocratic nose, high cheekbones, and cobalt blue eyes. Theodosia tended to call him Riley instead of Pete, and he called her Theo. It was what worked for them. And had for a couple of years now.

"I . . . I really am fine," Theodosia said again. "But Celeste . . ." She made a feeble gesture toward the collapsed structure. "Half of that greenhouse crashed down on top of her, and we had to pull her out from underneath . . . so her prognosis isn't good."

"I've got two Crime Scene investigators on the way," Riley said.

"Is this even your jurisdiction?"

"We're on the far edge of Charleston Country, but yes." Then Riley gripped her gently by the shoulders and said, "On the phone you said something about murder. Explain please."

Theodosia swallowed hard and nodded.

"Tell me exactly what happened, tell me what you saw."

"It's more like what I heard," Theodosia said. "This metallic *rat-tat-tat* ratcheting sound, as if some kind of chain had broken loose and was thrashing all around, smacking against metal, cracking glass. Then there was this awful end-of-the-world crash—shards of glass shattering and falling down, I guess—and we all rushed out to find the greenhouse almost totally collapsed."

"On top of . . ."

"Jamie, the groom, and Celeste, the bridesmaid." Theodosia stopped and swiveled her head, saw that the EMTs huddled over Celeste had suspended their lifesaving measures. "They're not going to transport her to the hospital, are they?" she asked Riley.

Riley looked over, took in the situation, then gazed at her with soft, blue eyes. "I don't know," he said. "Probably not."

Theodosia staggered a few steps away from him, suddenly aware that the sun was shining down and an undulating ocean of chrysanthemums and silver grasses were waving in the breeze. It was a perfectly beautiful day except for the fact that a young woman whom she'd said hello to an hour ago, a girl with dimples and emerald green eyes, who was bubbly, sweet, and upbeat, was now deceased.

Something deep inside Theodosia's heart began to ache as she thought about the dead girl . . .

Celeste, her name is Celeste.

. . . who was being gently lifted onto a gurney.

The two EMTs raised the gurney up on scissored legs and slowly bumped it across the grass toward the back of their ambulance. Their faces were unreadable as they transported the sheet-covered body. The crowd of people suddenly grew hushed.

Then a gust of wind caught a corner of the flimsy white sheet and flipped it up.

Celeste's lifeless body was turned to one side, and Theodosia caught a quick glimpse of a single dead eye. It was almost the exact same shade as the glass in the shattered greenhouse.

Theodosia turned away, wiped a tear, and squared her shoulders.

This isn't the end. Not by a long shot.

* * *

Two Crime Scene investigators arrived, huddled with Riley, and immediately began exploring the greenhouse wreckage. Wearing rubber boots, gloves, and safety glasses, they poured through the ruined building, shot videotape, then set up portable lights and took still photos. While one investigator continued to poke through the shattered glass and sodden greenery, the other walked along the side of the greenhouse, looking down for . . .

What? Theodosia wondered. *Looking for footprints, fibers, clues?*

When Riley got the okay to enter what was left of the greenhouse, he went in, stepping carefully over shards of jagged glass and scattered piles of trampled ferns and broken orchids. Theodosia ignored his stringent advice to stay outside and gingerly followed him in.

"Sometimes glass panels can slip or glazing clips pop off, other times there's structural failure," Riley said as he studied what was left of the interior.

"Sometimes, yes," Theodosia said. "But what about this time?"

Riley turned his gaze upward. "Just taking a cursory look at these overhead gears, I'd say it's possible somebody fooled with the mechanism. Loosened it or set it on a hair trigger so whoever opened that door would cause the overhead windows to tilt sharply and come crashing down."

"Is that easy to do?"

"I don't know. I'm not a structural engineer."

"But you think the collapse was caused by some*one*, not just the wind or the rainstorm we had a few nights ago?"

"I can't say for sure, but it might have been rigged."

"I saw that in a movie once," Theodosia said. "Maybe *The Hand That Rocks the Cradle*."

Riley dusted his hands together. "Well, there you go."

* * *

Back outside, Delaine was jumping up and down and screaming at the owners of the flower farm.

"How could you let something like this *happen*?" she shrilled as they cowered in front of her small but formidable presence. "This was outright *neglect*! You people need to be held accountable!" She was a tiny, skinny, dark-haired wraith in a well-tailored pink suit.

"Everyone, please try to remain calm," Sheriff Ambourn said, trying to insert himself between the two parties. The sheriff was a large man, well over six feet tall, with a friendly, hangdog face and sparse silver hair. Though his brown uniform still looked starched and pressed, the events of the day seemed to be wearing him down.

Bettina, who was still in shock over Celeste's death and embarrassed by Delaine's theatrics, saw Theodosia step out of the greenhouse and ran to her, practically flinging herself into Theodosia's arms. "This is so awful," she cried.

"Of course it is," Theodosia soothed.

"It was an accident, a terrible accident," Sheriff Ambourn intoned.

Theodosia gave a slight shake of her head, a gesture that was not missed by Bettina.

"You don't think it was an accident?" Bettina whispered, her eyes suddenly large and questioning.

Theodosia gazed at the collapsed greenhouse and said, in a quiet voice, "It could have been deliberate."

Bettina dug the heels of her hands into her eye sockets, rubbed hard, then took them away and blinked. "Deliberate?" she said. "You really think so?"

"We're not sure of anything right now," Riley said as he

joined them. "And we won't have any answers until there's been a thorough investigation." He put an arm around Bettina and led her over to where Reggie and another friend of Jamie's were standing around, looking glum. "Take care of her, will you?"

The two men nodded.

"I've got to get to the hospital," Bettina blubbered. "Jamie . . ."

"We'll take you," Reggie said.

Theodosia was keeping an eye on the Crime Scene techs. "If we're not sure of anything right now, why are the Crime Scene investigators hunting around, looking for clues?" she asked.

Riley smiled at her. "Because it's their job, that's what they do."

"Maybe we should do the same," she said.

"I don't think . . . ," Riley started to say. But Theodosia had already walked away from him and begun stalking the outside perimeter of the greenhouse, looking for whatever she could find.

When Riley hurried to join her, she was already pointing to a depression in the moss.

"Look," she said. "I told you somebody snuck onto this property and fiddled with those overhead gears. Here's where they hunkered down, biding their time." She took a few more steps. "And here, it looks like footprints—well, heelprints, anyway—in the mud." She continued on a few paces. "And over here the heelprints are spaced farther apart, probably from when he ran away."

"We'll have the Crime Scene techs shoot photos, make plaster casts, do the usual," Riley said.

But Theodosia was upset and in no mood to settle for the usual.

3

"No, we've got to keep looking," Theodosia insisted. "If the killer escaped this way, there have to be more clues. You once told me that the first sixty minutes after a crime is committed are a kind of golden hour. That's when you learn the most about suspects, motives, and the crime itself." She headed down a row of sunflowers, then turned and said, "Are you coming?"

Riley dutifully followed her another hundred yards, then another fifty. By that time they'd covered almost half the length of the flower field, which was when Theodosia stopped and said, "What's that over there?" She'd caught a glint of sunlight reflecting off a moving vehicle.

"Um . . ." Riley was studying Google Maps on his iPhone. "I think it's a park. Yeah, here it is. Kipley Park."

"A county park?"

"Right."

"Maybe we should go over there and look around."

"You're thinking your suspect came in that way?" Riley asked. "Started from the park and then cut across the fields?"

Theodosia put a hand to her head and scrubbed at her mass of auburn hair. "I don't know. Maybe. Maybe not. But if we don't look, there's always the chance we'll miss something important."

"Well . . ." Riley glanced back toward the greenhouse, where the sheriff, his deputies, and the Crime Scene techs seemed to have everything under control. "Okay then."

Theodosia arranged with Drayton and Haley, her young chef, to drive her Jeep back to Charleston, while she rode with Riley. Just as they were pulling away, she spotted another TV van, tricked out with aerials and satellite gear on its roof. This one was from K-BAM.

"Can you believe another TV crew showed up?" Theodosia said.

"It's that Ken Lotter guy," Riley said. "We figure he uses an illegal police scanner to catch all the emergency calls. Then he drives his stupid news van a hundred miles an hour."

"Either that," Theodosia said, "or he wears a flying monkey suit."

Over in Kipley Park the scene looked like a normal Saturday afternoon. There were grills, picnic tables, swing sets, a horseshoe pit, and at least a dozen families enjoying the park's hospitality. Moms unpacked picnic baskets, dads grilled hot dogs and hamburgers, kids played softball, while toddlers whooped and hollered on the swing sets. The day smelled like new-mown grass, burning charcoal, and sizzling meat.

"You see?" Riley said. "Nada. We're probably not going to find any answers over here."

"Not so fast," Theodosia said.

She climbed out of the car and looked around. The gravel

parking lot was relatively small, with a couple acres of grass stretching out from it like a green, undulating carpet. Beyond that was a fairly dense woodlot as well as a swampy area.

"Nothing nefarious that I can see," Riley said. "No clue to indicate the killer was even here."

Theodosia remained rooted to the spot, one hand shielding her eyes as she surveyed the area, making a slow and deliberate 360-degree inspection. Disappointment was slowly beginning to seep in, until a shady spot highlighted by a dapple of sunlight caught her eye.

"I see one possibility," Theodosia said.

"What's that?" Riley asked.

Theodosia pointed to a narrow opening in the woods. "There's a trail over there."

At the far edge of the picnic grounds, a path led into what was a fairly dense woodlot.

"A trail?" Riley said.

"You see that shady spot? That's the entrance."

"Okay, there's a trail," Riley said. "I mean, it *is* a county park, after all. People probably come here to go hiking and ride mountain bikes. Maybe trailer their horses in, too."

"We should still take a look."

"We can look," Riley said as he checked his watch. "But I'd rather it not turn into a ten-mile hike."

"What? You were never an Eagle Scout?"

Riley gave a rueful chuckle. "I was more chess club material."

"Analytical. Which probably makes for a good detective."

They followed the three-foot-wide, hard-pack dirt trail through stands of beech and ash, twisting along until the woods grew even more dense. Here, live oak and ash trees stood tall, and the ground underfoot began to feel boggy.

"Hate bogs." Riley did everything but shiver.

"Just spongy peat deposits," Theodosia said as they pushed on. "Good for the environment because they support so much plant and animal life."

The trail wound through a swampy area where tupelo and river birch grew. In the middle of a tea-colored pond, sitting atop a half-submerged log, three turtles—red-eared sliders—stuck their heads out, trying to capture as much of the sun's rays as possible.

"Love those turtles," Theodosia said as she paused to look at them. Ever since she was a kid, she'd had a soft spot in her heart for turtles and tortoises. She even had a small collection of ceramic turtles.

"You wouldn't love an alligator turtle," Riley said. "Get too close to one of those puppies and they'll chomp your hand off."

"I hear you." Theodosia had spent time at her aunt Libby's place, Cane Ridge Plantation, where she'd had a few encounters with snapping turtles and alligators.

Riley lifted an eyebrow. "Getting too close can be dangerous on any number of levels."

Theodosia ignored Riley, figuring it was an offhand reference to her getting tangled up in what he figured was his investigation. On the other hand, seeing as how she'd taken the lead in exploring this trail, it was *her* investigation for the time being.

The afternoon sun poured down like melted butter as they walked along, and Theodosia was glad of it. The weather guy on WSSX Radio had mentioned the possibility of rain for tonight, but so far not a single ominous cloud had bubbled up in a robin's-egg blue sky.

Then Theodosia's sharp eyes spotted something that made

her stop in her tracks and practically gasp. On a wooden post, silvered with age and half obscured by a tangle of kudzu, was a black box.

"Riley," she said, "I think there's a trail cam."

"What?" Riley looked around but didn't see anything. "Where?"

Theodosia pointed at the camera. "There, kind of hidden in that thicket of kudzu."

Riley walked over and pushed back a tangle of bright green leaves. "Darn stuff grows everywhere. Wants to take over." He leaned down, touched a hand to the trail cam, and said, "Okay, this is something. Probably put here by the South Carolina DNR, the Department of Natural Resources, to monitor wildlife. Lots of mink, nutria, and coyotes inhabit this area. Probably a few bobcats and wild hogs, too."

"Those hogs are especially super aggressive," Theodosia said, glancing around. Were there hogs? Nope, none that she could see.

Then her focus was back on the trail camera. "If this camera is motion-activated, and I'm guessing it must be, then it might have captured a shot of the intruder."

"Only if he came this way," Riley said. He stared intently at the camera, lifted a shoulder, and added, "This could be helpful."

"Here's what I'm thinking," Theodosia said, a little breathlessly. "What if the killer left his car in the parking lot and walked in this way? Crept down this path, then cut over to the flower fields?"

"Maybe." Riley didn't sound convinced.

"There's only one way to find out," Theodosia said. "Follow this trail a little farther and see where it comes out."

They did exactly that. And ten minutes later, after swatting their fair share of bugs and taking one wrong turn, emerged from the woods to find themselves staring at a field of purple lavender.

"I was right," Theodosia said, shielding her eyes and pointing. "Look over there. You can just see a corner of the greenhouse. See how the sun reflects off it?"

Riley squinted, finally saw the green glint for himself, and said, "You're right."

"So this could have been the killer's route in. And out." Theodosia continued to stare at the greenhouse, feeling a rush of accomplishment. This was *something.* This was practically proof positive evidence that an outside person had crept in and rigged the greenhouse. Her nose fairly twitched with anticipation as she turned to Riley and said, "Now what?"

"Now we leave it alone."

"What!" This wasn't what Theodosia wanted to hear. She envisioned hard-nosed detectives with probing questions, suspects buckling under stress, lie detector tests, and maybe even an arrest.

"We go back to Charleston and trust that Crime Scene will come up with some answers," Riley said. "That Sheriff Ambourn puts his investigators on this, too. Meanwhile, I'll call the DNR and see if we can take a look at that trail cam footage."

Theodosia tapped a foot. "What else?"

"I'll arrange interviews with witnesses, guests, whoever was at the wedding. Conduct a by-the-book investigation," Riley said.

"Uh-huh." Theodosia stared out across the purple field and felt another twitch of excitement, of restlessness. As if the hunt was about to begin for real. Yes, a by-the-book investigation was fine for law enforcement, but if she could cut a few corners, figure out a motive, and speed things up . . . then maybe, just maybe, she could help find a killer.

The idea thrilled her beyond words.

4

Sunday morning. Theodosia slid out of bed and did a few stretches and leisurely toe touches. She pulled on a cozy peach-colored sweater and a pair of faded blue jeans and padded downstairs to let her dog, Earl Grey, out into the backyard. She yawned as she filled a kettle with water, set it to boil, then grabbed one of her Yi-shing teapots and a tin of English breakfast tea. Once her tea had brewed, she carried her steaming mug out into the backyard to see what Earl Grey was up to.

Earl Grey was sniffing around, reveling in the fact that it was a sunny day with the distinct taste of fall in the air. Even bright-eyed grackles, flitting gracefully from leafy palmettos to a nearby boxwood hedge, looked as if they felt a seasonal upheaval.

Still, amid all the blue skies, pink scudding clouds, golden leaves, and bird chirps, Theodosia felt awful. She thought back on the words of an old Kris Kristofferson song, "Sunday

Mornin' Comin' Down." It seemed to capture her mood perfectly.

How could yesterday have gone so wrong? Turned so tragic? An innocent young girl had been killed, a bridegroom seriously injured, and a wedding totally derailed. And for what reason?

That thought niggled at Theodosia as her hand dipped into the pocket of her jeans and she pulled out her phone. She hit a button and, a few seconds later, Drayton came on the line.

"I feel awful," Theodosia said without preamble.

"So do I," said Drayton. "I woke up feeling sad and dispirited. Like I'm experiencing some kind of emotional hangover."

"Why don't we go to the hospital and visit Jamie? If he's awake, we can talk to him, see if he can shed any light on what might have happened. Maybe he saw something."

"In the split second before the roof collapsed?"

"It's possible," Theodosia said.

"You want to investigate," Drayton said. He'd known Theodosia long enough that he could practically read her mind.

"Well, maybe. There is that. But I'd also like to see how Jamie's doing. He looked as if he was banged up pretty bad. Maybe we could cheer him up with a basket of fresh-baked scones."

"Mmn, who wouldn't love that? But there aren't any scones left at the tea shop. Even in the freezer. We sold our last batch Friday afternoon."

"I'll call Haley, ask her to run downstairs and get cranking."

"If you say so. And I suppose, if push came to shove, I could bring along a thermos of fresh-brewed tea."

"Works for me," Theodosia said. "Pick you up in, what, forty-five minutes?"

"I'll be ready."

* * *

Drayton was as good as his word. When Theodosia pulled up to his house, he was waiting curbside with a silver thermos tucked in the crook of his arm. Dressed in dove gray slacks, a tweed jacket, and a bright yellow bow tie, he looked as if he were heading to brunch at Poogan's Porch or La Bonne Franquette instead of going on a serious, sedate hospital visit.

"You look like a very posh Southern gent," Theodosia told Drayton as he climbed into her Jeep. "Lord of the manor."

"Now you're making fun of me," Drayton said as he settled in and pulled his seat belt across his chest.

"Not at all," Theodosia said. "That's what came to mind when I saw you standing there in front of your fabulous house." Drayton's home was listed on Charleston's historic register. It had formerly been owned by a Civil War doctor but over the decades had been remodeled and added on to. When Drayton had purchased the home some twelve years ago, he'd spiffed up the outside, tuck-pointed the bricks, added a Chinese garden in back, and imbued the home's interior with touches of French elegance as well as fine English furniture. Now it was a showpiece that had been featured in magazines, as well as the residence he shared with Honey Bee, his adorable King Charles spaniel.

Theodosia drove down Church Street, turned on Cumberland, and bumped down the cobblestone alley that ran behind the Indigo Tea Shop. A sharp *toot* of the horn brought their chef, Haley, running out with an indigo blue bakery box full of scones.

"Apple scones, hot from the oven," Haley said as she handed the box to Drayton.

"The very best kind," Drayton said.

"So you're off to the hospital?" Haley asked. She was twenty-something, with stick-straight blond hair, blue eyes, and a pert nose. She looked like a college kid but could cook like Gordon Ramsay. She could swear like him, too.

Theodosia leaned across Drayton to talk to Haley. "It's the least we can do. And thanks for baking these scones."

"No problem," Haley said. "Gosh, I feel awful about Celeste. And poor Jamie, too." She shook her head. "Such shattered lives, in more ways than one. The whole thing—the wedding and reception—completely ruined."

"Who knows what will happen now," Drayton said.

Haley looked utterly forlorn. "Do you think Bettina and Jamie will still get married?"

"Hard to say," Theodosia said. She hoped they would. But yesterday had to have put a terrible damper on their outlook for the future.

Roper Hospital at the Medical University was practically deserted this Sunday morning as they checked in at the front desk, got Jamie's room number, and rode the elevator up to the fourth floor.

"So where exactly did you run off to yesterday with Riley?" Drayton asked as they walked down the hallway.

"We went over to Kipley Park," Theodosia said. "And walked a trail that led around a bog to the end of the flower fields."

"Because . . . ?"

"Because I think somebody snuck in that way yesterday and sabotaged the greenhouse."

"With the idea being what?"

"Kill Jamie? Kill Celeste?"

"So you were looking for clues?" Drayton sounded skeptical.

"Not just looking, we found one. Well, not an actual clue, but something that could produce a clue. We found a motion-activated trail cam."

"And you think this camera might have captured a picture of the intruder?"

"That's what we're hoping," Theodosia said. She looked around. "Jeez, what a maze, where is Jamie's room anyway?"

"Um, I think down and around that corner."

"Quiet up here," Theodosia said. They were walking past rooms where doors were open, but no patients were in sight.

"I suppose a lot of patients are released on Friday so doctors have the weekend off. They don't have to pop back in to check on their patients' status," Drayton said.

"Guess so," Theodosia said as they stepped around a linen cart that was sitting in the middle of the hallway. Beyond it was a meal delivery cart with dozens of hot meals under stainless steel domes.

"This is like an obstacle course," Drayton said as they walked around that cart, too.

Delaine and Bettina were standing outside Jamie's room talking in low whispers. Bettina was dressed in pale peach yoga pants and a matching hoodie; Delaine wore a bright blue skirt suit with pearl buttons and was clutching a matching Dior bag. They both looked fashionable, upscale, and deeply upset.

"Jamie's parents just left," Bettina said when she spotted Theodosia and Drayton. "They're on their way to church at St. Michael's over on Meeting Street, then they're coming back here." She gave a sad smile and added, "I don't know why I just told you all that. Guess my brain's still in a muddle."

"How's Jamie doing?" Theodosia asked in a sympathetic

tone. She saw how Bettina's shoulders sagged and deep worry lines were etched in her young face.

Bettina shook her head. "Jamie's in a lot of pain. He's got a fairly deep cut just above his right wrist. They had to bring in a microsurgeon to repair it. The doc had to do something like twenty-five stitches."

"There was a tendon involved," Delaine added.

"And Jamie's nose is broken. So he has to wear an ugly gray plastic splint," Bettina said. "And his ribs are banged up."

"But not broken," Delaine said. "Thank goodness."

"Maybe we should come back later," Drayton said.

"No, no," Bettina said. "You should go in now. I think Jamie would be happy to see you guys. His . . . his spirits are pretty low. He feels just awful about Celeste."

"Okay," Theodosia said. She pushed open the door to Jamie's room. "Knock knock. It's Theodosia and Drayton. May we come in?"

"Theodosia?" Jamie said. He struggled to sit up in bed as they entered his room, then fell back against his pillows as if the effort were too much and said, "Hi, guys."

Jamie looked awful. His face had the appearance of a cold, pale moon, his eyes were half-closed, and he definitely looked loopy from taking painkillers. His right wrist was heavily bandaged, and he did, indeed, have a strange-looking gray plastic splint on his nose.

"We just had to come check on you," Theodosia said.

Drayton touched two fingers to his forehead in a jaunty salute. "How you doing, sport?"

"Not too bad," Jamie said. Then he gave a tentative laugh. "Not too good, either."

"He's still woozy," Delaine said. She and Bettina had followed them into the hospital room.

"We brought scones," Theodosia said as she held up a box.

"And tea," Drayton said.

"That's great," Jamie rasped. His throat was still dry from the anesthesia. "But maybe I could have a glass of water first?"

"Coming right up," Bettina said. She hustled to his bedside, grabbed a pitcher of water, and poured out a glass. Then she handed it to Jamie along with a straw.

"Thanks." Jamie sipped a bit of water, then set down his glass. He gazed at Theodosia and said, "You know about Celeste? That she didn't make it?"

Theodosia nodded. "We know. And we feel terrible about it."

Jamie's eyes sparkled with tears. "That could have been me."

"But it wasn't," Bettina said with a touch of flint in her voice. "So all you have to worry about is getting better."

Jamie still looked distressed. "Not so easy."

Bettina took his good hand, laced her fingers through his, and said, "We'll get through this together, sweetie."

"Of course you will," Theodosia said.

They were all standing around Jamie's bed, giving little coos and making encouraging remarks, when a motherly-looking woman in a pink-and-white smock walked in carrying a meal tray. "Let's see now . . . ," she said as she checked the ticket that was stuck beneath the covered plate. "You're Jamie Wilkes, right?"

"That's me," Jamie said.

"I'm Deanie from food service." The woman smiled as she rolled his side table closer to his bed, then set his meal tray down on it. "I've got the lunch you ordered."

"I didn't order lunch," Jamie said.

"Well, I'm guessing you must have been admitted late yesterday," Deanie said. "So the kitchen sent up a standard lunch of soup, a sandwich, and applesauce. Here, let me give you a hand."

Deanie lifted the dome off the plate, gaped in surprise at what was sitting there, and promptly let out an ear-piercing scream.

"What on earth?" Theodosia murmured as Deanie's scream rose higher in volume until she practically hit high C.

"That's a that's a that's a . . ." Deanie was so undone her stammered words were running on a loop, even as her hand jabbed the air furiously, pointing at what was supposed to be Jamie's lunch. Theodosia followed Deanie's shaking finger to the meal plate she'd just uncovered. And there, sitting in the middle of that plate, was a human skull!

Delaine caught sight of it, too, and let loose a piercing shriek. She took a wobbly step forward, stumbled, and bumped hard against Jamie's bed.

Which hit the tray table, sending the thermos of tea crashing to the floor and setting off a cascading motion that caused the skull to rock back and forth while a beam of overhead light caught it just right, making it look as if one of the eyes were winking at them.

"There's something you don't see every day," Drayton said in a strangled voice.

And then Theodosia was there, grabbing the cover and slamming it back down on top of the skull. But not before it rocked sideways and two empty eye sockets fixed her with a wicked gaze.

5

Dead silence fell across the room until Drayton finally spoke up. "Excuse me, but is that thing even real?"

"I don't know," Theodosia said. If someone was playing a nasty trick on Jamie, it was about as welcome—and as out of place—as a rat perched on the edge of a punch bowl. "But I'm going to find out."

"H-how?" Delaine gasped. She was practically speechless, no mean feat for the usually motormouthed Delaine.

"I'll get an expert opinion," Theodosia said. She picked up the tray and carried it out to the hallway. Looking to her right, she saw a nurses' station at the end of the corridor and headed that way. When a gray-haired woman in blue scrubs and a name tag that said MARGIE BURNHAM, RN glanced up from her computer and smiled, Theodosia said, "I need your help with something."

"Sure," the nurse said. "What's up?"

Theodosia lifted the metal cover from the dish to reveal the skull. "Is this thing real?"

Unlike everyone else, the nurse gave the skull a cool, appraising look, then poked the jaw with an index finger. "It's plastic," she said as she turned toward Theodosia with a quizzical look. "Is this some kind of joke? Did that little twerp Ardie put you up to this?"

"It's somebody's idea of a joke all right, but not who you think. This skull was just now served up on a platter and delivered to our friend in room 427."

Margie Burnham blinked as she consulted her computer screen. "The hand surgery patient admitted last night."

"Right. Jamie Wilkes. It was on his meal tray."

"You're kidding." The nurse almost smiled but didn't quite. "That's pretty goldarned weird."

"My thoughts exactly. Do you by any chance have a bag I could put this in?"

"Sure. You're going to take it with you?"

"That's right."

Margie Burnham dug under her desk and pulled out a blue plastic drawstring bag. It was the kind given to patients to hold their clothing and belongings.

"Thank you." Theodosia dropped the skull into the bag and headed back to Jamie's room. When she got there, she said, "It's fake. Probably plastic. The kind of thing you buy in a trick shop."

"You're sure?" Delaine asked. She was jittering like an overcaffeinated Chihuahua and nibbling the ends of her French-tipped nails.

"I'm going to give this skull to Riley and see if his Crime Scene guys can pull prints off it," Theodosia said. "Because this is just way too weird."

"Who would do something like this?" Bettina quavered. "I mean, it's absolutely sick."

"Maybe somebody from the wedding party was trying to punk me," Jamie said.

"Like they did yesterday?" Delaine snapped.

Jamie looked subdued. "I guess not," he said, just as a janitor with a bucket and mop came into the room and said, "You need a cleanup?"

"Please," Bettina said.

Theodosia crooked a finger at Drayton and said, "We need to talk." When they were both out in the hallway, Theodosia said, "Let's go down to the coffee shop, get something to eat, and put our heads together."

"Do you think they'll have tea?"

"Tea bags anyway," Theodosia said.

"Then I'd best settle for a glass of orange juice."

Drayton got his orange juice while Theodosia got a Diet Coke and a peanut butter cookie. They carried their trays to a table in the far corner of the clattery, semi-busy coffee shop, where they could talk undisturbed.

"So," Drayton said, "what was that all about? How did the skull even get there?"

"I don't know. But short of it being a Halloween prank, which I don't think it was, that skull could be some sort of warning."

"Warning about . . . ?"

"Not sure. But someone seems very intent on targeting Jamie," Theodosia said.

"After yesterday's disaster, I figured they were after Bettina. You know, a jilted boyfriend . . . a jealous whomever," Drayton said.

"That's what I thought, too, but this kind of changes things. Somebody who's clever enough to sneak into a hospital, find out what room Jamie's in, and try to spook him with a skull—even though it's plastic—well, maybe Jamie *was* the intended target. Probably still is."

"Or yesterday's intruder, who's now attained killer status, was focused on both Bettina and Jamie."

Theodosia thought for a few moments. "Both of them. That's certainly possible."

They batted around ideas for another ten minutes. Then Theodosia said, "I think we should go back upstairs and talk to Jamie. Quiz him about what's been going on in his life. Has he had personal problems? Business issues? Has he ruffled someone's feathers and made a possible enemy?"

But when they went back upstairs, Jamie's eyes were closed and he was snoring softly. And Delaine and Bettina were nowhere to be found.

"Now what?" Drayton asked.

"We wake him up."

"Do you think that's wise?"

Theodosia was already standing at Jamie's bedside, so she reached out and gave his shoulder a gentle shake.

Jamie's eyes popped open and he said, "No." Then Theodosia's face swam into focus for him and he said, "Oh . . . hi."

"Do you feel well enough to answer a few questions?" Theodosia asked.

Jamie wiggled his shoulders and pulled himself up in bed. "Not really, but I'll try."

Theodosia slid a chair up to his bedside while Drayton stood behind her. "I'll try to keep this brief," Theodosia said.

Jamie gingerly touched a finger to his nose splint. "Okay."

"We think—that is, Drayton and I think—that somebody might be targeting you."

Jamie's eyes fluttered. "You mean somebody wants to *kill* me?" Now he looked scared.

"It's possible," Drayton said. "Have the Charleston Police talked to you about the greenhouse collapse?"

"Should they?" Jamie asked.

"Absolutely," Theodosia said. "Or maybe Sheriff Ambourn has been in touch?"

"Nuh, no," Jamie stammered. "Not yet anyway."

"Well, law enforcement will for sure be asking you some very pointed questions," Theodosia said. "But in the meantime, Drayton and I would like to do a little nosing around ourselves." She stopped, drew breath, and said, "Jamie, do you have any enemies?"

Jamie gave her a startled look. "I don't think so."

"Anybody who might be angry at you?"

"Not really."

"A rival at the brokerage firm where you work? Somebody from college?"

"Uh-uh."

"Maybe someone with a personal vendetta?" Theodosia said, pressing him a little harder. "Someone who believes you may have wronged him in some way and has decided to retaliate?"

Jamie shook his head. "No, I . . . well . . . I don't think so."

"You were about to say something, what was it?" Theodosia asked.

"I thought about one guy. But, probably not," Jamie said.

"May we inquire as to who this person might be?" Drayton asked.

"You wouldn't know him," Jamie said, shaking his head.

Drayton offered a mild smile. "Try me."

Jamie hemmed and hawed for a while, then finally blurted out, "I know for a fact that Martin Hunt is super mad at me."

"Martin Hunt," Theodosia said. "Why do I know that name?"

Jamie swallowed hard and said, "He owns . . ."

"Hunt and Peck," Drayton said, filling in the blanks. "That upscale men's clothing store over on King Street that caters to the polo and yachting crowd."

"Got it," Theodosia said. She stared at Jamie. "Okay, can you think of any reason why this Martin Hunt fellow might want to *kill* you?"

"You know I'm a licensed broker now . . ." Jamie licked his lips before he continued. "Well, Hunt was one of my very first customers at Hamilton and McLaughlin."

"And there was a problem?" Theodosia asked.

"You could say that," Jamie said.

"Can you tell us what happened?"

"Hunt likes to think of himself as a high roller," Jamie said. "So he came to me one day looking for a super quick way to double his money."

"Oops," Drayton said.

"Right, there is no quick way," Jamie said. "And I told Hunt exactly that. And then he blew me off and said he really needed a fast payoff and wanted to invest in leveraged ETFs and crypto. I told him there was too much risk involved, but Hunt said he wanted to go ahead and roll the dice anyway."

"So you rolled the dice," Theodosia said. "And Hunt lost his shirt."

"Most of his investment, anyway," Jamie said. "I warned Hunt these were high-risk investments, but he wouldn't listen. Didn't listen. He believed he could double his money, but most of it went south."

"And after this happened, Martin Hunt actually threatened you?" Theodosia asked.

"Yeah."

"How so?"

"Physically, verbally, any way he could. And believe me, he meant it," Jamie said. "You don't know this, but Martin Hunt was a Golden Gloves champion in Alabama, in the Southeast Golden Gloves. This was right after he graduated from Auburn. Fought in the superheavyweight division and won a diamond belt. Hunt still works out at Greebe's Gym over on Laurens Street. He boxes, lifts weights, does Nautilus, and supposedly has a Peloton bike in the back of his store. For all I know he does the whole 'roid thing, too. I mean, Hunt is super hard-core."

"So Hunt actually harmed you physically?" Drayton asked.

"He gave me a black eye once," Jamie said. "Does that count?"

Theodosia pursed her lips. "I'd say that definitely counts."

6

Earl Grey greeted Theodosia with tail wags and excited barks when she walked in the back door.

"Hey, boy," she said, getting down on her hands and knees to give him a hug and a kiss on his muzzle. "You miss me?"

Rowrf.

"I know, and I'm sorry. There was something I had to take care of. But we'll go for a run tonight, okay? I promise."

Earl Grey was a smoky gray Dalbrador (half dalmatian, half Labrador) that Theodosia had adopted a number of years ago. Since then they'd coexisted as roommates, best friends, and running partners. Under Theodosia's gentle tutelage, Earl Grey had also become a registered therapy dog, welcome to give kisses and spread doggy cheer in any number of children's hospital wards and senior living homes.

Theodosia gave Earl Grey a fresh dish of water, then grabbed a bottle of Fiji water out of her refrigerator for herself and headed for the living room. Passing through the dining room, she glanced at the smoked mirror that hung over her Sheraton buffet, put a hand to her hair, and said, "Eek."

Then she promptly forgot about how abundantly curly her hair looked and plopped down in a chintz-covered armchair. She took a hit of water, looked around her small but cozy living room, and smiled. Even when everything went paws up, she could always come home to this.

Theodosia had bought her home, a small cottage with the adorable name of Hazelhurst, several years ago. From outside it looked like a place Hansel and Gretel might have lived in, especially with its brick and stucco walls, wooden cross gables, cedar shingles that replicated a thatched roof, and curls of ivy. On the inside, she'd refinished the pegged wood floors, put the brick fireplace in working order, and filled it with plush furniture and overstuffed cushions. Oh, and a supersoft rug for Earl Grey.

Earl Grey was sprawled on that rug right then, looking content and ready to ease into a good snooze, when Theodosia's phone rang. He lifted his head just as Theodosia reached into her pocket and pulled out her phone. Checking the screen, she said, "Riley," then pressed Answer and said, "Hey there."

"Hey there, yourself," Riley said. "You feeling any better today?"

"Actually, I'm a little puzzled . . . worried maybe."

"What's wrong?" he asked.

"Something very weird happened when Drayton and I went to the hospital to check on Jamie."

"What's that?"

Theodosia quickly told Riley about the skull that had been delivered to Jamie's room.

"A skull!" Riley seemed a little freaked. "Are you kidding me?"

"Nope."

"Put there on purpose?"

"I think so."

"Please tell me it wasn't real."

"It was cheap plastic, the kind you'd buy in a novelty store. Or one of those specialty Halloween stores that seem to spring up out of nowhere in late September."

"Where's this skull now?"

"I have it. I brought it home with me."

"If this fake skull was meant as a threat to Jamie, maybe I should run it for prints."

"I was hoping you'd say that. Speaking of which, is there any news on the trail cam yet?"

"No, but we'll probably have something by tomorrow."

"Then maybe we'll know who tried to kill Jamie."

"Now you think Jamie was the intended victim?"

"Yesterday, I wasn't sure if it was Bettina or Jamie. But with that skull showing up today . . . Well, it sure feels as if Jamie is being targeted. And with him in the hospital and Celeste in the morgue, it makes me want to find the culprit and beat his sorry ass to a pulp."

"Easy, tiger. You really should let law enforcement handle this," Riley said.

"You're on this, right?"

"Me and a few others, sure. And I don't mind running prints on the skull, but I can't be sharing inside information with you."

"Sure you can," Theodosia said.

"Hah, no. Maybe you can pry something out of Sheriff Ambourn."

"Oh please. How many murder cases would you say Sheriff Ambourn handles in a year?"

"I don't know. Three or four?"

"How many do you get involved in?"

"Well, homicide and ag assault have seriously bumped up this year so . . . hmm . . . homicides? Maybe twenty-five or thirty."

"I rest my case. You're my best bet."

"No, sweetheart. Not this time," Riley said.

"But you'll let me know as soon as you get the stills from the trail cam, right?"

"That I can do. And be sure to drop off that skull on your way into the Indigo Tea Shop tomorrow, will you?" Riley said.

"Count on it."

Theodosia was a little worried that Riley was going to play this investigation close to the vest—and that wasn't good. She had to find a way to gather more information. Maybe if she interviewed some of the witnesses herself. And, of course, spoke with Bettina. As Jamie's fiancée, Bettina had to have the inside track, right?

With thoughts of a faceless killer swirling in her head, Theodosia ran upstairs to her combination bedroom / sitting room and changed into a hoodie, jogging pants, and running shoes. Then she headed out the back door with Earl Grey for a late afternoon run. She figured she'd either clear her head completely—or come up with some fantastic insight.

But by the time she hit White Point Garden at the tip of the peninsula, no brilliant ideas had popped like kernels of corn in her brain.

Come on, brain, do your thing.

But, no, nothing seemed to light up in her prefrontal cortex.

Oh well.

Earl Grey, on the other hand, was suddenly invigorated by the waves crashing along the shore, by the salty sea breeze rushing in, and several other dogs up ahead of them, and he fairly pulled Theodosia along.

Theodosia decided to go with the flow and let him take the lead. After all, White Point Garden was one of her favorite places. Charleston Harbor encircled most of the point, giving the almost six-acre park a slightly untamed atmosphere. Marauding pirates had been hanged here. Now cannons and stacks of cannonballs were on display, as well as statues, a gazebo, and a World War I howitzer. Waves crashed onto the shore, depositing sea glass and broken shells. Once, years ago, Theodosia had even found a shark's tooth. She'd had a marine biologist at the South Carolina Aquarium look at it, and he'd determined it was from the Pliocene epoch, some four million years ago. Haley had urged her to wear the tooth around her neck on a gold chain like a surfer; Drayton had been horrified by the idea. Drayton had won out.

Theodosia and Earl Grey changed course and ran down South Battery Street, then turned on Legare Street. Here were fantastical old homes built in the Federal, Georgian, Italianate, and Classic Revival style. Most were three stories; many featured columns and capitals, hipped roofs, pointed arches, and porte cocheres built as side entrances for a horse and carriage.

In late fall, when the traditional Lamplighter Tour was held, many of these homes were opened to the public. Over the years, Theodosia had been tapped to serve tea at several of these homes, so she'd been privy to exploring their interiors and had seen dramatic free-flying staircases, French marble fireplaces, gorgeous woodwork, private libraries, and backyards that featured elaborate gardens, fountains, and statuary.

As the sun began to set and the horizon was smudged with

purple and blue, a few of these homes turned on the lights of their elaborate Halloween displays.

One of the homes was decorated to the nines. It had a rickety fence in the front yard that surrounded a dozen fake tombstones, a machine that puffed out streams of purple fog, and at least a dozen skeletons dressed as pirates. These bony creatures were clustered on the main portico as well as on the second- and third-floor balconies. And up on the roof—was that Jack Sparrow leering down?

Theodosia was pretty sure it was as she hurried home.

7

Monday morning at the Indigo Tea Shop found Theodosia, Drayton, and Haley sipping cups of jade green Ambootia Estate organic tea and rehashing the bizarre events of Saturday before they opened for the day. Everyone seemed to have a different theory about what had happened and why, though they all shared the feeling of being upended by Celeste's death and Jamie's injuries.

"I didn't really know Celeste all that well," Haley said. "But I used to see her working out at Core Yoga, and she seemed super nice."

"She *was* nice," Theodosia said. In the few times she'd talked to Celeste, the girl had seemed smart, wickedly funny, and full of life.

"It kinda rocks your world when somebody is killed like that. Somebody you *know*," Haley said.

"It shows that life can turn on a dime," Drayton said.

"But we're not talking about life," Haley said. "We're talking about Celeste's *death*."

"It was merely a figure of speech. I meant no harm," Drayton said. He touched a hand to Haley's shoulder. "I feel as awful as you do."

"And the wedding, that beautiful outdoor wedding, was completely ruined," Theodosia said.

Haley bobbed her head. "I know. I'd never been to a wedding at a real-deal flower farm before. It would have been incredible. I mean, did you see Bettina's dress?"

"Brand new but constructed of antique lace," Theodosia said. "Custom designed just for her."

"Gosh, I sure hope that sheriff guy is hard at work on this case," Haley said.

"Sheriff Ambourn? I'm sure he is. He and his deputies seemed quite capable," Theodosia said.

"Have you heard anything about that DNR trail camera?" Drayton asked.

"I'm still waiting to hear from Riley," Theodosia said.

Haley looked suddenly interested. "What trail camera?"

So Theodosia told Haley about how she and Riley had gone to Kipley Park, walked down the trail, and found a camera.

"Do you think the killer's face was caught on camera?" Haley asked. "That would be great if the police could identify him."

"Fingers crossed," Theodosia said.

"For sure," Haley said. When she started to get up from the table, Drayton touched a hand to her arm. "Hang on a minute. There's more."

Haley looked flustered. "There's more?"

"Tell her, Theo."

So Theodosia told Haley about taking their trip to the hospital yesterday, talking to Jamie, and the skull being delivered on Jamie's luncheon tray.

"Whoa, whoa, whoa," Haley cried, her baby blue eyes

opening wide as she reared back in her chair. "A real skull? Like, dug up from a grave?"

"It turned out to be plastic," Drayton said.

"How do you know that?" Haley liked to be scared, but not too scared.

"I got an expert opinion," Theodosia said. "From a nurse."

"That's crazy. Who would sneak into a hospital and leave a skull like that?" Haley said. "You're sure it was intended for Jamie? That it wasn't just a Halloween prank?"

"I think it was definitely put there to frighten Jamie," Theodosia said.

"So the killer is out there, waiting and watching," Haley said. "That's kinda scary." She gave a little shiver as her Apple Watch suddenly chimed. "My scones!" she said, suddenly all business. "I gotta take my cinnamon scones out of the oven."

Haley disappeared into the kitchen while Theodosia and Drayton lingered over a second cup of tea.

"I know you've pulled Riley into this murder, but are you going to get involved yourself?" Drayton asked Theodosia.

"I'd say I'm already involved."

"You know what I'm talking about, I mean *involved* involved."

"I don't know. I have to admit it's a strange case."

"And right up your alley," Drayton said. "The kind of thing that lets you do some amateur investigating." He considered his words for a few moments, then frowned. "Although we do have a rather hectic week ahead of us."

"Every week is busy," Theodosia said.

"But this week is going to be even more hectic," Drayton said as Haley wandered back into the tea room with a tray full of scones.

"You want me to stick these in the glass cake saver on the counter?" Haley asked Theodosia.

"Please," Theodosia said. "And, Haley, they smell delicious."

"Thanks."

But Drayton was still in deep worry mode. "We've got our Under the Tuscan Sun Tea tomorrow, our Victorian Halloween Tea on Wednesday, and our Harvest Tea on Friday."

"Don't forget we're supposed to serve tea, scones, and cookies at the cemetery crawl on Wednesday night," Haley said. "Although I think the historical people are calling the event something else."

"The official title is A Walk Among the Tombstones," Drayton said. "And it's happening citywide. There'll be guided candlelight tours through all of Charleston's historic cemeteries. Magnolia Cemetery, St. Philips, St. Michael's, St. Lawrence, and the Unitarian Church Graveyard."

"Which cemetery are we going to?" Haley asked.

"St. Philips," Theodosia said.

"So just down the block from us," Haley said. "Should be easy-peasy." She stopped short and added, "Unless something weird happens."

"We're serving tea and scones in what's been called one of the most haunted places on earth," Drayton said. "What could possibly go wrong?"

They got ready for morning tea then. Drayton stepped behind the front counter to survey his floor-to-ceiling shelves of tea tins while Theodosia bustled about the tea room, readying her tables.

"I'm thinking Grand Keemun and Earl Grey for morning offerings," Drayton said as he deftly plucked tea tins off the shelf. "Unless you have an opinion otherwise."

"You know I always leave tea choices up to you," Theodosia

said. In the six or so years they'd worked together, Drayton had never had a misstep when it came to tea. No, he was a true expert and aficionado, able to discern between Goomtee Garden Assam and Namring Garden Assam, as well as between China's Mao Jiang and traditional Gunpowder green teas. And should a tea exhibit a hint of bakiness or the smallest loss of flavor, it was tossed out immediately.

Theodosia placed woven bamboo place mats on all the tables, then opened one of her antique highboys to study her various sets of dishes. Because it was kind of a down day, she chose Apple Blossom by Haviland. It was a lovely pattern that always brought a smile to her face. And the teacups were particularly cute with their small round handles.

For Theodosia it was a joy to work in her tea room. She placed cups, saucers, butter knives, spoons, pitchers of cream, and bowls of sugar on the tables.

Let's see, what else?

Candles. Another peek in one of her cupboards and she pulled out tall silver candleholders with white tapers. Perfect and elegant. That done, she gazed around her tea room with a renewed sense of pride. The French crystal chandelier that hung overhead imparted a sort of warm Rembrandt lighting, as Drayton liked to call it. The pegged heart pine floors were covered with slightly faded Oriental rugs, the leaded windows were swagged with blue toile curtains, and a small stone fireplace added an extra touch of coziness. The brick walls held framed etchings of Charleston Harbor as well as grapevine wreaths that Theodosia had decorated with ribbons and small, colorful teacups. All told, the Indigo Tea Shop was a quasi-British, semi-country-French affair that drew locals as well as tourists who flocked to the elegant B and Bs in the surrounding Historic District.

* * *

At precisely nine o'clock Theodosia hung out her hand-painted, curlicued sign that said OPEN FOR TEA AND LIGHT LUNCHES. And at nine oh two customers began to arrive. Theodosia greeted her guests, seated them, and gave a quick rundown on the day's baked offerings, which included cinnamon scones, lemon tea bread, and British-style crumpets. Then Theodosia ran the orders into the kitchen while Drayton prepped tea orders.

Business remained steady this morning, and Theodosia was so caught up in answering questions about tea—and how to properly slice a scone (lengthwise, of course)—that she almost forgot about Saturday's tragedy.

Until a woman walked through her front door, looked around the tea room with a certain amount of intensity, then rested her gaze on Theodosia. A woman that was the spitting image of Celeste!

Theodosia felt as if she'd been jolted by a bolt of lightning. What was going on? This couldn't be Celeste, could it? Unless Celeste had somehow pulled off a miracle and risen from the dead!

8

"Theodosia?" the woman said.

Feeling as if the world had suddenly tilted on its axis, Theodosia struggled to regain her composure as she walked toward the Celeste look-alike. "I'm sorry," she said. "You startled me for a moment. You look exactly like . . ."

"Like my sister, Celeste?"

Theodosia's answer was a sharp "Oh," accompanied by a small puff of air.

The woman offered Theodosia a faint smile. "I didn't mean to scare you. Celeste and I were often mistaken for twins even though I'm a year older."

"Your poor sister, you . . . you have my heartfelt sympathy."

"Thank you, I appreciate your condolences. And I suppose I should introduce myself. I'm Sabrina Haynes."

"Won't you come in?" Theodosia said. "And, oh, please sit down. Let me bring you something." She was babbling slightly and knew it. "And, Drayton . . ." She held up a hand and gave Drayton the high sign. "A pot of strong tea?"

Drayton nodded. "Coming right up."

Once Theodosia had brought Sabrina a pot of black orchid tea and a cinnamon scone, she sat down at the table across from her. Most of her guests were busy eating and sipping tea, so she had a few moments to spare.

"Again, I'm so very sorry for your loss," Theodosia said.

Sabrina nodded. "I drove to the flower farm Saturday, all primped and prettied, ready for Bettina and Jamie's wedding. And when I arrived, all I saw were two ambulances pulling away, lights and sirens going like crazy. When I was finally able to corner one of the deputies, he told me what had happened. He also told me that you were the one who'd rushed in to help. That you moved heaven and earth to pull Celeste out of that . . . disaster area." Sabrina's eyes glistened with tears. "I wanted to talk to you then, but I thought it was more important to follow the ambulance to the hospital."

"Absolutely," Theodosia said. She reached over and patted Sabrina's hand.

"Not that it did any good. When I got to the ER, she was already gone," Sabrina said.

"I'm so sorry," Theodosia whispered. "I wish I could have done more. We had all hoped for a better . . ." She fished around for the right word. "Outcome."

"From what Sheriff Ambourn told my family, you and the EMTs did all you could." Sabrina paused as she pulled out a hankie and wiped her eyes. "The sheriff also told us that he believes the greenhouse might have been sabotaged."

"I have to say, that's my opinion as well," Theodosia said. "It was too horrific a crash for it to have happened on its own."

"So you think someone in the wedding party was being targeted?"

"I suppose you could look at it that way, though it would

have been difficult to predict who'd walk through that door first. Someone from the wedding party, one of the guests, maybe a server."

"Do you think Jamie was the intended target?" Sabrina asked. Her tears had dried and her voice had suddenly taken on a sharp edge.

"Why do you think it was Jamie?" Theodosia asked.

"I live nearby in Moncks Corner, so I've run into Jamie from time to time. Mostly at trendy bars like Ichabod's and the Pickled Parrot. And because, back in the day, Jamie had a reputation as a bit of a *player*."

A player? In Theodosia's mind that meant Jamie was a ladies' man, a serial dater. Maybe a one-night stand kind of guy.

"From what I've seen, Jamie has always been totally committed to Bettina," Theodosia said. For some reason she felt the need to defend him.

"I'm sure he is. Now." Sabrina hesitated for a moment, then added, "The other thing I wondered about . . ."

"Yes?"

"Celeste has a rather nasty ex-boyfriend, a guy by the name of Karl Rueff. His name is pronounced *roof*, like the roof of a house. He's what you might call *rough trade*."

That didn't sound good to Theodosia. "Rough enough to kill someone?"

"Maybe."

"But how would this ex have predicted that Celeste would be the first to rush into the greenhouse?"

"Maybe because Celeste has always been flighty and impulsive?" Sabrina said. "Always snooping around, always trying to be first in line for everything."

"I hear you, but it still sounds awfully far-fetched."

"Yes," Sabrina said. "You're probably right." She sighed,

then shoved her untouched scone aside. "I'm sorry, I guess I'm not particularly hungry."

"Don't worry about it," Theodosia said.

"What I really wanted was to come here and thank you."

"Like I said, I wish I could have done more."

"You did what you could." Sabrina pushed back from the table and stood up. "Now I'm off to the airport to pick up my parents. They're flying in from Chicago. The plan, as of this moment, is to hold a visitation here in Charleston tomorrow evening, then fly Celeste's body back to Chicago for a proper funeral and burial."

"Will you let me know when the visitation details are finalized?" Theodosia said. "I'd like to come."

Sabrina gave a sad smile. "Of course."

"She didn't touch her tea," Drayton said once Sabrina had left.

"Nor her scone," Theodosia said. "Too upset, too sad."

"Yes, I overheard most of your conversation. Such an awful thing, her sister's young life cut so short."

"Sabrina wondered if maybe Jamie was the intended target and not Celeste."

"It's certainly a plausible theory, though there's still no actual proof. For all we know it could have been a random thing," Drayton said as he measured six scoops of Pouchong into a bright orange teapot.

"Maybe."

But deep down, Theodosia didn't think it had been random at all. And that worried her. Especially in light of the fake skull yesterday. It felt like someone very crafty and super nasty was targeting Jamie Wilkes.

"Sabrina also mentioned a guy by the name of Karl Rueff,

who is Celeste's ex-boyfriend. She said he was kind of a hard case."

"Meaning?" Drayton said.

"Sabrina didn't go into the particulars, and I didn't ask." Theodosia gazed at Drayton. "Maybe I should have."

"And maybe Sabrina is just terribly sad and everything looks bleak to her," Drayton said.

"You're probably right. But now that I know about Karl Rueff, I wouldn't mind knowing a little more."

"See?" Drayton said. "You're investigating."

Some thirty minutes later, when the Indigo Tea Shop was redolent with spicy aromas and kettles chirped like anxious birds, Delaine and Bettina came bursting in.

"How's Jamie?" was Theodosia's first question.

"Much better," Bettina said, taking a deep, shuddering breath. "He's getting out of the hospital tomorrow. And I just got a call from Celeste's family. Apparently, the medical examiner determined that she died from a shard of glass that punctured her chest and collapsed a lung."

"Sliced right through her collarbone," Delaine said in a harsh voice.

"Celeste's sister was just here," Theodosia said.

"You're talking about Sabrina?" Bettina said. "I hope you don't mind, but I told Sabrina that you were, like, a first responder. That you rushed in to help before anyone else did."

Delaine made a noise in the back of her throat. She knew darn well that she'd stood there like a statue. Paralyzed with fear.

"Delaine?" Theodosia said. "You seem awfully upset."

Delaine shook her head fiercely. "Because I really can't bear to talk any more about the accident."

"Stop calling it an accident," Bettina hissed to her aunt as Theodosia led them to a table. "I for one am spitting mad about this and intend to get to the bottom of it. I mean, was Jamie the intended target or was it Celeste? I need to *know*!" She pulled out her chair and plopped down hard.

"Just off the top of my head I'd probably say Jamie," Theodosia said.

Which caused the normally stiff-upper-lip Bettina to burst into tears.

"Shush," Delaine warned as she took a quick look around, then sat down. "Please don't make a scene."

Tears streaming down her face, Bettina fixed Delaine with an incredulous look. "Don't make a *scene*? My wedding was a total catastrophe, my best friend is dead, and my fiancé is in the hospital. Now *you're* telling *me* not to make a *scene*?" Bettina dabbed at her reddened eyes with a hankie. "You're one to talk. You're the Queen of Scenes. You throw a hissy fit if your pantyhose gets a run, if you lose an earring."

"I do not," Delaine pouted.

"Ladies," Theodosia said. "Let's stick to the issue at hand, shall we?"

"Sure, okay," Bettina said with a sniffle. "The thing is, why would someone want to hurt Jamie? Or, worse yet, try to *kill* him? It doesn't make any sense."

"Not a bit," Delaine said.

"And that skull yesterday? What was *that* all about?" Bettina said.

Delaine gave a little shudder. "So creepy."

"I don't know what the skull was for," Theodosia said. "Unless someone wanted to frighten Jamie."

"But who?" Bettina asked. "And why? Jamie's a pussycat, the sweetest guy you'd ever want to meet."

Delaine nodded. "Sweet."

Theodosia wondered about Sabrina's assessment of Jamie. She'd called him a player. Was Jamie a player, a ladies' man? Was there an ex-girlfriend out there who wanted to target him? Or what about Martin Hunt, the man Jamie mentioned yesterday? Hunt might still have been smarting over his financial losses and finally decided to retaliate. Lots of theories were swirling in Theodosia's brain, but nothing had started to gel yet.

"I have to tend to my guests right now," Theodosia said. "But if you two ladies want to stick around for lunch, we can talk more afterwards."

"Well, I . . . ," Delaine started to say.

"Absolutely," Bettina said.

Taking a page from *Downton Abbey*, Haley had come up with three prix fixe luncheon choices: the Mrs. Patmore, the Mrs. Hughes, and the Lady Violet Crawley. All included a cinnamon scone and a bowl of tomato bisque, but they differed on entrées. The Mrs. Patmore entrée was a ploughman's lunch of turkey meat loaf, cheddar cheese, and sourdough bread. The Mrs. Hughes a chicken salad and grape tea sandwich. And the Lady Violet Crawley a crab salad tea sandwich.

Theodosia took orders, delivered tea, and checked in with Haley.

"Our guests are going wild for your luncheon specials," she told Haley. "They all love the *Downton Abbey* characters so much and think you've perfectly matched the food to their personalities."

"Good to hear," Haley said as she ladled tomato bisque into six waiting bowls. "And kind of easy to do, too." She dusted her hands together and said, "Okay, what else?" Then, "Croutons.

How could I forget croutons?" She grabbed a plastic container full of homemade croutons and liberally sprinkled them on top of the bisque. "Say, I saw Delaine and Bettina out there, what do they want for lunch?"

"Why don't you make up two orders of the Lady Violet Crawley," Theodosia said. "They'll for sure love that."

As their guests sipped tea and enjoyed their luncheons, Theodosia and Drayton both made the rounds, pouring refills on tea and chatting away. Finally, Theodosia had a chance to sit down with Bettina and Delaine again.

"How's lunch?" Theodosia asked. "Is there anything else I can get you?"

Delaine tapped a scarlet-tipped fingernail against the table and said, "How about a little help?"

Theodosia's brows shot up. "Excuse me?"

Delaine nudged Bettina with an elbow. "You ask her."

"Look, I'm just going to come right out and say this," Bettina said. "We need your expertise."

"Regarding . . . ?"

"Celeste's murder. And Jamie. Especially Jamie."

"I'd say you've probably got all the help you need," Theodosia said. "Sheriff Ambourn is undoubtedly interviewing witnesses, and Riley promised to follow up on the footprint casts, trail cam video, and skull—as well as conduct some of his own interviews."

"That's all well and good, but we want *you*," Delaine said emphatically.

Theodosia shook her head. "No, you really don't." It was an interesting case—well, actually it was downright fascinating—but she had a lot on her plate. Didn't she?

"Excuse me," Delaine said. Suddenly, she'd morphed into

full Miss Bossy Pants mode. "But *you're* the one with the rather stellar track record when it comes to solving strange cases."

Theodosia shrugged. "I'm not exactly Miss Marple. All I did was get lucky a few times."

Delaine waved an index finger at her. "No, sweetie, you got smart! You've got a computer for a brain, an investigator's curiosity, and a killer instinct."

"It's a tricky case, I wouldn't want to get in the way," Theodosia said. *In fact, I've been warned not to.*

"Please reconsider," Bettina begged. "You saw how distraught Sabrina is and how badly Jamie was hurt. Just go have another conversation with Jamie, will you? He's feeling better—thanks to a boatload of pain pills, I guess—but maybe you could ask him a few more pertinent questions. See what's really going on with him, figure out if he has any serious enemies out there."

I know he does, Theodosia thought to herself, but said to Bettina, "I would think you'd know more about that."

"No, I . . . I've been so focused on my wedding that I kind of defocused on Jamie. If that's an actual word."

"Oh, it is," Delaine assured her.

"Okay, tell me what you know about Martin Hunt," Theodosia said.

"Who?" Bettina asked.

"Hunt owns Hunt and Peck," Delaine said. "A men's shop geared toward men who don't actually own a yacht or a polo pony, but are into that stuck-up, high-end sporty look."

Bettina looked nervous. "Why are you asking about this Martin Hunt person?"

"Because Jamie told me that Hunt lost a pile of money with his investments at Hamilton and McLaughlin."

"I didn't know that," Delaine said.

"Neither did I," Bettina said. Then, "Jeez, since when is losing money a reason to kill somebody?"

"Are you serious?" Delaine said. "These days people are shot and killed for less than twenty bucks." Her eyes grew bigger and her voice more strident. "I mean, cars are hijacked for the sake of a joyride. Flash mobs invade drugstores just to steal cold medicine and razor blades. *Razor blades*, for heaven's sake!"

In the end, after all Bettina's pleading and Delaine's histrionics, Theodosia agreed to look into things. Promised to talk to Jamie again, put out a few feelers, and try to get a meeting with Martin Hunt.

Bettina and Delaine thanked Theodosia profusely and left, seemingly satisfied by her promise of a semi-shadow investigation. But once they were gone, Theodosia wondered exactly how she was going to manage her tea shop along with all that investigating. Which was precisely when Pete Riley walked through the front door.

Was this perhaps a light at the end of the tunnel? Did he have some good news for her?

9

"Hey there," Theodosia exclaimed. "What a lovely surprise." She sprinted to the door, grabbed Riley by the hand, and pulled him to one of the tables. "I'm guessing you have something for me?"

"It's something all right," Riley said as he plopped down in one of Theodosia's antique captain's chairs.

"The stills from the trail cam?" Theodosia felt a flutter of anticipation as she sat down across from him.

Riley stuck a hand inside his leather jacket and pulled out three four-by-six photos. "The DNR was able to pull three blurry stills from that trail cam footage. But I don't think they're going to solve any mysteries."

"Let's take a look," Theodosia said.

Riley spread them out on the table like a blackjack dealer flipping out cards. "You see? There was a person walking by, but it's hard to tell what's going on, or even if it's a man or a woman."

Theodosia studied the three stills. "You're right." They were grainy black-and-white, blurry to the point of being practically abstract. Still, she could discern that a human form had been caught from the side at a low angle. She could make out the head and shoulders, one arm, legs.

"Can't even tell what they're wearing," Riley said.

"Not really." But as Theodosia scanned the images more carefully, her eyes were drawn to one small thing. "Except for his shoes."

Riley wrinkled his brow. "What are you seeing that I'm not?"

Theodosia touched one of the blurry stills. "You see where the bottom half of this still is slightly more distinct? Down near his feet? I'd almost bet this person was wearing Sorel boots. You see that little white squiggle? I think it's their polar bear logo."

Riley squinted at it. "Okay, maybe it's a bear. But how can you be sure?"

"For one thing, I own a pair of Sorel hiking boots with the exact same logo on them. And I'll wager you a hundred bucks that if you check the photos and plaster casts that the Crime Scene techs pulled from behind the greenhouse, you'll find they match the waffle sole of a Sorel boot."

"Okay, that's something," Riley said. "A killer who wears Sorel boots. That should narrow it down. Not."

"Hey," Theodosia said. "What do you want? At least it's *some* kind of clue."

"I suppose you're right. Okay, I'll shoot these over to Sheriff Ambourn so he can follow up on his end as well."

"Have you started interviewing witnesses?" Theodosia asked.

Riley shrugged. "Working on it."

"Anything interesting turn up yet?"

"Nope. How about you?"

Theodosia gave a dimpled smile. "Wouldn't you like to know?"

"Is your Detective Riley onto something?" Drayton asked once Riley had been packed off with a take-out cup of tea and a bag of scones.

"He had three blurry stills that the Department of Natural Resources people pulled off a trail cam in Kipley Park. You could kind of see a human figure, but what interested me most was the fact that you could make out a Sorel logo on one of the guy's boots."

"That sounds promising."

"Riley wasn't all that impressed, but I think it could lead to something," Theodosia said.

"Like the actual killer?" Drayton asked.

"Not yet, but it's a step in the right direction." She thought for a minute, then pulled out her cell phone and wandered back to her office. Maybe Sheriff Ambourn had something to add to the Sorel boot clue?

Theodosia called the sheriff's office, asked to talk to Sheriff Ambourn, and was put on hold for almost five minutes. When the sheriff finally came on the line, she identified herself and asked how the investigation was going.

"Who is this again?" Sheriff Ambourn asked.

"Theodosia Browning. We met Saturday. I was the one who crawled under the table and pulled that girl out?"

"You're the woman with the curly auburn hair."

"That's me."

"Heck of a thing you did there," Sheriff Ambourn said. "Fast thinking."

"Not fast enough. Sheriff, I was wondering if you've come up with anything new."

"Nope, not yet. Me and my boys are working it, though. Thanks so much for calling."

And with that he hung up.

"Did the sheriff have any new information?" Drayton asked as Theodosia walked back to the front counter.

Theodosia shook her head. "The sheriff was extremely tight-lipped. I got the feeling that even if there *was* a break in the case, he wouldn't tell me."

"He blew you off?"

"Essentially."

"That's Johnny Law for you. But maybe . . ." Drayton stopped short as the front door flew open and Bill Glass came stomping in.

"*You*," Glass said, pointing an accusing finger at Theodosia. "I need to have a serious conversation with *you*."

"Glass," Theodosia muttered under her breath. "I should have known." Bill Glass was the editor and publisher of *Shooting Star*, a local gossip rag. Which meant he was always on the prowl for society scuttlebutt, news of the weird and wacky, and, in this case, details over a suspected murder.

"I heard what happened at that flower farm and I want the story," Glass demanded. "The whole story."

"I don't have the whole story," Theodosia said.

"Bull wacky!" Glass thundered.

"Say now," Drayton said in his sternest tone. "Kindly restrain yourself, there are ladies and gentlemen present in this establishment."

"Okay, okay," Glass said in a conciliatory tone. "Sorry. It's just that I'm on deadline." He unslung a camera from around his neck and stared at Theodosia.

Theodosia stared back. Mostly because Glass looked so crazy-awful today. He wore a brown corduroy jacket with a rip on the right shoulder seam, bilious green slacks, and sloppy high-top tennis shoes. He wasn't a bad-looking man, with his olive complexion and dark slicked-back hair, but his taste in clothes ran the gamut from ragamuffin to ruffian. Theodosia wondered, once again, how Glass managed to pick up as much society gossip as he did, since he basically had the charisma of a reptile. On the other hand, he was so outlandish that people probably fed him juicy tidbits just to make him go away. Yup, that had to be it.

"I'm afraid we have nothing for you, Glass," Drayton said.

"Aw, not even a cup of tea?" Glass had switched to whiny mode.

"Only if it's to go," Theodosia said.

Glass's face crumpled. "Sounds like a bribe."

"Because it is," Drayton said.

"Take it or leave it," Theodosia said.

"Awright, I'll take it," Glass said. "But you gotta give me something."

"The greenhouse collapsed and poor Celeste Haynes was killed," Theodosia said.

"That's it?" Glass had a cagey look on his face. "Then why are the police involved?"

"Are they?" Theodosia said. She was all innocence.

"That's what my contact in the department says." He accepted the cup of tea that Drayton handed him and added, "I know you're up to something, Theodosia Browning, and I'm going to find out what it is."

"Good day," Drayton said. "Nice of you to drop in."

Bill Glass lifted his cup in Theodosia's direction and said, "But I'll be back."

* * *

With the afternoon fading away, Theodosia took a quick peek at her watch and said, "Drayton, can you hold down the fort for a while?"

"What are you up to?"

"I want to run over to Hunt and Peck and talk to Martin Hunt."

"The guy who lost all the money in the stock market?" Drayton said.

"The one who smacked Jamie in the eye," Theodosia said.

"Okay. But if he swings at you, be prepared to duck!"

Theodosia jumped into her Jeep and drove over to King Street. She lucked out and found a parking spot just two doors down from Hunt and Peck. As she walked toward the men's shop, she happened to peek in the window of Cornucopia Antiques. And there, in the front window, was a perfect blue-and-white Meissen teapot.

Be still my heart, was her first thought. As well as, *I wonder if I can afford it.*

Asking was free, so Theodosia went inside. And found herself in an antique shop that was tiny, tidy, and glittering with Majolica porcelain, French Sèvres bisque statues, bronze sculptures, jardinieres, and Chinese lacquer. Chandeliers dangled from the ceiling, and glass cases held jewelry and antique perfume bottles.

How is it I've never been in here? Theodosia wondered. Although there were so many delightful antique shops in Charleston that she'd barely scraped the surface.

A silver-haired woman in a silver-gray dress looked up from a spinet desk in the back of the shop and smiled. "Can I help you?"

"I couldn't help but notice the Meissen teapot in your front window," Theodosia said.

"Yes, that one's a honey," the woman said. She stood up and said, "I'm Grace Warner by the way, welcome to Cornucopia Antiques."

"Theodosia Browning," Theodosia said.

Grace studied her for a moment, then snapped her fingers. "You're the tea shop lady, aren't you?"

"Guilty as charged."

"No wonder you have an eye for the Meissen," Grace Warner said. "Here, let me pull it from the display so you can take a nice up close look at it." Grace lifted the teapot out of the window, spun about, and handed it to Theodosia. "As you can see, it's in remarkable condition."

Theodosia studied the teapot. It was an exquisite blue-and-white porcelain teapot with metal mounts securing the handle. When she turned it over, there was the maker's mark of crossed swords and a price tag that said four hundred dollars.

"Authentic and it has some age on it," Theodosia remarked.

"Early eighteenth century," Grace said. "Maybe you'd like to add it to your collection? I'm assuming you have a collection."

"Enough to fill a warehouse," Theodosia said. "But this one . . . this would be special."

"The jewel in the crown, perhaps?"

"Perhaps," Theodosia said. With some reluctance she handed the Meissen teapot back to Grace Warner. "Let me think about it." *And wish upon a star for an extra four hundred dollars.*

"Of course."

Theodosia thanked Warner for her help, then, still thinking about the Meissen teapot, dashed down the street and ducked into Hunt and Peck. Drayton and Delaine had both been spot-on in their description of the place, because Hunt and Peck looked like a spiffy men's club. The carpet was a dark hunter green, oil paintings of yachts and polo ponies hung on the walls, and there was rack after rack of hunting vests, tweed jackets, wool slacks, Barbour jackets, and handsome shirts. The place smelled like Cuban cigars, old books, and rugged leather, though Theodosia was pretty sure the scent came compliments of an aroma diffuser.

A young male clerk approached her immediately. He was slim, wore a tailored camel-hair sport coat and dark green twill slacks, and had the look of money about him. Theodosia pegged him as a scion from one of the old Charleston families.

"May I help you?" The young man's voice was melodic and his diction private-school precise.

"I'm looking for Martin Hunt," Theodosia said.

His eyebrows rose a notch. "You have an appointment?"

"Not really, I was in the neighborhood and thought I'd drop by."

"In that case, may I tell him who's calling?"

"Theodosia Browning."

"I'll be right back."

The clerk returned almost immediately. "You'll find Mr. Hunt's private office upstairs on the mezzanine," he said, then indicated the stairway on the sidewall. "Go on up."

"Thank you."

Theodosia climbed stairs covered in a whisper-soft carpet with a horseshoe pattern and found herself on the mezzanine. Here, fine wool suits and handsome tuxedos were on display, and there were leather and hobnailed club chairs for relaxing in, as well as two large three-way mirrors. She figured most of the tailoring was done up here.

"Miss Browning?" Martin Hunt emerged silently from behind a rack of shooting jackets. "You wanted to see me?"

"Yes, thank you," Theodosia said. She smiled at Hunt and decided he definitely had the look of a serious gym rat. His shoulders were so bulked up that his jackets must undoubtedly have been super tailored to fit a body that tapered to a narrow waist. He had short dark hair, piercing amber eyes, and a thin mouth poised over a square chin. The word *thug* danced in Theodosia's brain for a split second.

"How may I help you?" Hunt asked.

Theodosia decided to take a direct approach. "I'm here because I'm looking into the recent tragedy involving Celeste Haynes and Jamie Wilkes."

There was a hint of a smirk on Hunt's face when he said, "I heard what happened at that flower farm this past Saturday. Some bridesmaid chick got offed."

"And the groom, Jamie Wilkes, was seriously injured as well. I believe you know Mr. Wilkes?"

"Know him and would trust him about as far as I could spit a rat."

"I think Jamie might have been directly targeted," Theodosia said. "By whom, I don't know, but I'm checking all angles, talking to everyone who knew him."

Now Hunt showed a hint of a smile. "I'll bet that little weasel sent you sniffing in my direction, didn't he?"

"Jamie might have mentioned your name, yes."

"Well, I don't have any idea what happened. Who rigged that greenhouse or who was the intended target."

"You're quite sure about that?"

His jaw hardened. "Absolutely."

"Because Jamie mentioned that you—"

"Look, what's your interest in all this?" Hunt asked, cutting her off. "Are you some kind of private investigator?"

"Actually, I own the Indigo Tea Shop over on Church Street. But I'm a close friend of Bettina and Jamie's."

"Good old Bettina, the heartbreaker."

Theodosia narrowed her eyes. There was something peculiar about the way Hunt said that. "Heartbreaker. Why would you use that particular word? Were you two romantically involved?"

"No way, not me. As far as *Bettina*'s romances go, that's another story."

"How so?" Theodosia asked.

"Bettina. Where do I start?" Hunt rocked back on his heels. "Okay, if you want to run around playing amateur Sherlock Holmes—and it seems like you do—you need to take a look at Adam Lynch."

"Why is that? *Who* is that?"

"Lynch is Bettina's most recent ex-fiancé."

Theodosia's mouth opened in surprise, but no words came out.

"Oh, you don't know about that, huh?" Hunt said in a snarky tone. "The blushing little bride didn't happen to mention Adam Lynch?"

"No, she didn't."

"Adam Lynch, the poor sap, thought *he* was engaged to Bettina right up until the bitter end. When he finally found out—secondhand, I might add—that Bettina was engaged to Jamie Wilkes, Lynch went apeshit. Tried to win her back with bouquets of roses, candy, love notes . . ." Hunt chuckled. "When that didn't work, Adam Lynch slashed her tires, stalked her, and bombarded her with threatening calls."

"So he tried to harass her into loving him?" Theodosia said.

"Crazy, huh? Anyway, Lynch finally talked Bettina into getting together with him for a big come-to-brass-tacks meetin'. When Bettina showed up, he begged, cajoled, and screamed at her. When Bettina said no way was she getting back with him, Lynch hauled off and hit her. Popped her so hard he knocked out a tooth."

"Holy crap," Theodosia said. "So you're telling me this guy is dangerous?"

"Are you kidding?" Hunt said. "Adam Lynch is a freaking maniac."

10

"What do you think a blue-and-white Meissen teapot should cost?" Theodosia asked Drayton once she was back at the tea shop.

"I don't know. Maybe four or five hundred dollars?"

"You're right in the ballpark."

"Why? Do you intend to buy one?"

"Thinking about it. There was one in the window of Cornucopia Antiques just down the street from Hunt and Peck," Theodosia said.

"So what was the upshot of your errand? Time well spent discovering a coveted teapot or having a chat with Martin Hunt?"

"Both. And did I ever learn something important."

"I'm intrigued," Drayton said. "Do tell."

Theodosia quickly told Drayton about her conversation with Martin Hunt and how he'd revealed Bettina's former relationship—really, engagement—to a man by the name of Adam Lynch.

"Never heard of him," Drayton said. "What does he do?"

"No idea," Theodosia said. "But Hunt called this guy Lynch a 'freaking maniac.' Which is why we need to pay another visit to Jamie."

They finished up at the tea shop, pouring final cups of tea for a few lingering guests, then cashed them out, cleared tables, and swept the floor. By four o'clock they were on their way back to Roper Hospital. The sun's last rays were a bright orange smudge on the horizon as they traversed their way through the Historic District.

"This is one of my favorite times of day," Drayton said as they drove past a half dozen historic mansions. "The lights in these old homes are coming on, and you can peek in and see antique chandeliers dangling over dining room tables, fires being lit in cozy libraries, and folks sitting down to glasses of sherry."

"If the Great Gatsby lived in Charleston . . ."

"Exactly," Drayton said. "See how the sky has transformed into a marvelous purple haze—and when you gaze all the way down the street, golden lamps in wrought iron streetlights look like a string of rosary beads."

"I think that haze is compliments of Charleston Harbor," Theodosia said. "The rush of the Atlantic into the harbor shoots tiny beads of water into the air and—poof—suddenly they turn the landscape into a kind of pointillist painting."

"That's a lovely way to describe a pesky mist," Drayton said. "Though the humidity does seem to keep our flora and fauna well hydrated and . . . will you look at that!"

"What?"

"House up there on the corner."

Theodosia slowed down as they approached the corner of Montagu and Rutledge.

"Wow," she said. "I've never seen so many pumpkins." At least two hundred carved pumpkins lined the curb as well as the sidewalk leading to a quaint Victorian home with an enormous glass skylight on the third floor. "They're basically going to use pumpkins as luminaries. On Halloween night they'll undoubtedly light them all up."

"That will be quite the sight," Drayton said.

When they arrived at the hospital, Theodosia parked her Jeep in the underground garage, and they took the elevator up to Jamie's floor.

"You're sure he's still in the same room?" Drayton asked as they walked down a corridor that buzzed with nurses, respiratory techs, and aides. Probably all at the end of their shift.

"Pretty sure," Theodosia said. "Bettina and Delaine didn't mention a room change when they stopped by for lunch today."

"Good point."

Jamie was in his same room, sitting in a beige plastic recliner with a blanket folded across his lap. Bettina was sitting next to him, looking upbeat in a hot pink sweater and denim jeans.

"You came!" Bettina cried, a big smile lighting her face. "Theo, Drayton, thank you so much!"

"We're still very concerned about Jamie," Theodosia said.

"How are you feeling today?" Drayton asked Jamie. "Some better?"

"I guess," Jamie said. Some of the color had returned to his face, and his voice sounded stronger. "My parents were just here, and my mom thought I seemed better."

"You *look* better," Drayton said. "All perked up, which is always an excellent sign."

Bettina was still ebullient about their showing up. "I bet you've already done some investigating," she said to Theodosia. "I know there's not a whole lot to go on, but Aunt Delaine keeps telling me you're a regular Nancy Drew."

"I spoke with Martin Hunt today," Theodosia said. "Explained to him that I was interviewing anyone and everyone who'd had dealings with Jamie."

Bettina reached out and squeezed Jamie's hand. "See, I told you Theodosia was hot on the trail."

"And a few things came to light," Theodosia said.

"Uh-huh," Jamie said.

"We've been going on the supposition that Jamie was the intended target," Theodosia said. "When maybe Bettina's the one who's in danger."

"Me?" Bettina sat up as if she'd been touched with a hot poker. "Why would I be in danger?"

"Do you want to tell us about Adam Lynch?" Theodosia asked.

"What!" Bettina cried.

From the look of shock on Bettina's face, Theodosia knew she'd hit a nerve.

Jamie looked confused. "Who's Adam Lynch?"

"He's the man Bettina was engaged to before you," Theodosia said.

"*What?*" Jamie's jaw literally dropped.

"Oh, you didn't know?" Drayton said.

"I had no idea," Jamie said, throwing a questioning look at Bettina, who had now shrunk back in her chair, a flustered look on her face.

"You want to tell us about your Mr. Lynch?" Theodosia asked Bettina.

Bettina sat quietly for a few moments, plucking at her

engagement ring and rolling it around. "Maybe I should have brought this up earlier," she said, giving Jamie a searching look. "But I didn't want to upset you."

"You mean scare me off," Jamie said. He suddenly didn't look so drug addled and tired anymore.

"Well, that could be a part of it," Bettina admitted. "The truth of the matter is, I *was* engaged to Adam Lynch. But only for a few short weeks." Her eyes fluttered as if she'd been caught in a lie, which she kind of had been. "Then I met you and it was love at first sight. Obviously."

"Tell him about the breakup with Lynch," Theodosia said.

Bettina scrunched up her face. "It didn't go well."

"Give Jamie the whole story. Tell him what Lynch did when you told him you never wanted to see him again," Theodosia prompted.

"Long story short, he stalked me, harassed me, and knocked out my tooth," Bettina said.

"He *hit* you?" Jamie was aghast.

"You might say that," Bettina said in a small voice. Clearly, she was embarrassed beyond words.

Jamie sank back in his chair, trying to absorb what Bettina had told him. Then he said, "If this Lynch guy is still angry at Bettina, *he* could have been the one who rigged the greenhouse." He stared at Theodosia. "Right?"

"It's certainly a possibility," Theodosia said.

"How on earth did you meet this crazy person?" Drayton asked Bettina.

"I met Adam Lynch through Aunt Delaine," Bettina said. "Lynch was in charge of the Cotton Duck website. Did updates, videos of her fashion shows and events, things like that."

"Wait a minute, does Lynch *still* handle the Cotton Duck website?" Jamie asked.

"Um, maybe?" Bettina said. She started crying and hiccupping at the same time, flailing an arm out to try and grab a tissue.

"Seriously?" Jamie said. He passed Bettina a box of tissues but seemed stunned by her rather unsettling revelation.

"But I know Lynch has other accounts as well," Bettina sniffled.

"Wait a minute, time-out," Jamie said. He touched a hand to his head as if trying to organize and compress his thoughts, then said, "So Adam Lynch could have been targeting Bettina at the wedding?"

Bettina was shaking her head. "No, no. If that was the case, how would Lynch know *I'd* be the one to walk through that door first?"

"I have an answer for that," Theodosia said. "The logical assumption is that, at the conclusion of your wedding ceremony, you and Jamie would walk down the aisle and head into the greenhouse for the reception. And Jamie, being a fine Southern gentleman with impeccable manners, would've held the door open so you could enter first."

"Oh man, I would have!" Jamie cried. He reached a shaky hand over to grab a glass of water, spilled some, managed to gain control, and took a drink. Finally, he set the glass down and said, "What happens now?"

"For one thing, I'd like the key to your apartment," Theodosia said.

"Okay," Jamie said, pointing to a set of built-in drawers. "It's in there with my wallet and stuff. But why?"

"Just to take a look around," Theodosia said. "Is that a problem?"

Bettina reached over and touched a hand to his knee. "Remember, sweetie, Theodosia promised to dig into things for us." She dabbed at her eyes. "Even though they're not always pleasant things."

"Isn't that what the police are doing?" Jamie asked.

"Sure," Bettina said. "But Theodosia is attacking this from a completely different angle." She wiped away a few more tears and added, "But I still have a hunch about who rigged the greenhouse."

Theodosia gazed at her. "You do? Who do you think it was?"

"I believe that Martin Hunt is guilty as sin. Hunt lost a lot of money and he's always going to blame Jamie. He's never going to let it go!"

"Well, that was a joy," Drayton said as they descended in the hospital elevator. "I actually felt bad for Bettina."

"It had to be done," Theodosia said. "Jamie needed to know about Bettina's involvement with Adam Lynch. And what he did to her."

"You think he'll change his mind about marrying her?"

"No idea," Theodosia said as a bell *dinged* and the elevator door slid open. "Might make them both take their relationship a little more seriously."

"And that's a good thing?" Drayton said.

"I think it's more important than worrying about veils, flower bouquets, and what your signature color's going to be."

"All this intrigue has made me hungry," Drayton said. He glanced at his watch, a vintage Patek Philippe that seemed to run perpetually slow. "We have time for a light supper, don't we? Before we go rummaging through that boy's apartment."

"Works for me," Theodosia said. "Where would you like to go?"

Theodosia and Drayton ended up at Magnolia's on East Bay

Street. It was dark and clubby, a little bit casual, but with flickering candles and white linen tablecloths.

"This is perfect," Drayton said as they scanned their menus. "Good South Carolina staples, but from a chef who's cooked all over the world."

Theodosia ordered the blue crab bisque for her appetizer and the blackened catfish for her entrée. Drayton opted for an appetizer of sea scallops with johnnycakes and low-country bouillabaisse for his entrée. They talked about splitting a bottle of wine, but Theodosia decided she'd rather have bottled water, so Drayton ordered a glass of Russian River chardonnay.

As they enjoyed their dinners, they talked about the two suspects, Martin Hunt and Adam Lynch.

"You think there'll be more?" Drayton asked. "Suspects, I mean."

"We've only been investigating for about a day and a half, and look what we've come up with."

"What *you've* come up with," Drayton pointed out.

"Oh no, you're in this up to your eyeballs, too. As long as we keep poking around, more suspects are bound to crawl out of the woodwork."

"Which will make it even harder to solve this mystery, because that's surely what it is. A murder mystery."

"It's tricky though," Theodosia said. She took a piece of sourdough from the bread basket and spread it with butter. "Because we're still not sure who the intended victim was. As things stand right now, it could have been Bettina, Jamie, or Celeste."

"Even though Celeste was the victim, something tells me she was an *unintended* victim," Drayton said.

"Simply collateral damage," Theodosia said, nodding. "Which means figuring this out is even more critical."

"How so?"

"If there's a stone-cold killer intent on murdering either Bettina or Jamie, there's a good chance he'll try again."

Drayton took a sip of wine, gazed at Theodosia, and said, "Mercy."

11

The night sky was dark when Theodosia and Drayton arrived at Jamie's apartment on America Street. Per his directions, his place was a small one-bedroom unit on the back side of a three-story wood-frame building.

"This has to be it, right?" Theodosia said to Drayton as they pulled to the curb.

Drayton peered through the gloom. "Appears to be an old Charleston single house that fell into disrepair and was cut up into a crazy quilt of apartments. Probably by a slum landlord," he added.

"There are lots of sketchy buildings in this area because of the student population," Theodosia said. "With landlords charging sky-high rents just because they can." She stared at the building and felt a frisson of worry. Paint peeled off in long strips, and the place looked like it was ready to collapse. Then she shook off her feeling of nervousness and said, "Okay, let's do this."

They climbed out of Theodosia's Jeep, stepped through a

wrought iron gate that creaked like a rusty coffin lid, and followed a cracked cement walk around to the back just as Jamie had instructed.

"No lights on," Drayton commented. "Except for the third floor." He glanced around the backyard. "But not terrible back here. Two decent parking spaces for cars as well as a nice grove of palmettos and dogwoods."

"And a brick barbeque that someone built."

"I hope whoever did it used refractory bricks," Drayton said. "You choose the wrong kind of brick, the porous kind, and when they heat up, they tend to go boom."

"That'll add some pizzazz to your wood-fired pizza."

Drayton touched a hand to a battered-looking back door and said, "You have the key Jamie gave you?"

"Got it right here," Theodosia said.

"This door is all crooked and cockamamie. And look, the hinges are barely on at all. Any idiot could break in here if they wanted."

"The joys of living in an old building," Theodosia said as she stuck the key into the lock. The lock was sticky and obstinate at first and didn't want to release, but then she jiggled the key harder and something clicked. The door swung open. "Okay, finally."

"Let's see what we've got here," Drayton said.

The back door led directly into a small kitchen. Theodosia fumbled around for a light switch, found it, and turned on a yellow overhead light. Which sent a small flotilla of bugs scrambling for cover.

"Not exactly a gourmet kitchen like you'd find showcased in *Southern Living*," Drayton said.

"It's awful," Theodosia said. The linoleum flooring was warped, appliances were nineteen seventies avocado green, and the kitchen cupboards and counters were made of cheap plywood. She couldn't imagine cooking a meal in a place like this.

"Once they were married, was Bettina actually going to move in here?"

"I sincerely hope not," Theodosia said. "This place is a disaster zone." She opened the cupboard under the sink, found a can of bug spray, and gave the floor a spritz.

"More like a toxic waste dump," Drayton said. "I thought stockbrokers pulled down a fairly decent salary."

"Salary plus commissions. Maybe Jamie was scrimping and saving so he could buy a nice condo for him and Bettina. This . . ." She looked around. "Maybe it was only temporary."

"Let's hope so." Drayton walked over to the refrigerator, pulled open the door, and said, "Goodness me, it would appear Jamie is cultivating some odd strains of penicillin on his assortment of cheeses."

"That bad?"

"Don't ask. But if Jamie ever offers to make you a grilled cheese sandwich, take a pass. On a more hopeful note, the living room has to be an improvement."

It wasn't.

In the gloom they could make out a lumpy maroon sofa and matching chair parked in front of a flat-screen TV. Bookcases were your basic bricks and boards, and there was a strange odor.

"Mildew?" Theodosia wondered.

"Or mold," Drayton said.

"Aren't they the same thing?"

"Having opted not to pursue my PhD in mycology, I'm not sure I know the difference," Drayton said. "Here, let's turn on a light so we can see what we're dealing with." He took a few steps in, caught his toe on a scatter rug, and practically stumbled.

"Do you want me to . . . ?"

"I've got it," Drayton said as he switched on a seventies-looking floor lamp, a brass pole with three white globes.

The room was instantly flooded with light, revealing . . .

"Another skull!" Theodosia yelped.

"Sweet Fanny Adams," Drayton said as he stared at it. The skull was sitting in the center of a smoked-glass coffee table. And it looked identical to the one that had shown up in Jamie's hospital room. "Is it plastic?"

Theodosia tapped the top of the skull with a finger. "Yup. Feels like plastic, looks exactly like the other one, too."

"Maybe there was a two-for-one sale," Drayton joked.

But Theodosia shook her head. "This is just plain weird. I mean, somebody must have left it here, right? To scare Jamie when he got home from the hospital?"

"It could explain why the door was off-kilter in its frame. Somebody must have jimmied it open so they could come inside and plant this nasty thing."

"When you're right, you're right," Theodosia said.

"Now what?"

"Now we do what we came here for. We look around and see what else we can find."

"You mean like a clue?" Drayton asked.

"I don't think there's going to be a big red *X* marking the spot, but maybe something will turn up. Something that spills a little light on why Jamie is being threatened and harassed."

"So now you're definitely thinking that Jamie is the prime target?" Drayton asked.

"Yes. No. Actually, I'm still not sure."

"Okay then, we poke around anyway."

They spread out, Theodosia stepping into the small bedroom, Drayton searching the living room.

"Got a baggie here," Drayton called out. He held up a baggie filled with crumpled dark green leaves and said, "Somehow, I don't think it's his morning blend of herbal tea."

Theodosia came out, took a look, and said, "Whatever." She really didn't care if Bettina and Jamie toked up once in a while. "You find anything else?"

"Old magazines, some paperbacks, a *Monopoly* board game." Drayton shrugged, walked into the kitchen, and pulled open a few drawers. "There's a pocketknife mixed in with the forks and spoons."

"Just a pocketknife? Not a stiletto or a switchblade?" Theodosia called.

"It's more the Boy Scout variety."

"No other weapons? No guns or hunting knives?"

"None that I can see."

"What about tools?"

"Haven't seen those, either," Drayton said. "Which leads me to believe nothing gets fixed around here. By Jamie or the landlord." A few seconds went by, and Drayton said, "Ho boy."

"What?"

Drayton came out of the kitchen holding a pair of brown leather boots. "These were tucked between the stove and the back door. I think they're the brand you were talking about the other day. Sorels."

"Damn," Theodosia said, looking at the pair of scuffed boots. "That's just plain weird."

"Maybe a coincidence?"

"Let's hope so. But all the same, let's bag them and take them with us."

"What about the skull?"

"Let's bring that, too."

Back in the bedroom, Theodosia found Jamie's checkbook

and financial papers in a drawer. She hurriedly scanned as much as she could and determined that Jamie had a balance of three thousand two hundred dollars in his checking account and owned something like twenty-nine thousand dollars' worth of stocks and mutual funds. So certainly enough to put a down payment on a condo and move out of this rattrap.

In another drawer, Theodosia found a few pieces of correspondence. But they were of the postcard variety—no threatening notes that hinted at violence.

Theodosia wandered back out into the living room, where Drayton was perusing the bookshelf, and said, "Jamie's got some money. Enough to move out of here and buy a condo."

"Good to hear," Drayton said as he dusted his hands together. "Now can we leave?"

They locked the door behind them and headed toward Theodosia's Jeep. It was darker than a coal bin now, so they took care as they stepped along the broken sidewalk.

"Why don't we . . . ," Theodosia began, then suddenly stopped talking. She'd picked up a low noise, not just the skitter of dry leaves against pavement, but a throaty *putty-putt.* She looked across the street, where a car idled at the curb. "Drayton, there's a car over there," she whispered.

"Hmm?"

"Across the street. I think somebody's been watching us."

Drayton seemed unconcerned. "Maybe the driver is here to pick somebody up. Could be one of those Uber things."

Still, Theodosia's spider sense had been tickled. Something felt off. "I'm going to check it out," she said. She passed the bag with the skull and Sorels to Drayton. Then, stepping off the curb and into the street, she hurried in the direction of the waiting car. It was black or dark blue, and the headlights cast dancing beams down the street while the taillights glowed red, which was probably enough to illuminate the car's license plate. But just as Theodosia came up behind the car, ready to make note of the plate number, the car's lights winked out and its engine roared. Then the car accelerated fast, pulling away like a drag racer laying rubber and plunging the street into complete darkness.

"Whoa," Theodosia said as she watched the mysterious car recede into the distance. "That thing is smokin'."

"You okay over there?" Drayton called.

"I'm fine," Theodosia said. But she was still looking down the dark, deserted street, wondering just who had been spying on them.

12

Theodosia still felt strangely unsettled this Tuesday morning as she bustled about the Indigo Tea Shop. She'd had weird dreams all night long. Some involved Martin Hunt; others featured Adam Lynch, whom she'd yet to meet. The upshot of her dreams was that those two men had been skulking outside Jamie's apartment, peering in as she took a look around. Then the images turned muddy, faded, and were no longer there. But when she rushed across the street, the pavement feeling like sticky molasses, to investigate the car (still dreaming now), the vehicle had magically disappeared in a puff of purple smoke.

Theodosia shook her head and allowed herself a faint smile. Just too much stress mingled with too much Halloween on her mind, she decided, though the days were still building toward Charleston's big Halloween bash on Saturday.

"Did you do anything with the skull and Sorel boots we found in Jamie's apartment?" Drayton asked when Theodosia came to the counter to grab a pot of Tregothnan tea, a blend of black tea and Assam that a table of guests had requested.

"I dropped them off at Riley's office. But now that I think about it, in the cold, clear light of day, the boots are probably just a strange coincidence."

"Okay."

Theodosia raised a single eyebrow, one of her unique talents. "That's all you're going to say?"

"No, I wanted to ask you about someone else." Drayton reached up and grabbed a tin of silver needle tea. He tapped the top of it with an index finger. "I know this is going to sound strange coming from me, but have you done an online search to see if Adam Lynch is still working as a website developer?"

"That's a smart idea and one I wish I'd come up with myself," Theodosia said. She glanced around the tea shop, where six tables of guests were enjoying morning tea. "In fact, I'll check right now, if you can handle things for a few minutes."

"Child's play," Drayton said.

Theodosia delivered her pot of tea, then scurried down the hallway, pushing aside the celadon green velvet curtain that separated the back office and kitchen from the tea shop. She ducked into her office, fully cognizant that it was a messy affair and would probably stay that way for some time. Between favors and decor for upcoming event teas, and a holiday giving season that was fast approaching, her office was piled with boxes of tea strainers, teacups and saucers, jars of honey, and her own proprietary brand of T-Bath products—all lotions and potions that were infused with actual tea. She picked her way past stacks of *TeaTime* and *The Tea House Times* magazines and slid into her desk chair. Then her fingers were flying across the keyboard in search of Adam Lynch's website.

Which was a snap to find.

His splash page was a series of red-and-purple animated

graphics with the headline THE LYNCH MOB and beneath that STUNNING WEBSITES FROM CONCEPT TO CODE.

Nicely done, Theodosia decided. She'd spent several years at a marketing firm, so she had more than a working knowledge of what was needed to create effective TV spots, print ads, and online advertising. She immediately went to the MENU and clicked on PROJECTS, which took her to a dozen websites that Lynch and his team had created.

Let's see now . . .

Adam Lynch and his Lynch Mob crew had created websites for Southern Federal Bank, Alabaster Software, Lewin's Sportswear, Ricky's Automotive and Tire, Cotton Duck Boutique (yes, she knew about that), and . . .

What? The cemetery crawl? No way.

Theodosia stared harder. Yes way. It wasn't just her imagination playing tricks on her; Lynch had actually created a website for the cemetery crawl. The splash page had a shifting green-and-purple background with images of ancient tombstones fading in and out. The headline said A WALK AMONG THE TOMBSTONES, with the subtitle RUB SHOULDERS WITH THE GHOSTS AND SPIRITS OF OLD CHARLESTON.

Heels clicking like castanets, Theodosia hurried back into the tea room to tell Drayton about this. She found him measuring tea into a pink Shelley Duchess teapot.

"Drayton," she said almost breathlessly, "guess what website Adam Lynch created?"

Drayton, a confirmed Luddite, cocked his head like an inquisitive magpie and said, "I couldn't possibly guess."

"Lynch did the website for A Walk Among the Tombstones."

"No?"

"Yes," Theodosia said. "Can you believe it?"

"Well, if he's skilled at what he does . . ."

"He's got talent, that's for sure. But Lynch creating that website, it feels a little too close for comfort."

"The Cemetery Historical Society is just another client."

"Maybe so, but I'd like to know more about this guy. After all, his temper is supposedly so off the charts that he knocked Bettina's tooth out."

"Are you thinking of paying him a visit?" Drayton asked.

"I wasn't, but now you've given me another good idea."

"Just be careful."

"You know I will."

Drayton shook his head. "I *don't* know that. You have a strange habit of disregarding any sign of doom or danger. Even when it's staring you in the face." He was about to continue his warning when the phone rang.

Drayton picked up the phone, listened, and said, "Yes, she's right here." He handed the phone to Theodosia. "For you. A Charlie Skipstead?"

Dang it, the podcast lady. I wonder what she wants. Wait, I know what she wants.

She clutched the phone and said, "This is Theodosia."

"Theodosia, this is Charlie Skipstead. Remember me? I do the *Charleston Shivers* podcast."

"I remember," Theodosia said. *Do I ever.* Charlie Skipstead was constantly upbeat and always talking a mile a minute. Theodosia wondered if the woman ever paused long enough to take a breath.

"I've been *dying* to get you on the air, and this seems like the absolutely *perfect* time!" Charlie said. She was another one, like Delaine, who talked in italics and exclamation points.

"Because . . . ?"

"Because of the murder at that wedding you catered! Or

should I say, you were *supposed* to cater. I'll wager that, after that terrible accident, you've been doing some investigating on your own. It's what you do best, after all."

"Well, I . . . I suppose I am looking into a few things."

Charlie laughed. "By 'looking into things' you mean running a shadow investigation, right? Interviewing any and all possible suspects?"

"Um, maybe." *Why am I such a bad liar?* Theodosia wondered.

"Sure you are, and my listeners would *love* to hear all about it. When can we get together? How about this coming Thursday afternoon, does that work for you?"

"That soon?"

"Why not?" Charlie said. "We'll do our interview live in studio, but I'll also tape it and archive it."

"So our interview will always be out there in the netherworld? Whirling around for anybody to listen to?"

"Sweetie, that's basically the point of a podcast," Charlie said. "You listen when you *want* to listen, when you have time. So this Thursday, okay? Meet me at Air Supply Studio over on Bogard Street at three o'clock and we'll take it from there."

"Right," Theodosia said. "See you."

"What was that all about?" Drayton asked.

"Podcast." Theodosia wasn't sure how much to tell him.

"It's that crazy mystery podcast lady, isn't it? I'll bet she wants you to go on the radio . . ."

"Not the radio, a podcast."

"Whatever . . . and spill your guts about how you've been investigating Celeste's murder."

"I'd reference it more as a mysterious death."

"And here you promised me you'd be careful," Drayton said. "That you wouldn't rush in where angels fear to tread."

"You worry too much," Theodosia said.

"And you, my dear, don't worry enough."

Right on the dot of ten thirty, Miss Dimple arrived, ready to help out in the tea room. She was Theodosia's freelance bookkeeper, who loved nothing more than to put on an apron and serve tea.

"Pouring tea is lots more fun than poring over columns of numbers," Miss Dimple had told Theodosia. And so she was asked to help out whenever there was an event tea. Like today.

"What are we celebrating?" Miss Dimple asked Theodosia. She slipped out of her pink chenille sweater, hung it on the brass coatrack, and put on a black Parisian waiter's apron.

"We're having our Under the Tuscan Sun Tea," Theodosia said.

"You've never done an Italian-themed tea before, have you?" She pronounced it *Eye-talian.*

"We've mostly stuck to British Teas, Chocolate Teas, Downton Abbey Teas, and Sugarplum Teas. So this will be a first for us."

"Smart that you keep branching out," Miss Dimple said.

Barely five feet tall with pink cottony hair, Miss Dimple looked like your sweet old granny but was so skilled with numbers and spreadsheets she could have been a bookkeeper for the mob.

Approaching the front counter, where Drayton was brewing tea, she sang out, "Top of the morning to you, Drayton."

"Welcome, dear lady," Drayton said in his courtliest manner. "We're delighted you're able to step in and assist us."

"Always happy to help," Miss Dimple said.

"And how are the cats?" Miss Dimple had two Siamese cats.

"Purr-fectly lovely," Miss Dimple giggled. Then she turned serious. "You have some tea for me to deliver?"

Drayton pushed two pots of tea across the counter. "The Moroccan mint in the Brown Betty teapot is for table two. The white teapot goes to table six. But kindly tell them their tippy Yunnan needs to steep another two minutes."

"Got it," Miss Dimple said as she grabbed the two teapots and toddled off.

Theodosia was stocking her highboy with tea towels and mini bamboo strainers when Sabrina Haynes walked in. She looked around the tea shop, saw Theodosia, and gave a quick wave.

Theodosia hurried over to greet her. "Sabrina, hello. How nice to see you again."

"I have news," Sabrina said. "Celeste's visitation is set for tonight at Strait's Funeral Home over on Calhoun Street." Sabrina's eyes misted up as she touched a hand to her heart and said, "It begins at seven. And I sincerely hope you'll come."

"Absolutely," Theodosia said. "Drayton and I were both planning to be there." She glanced over at Drayton, who was busy cashing out a guest. "Do you . . . do you have time for a cup of tea?"

"I would love a cup of hot tea, preferably something strong."

Theodosia glanced over at Drayton again as he finished at the register. "Drayton?" She was pretty sure he'd been listening. Drayton had a knack for multitasking.

"I have a pot of English breakfast tea brewing right now," Drayton said.

"Come sit down." Theodosia led Sabrina to the small table by the stone fireplace, where they both took a seat. "Tell me what's going on."

"We've been staying in touch with law enforcement," Sabrina said. "Sheriff Ambourn and his investigators as well as Charleston PD. Both agencies have been fairly diligent about keeping us up-to-date on the investigation."

"Any news?" *Since they're not telling me anything.*

"Mostly they're still conducting interviews. But on the plus side, I found out that *you* were looking into things."

"Oh, I've just been asking around," Theodosia said, trying to downplay her role.

"That's not what Bettina told me. She said you're hot and heavy into your own investigation. That you've done this kind of thing before."

"Well . . . some," Theodosia said.

Drayton was suddenly at their table with a pot of tea. "Don't let Theodosia fool you," he said, giving Sabrina a knowing wink. "Theo has actually solved a number of crimes. You might say she's Charleston's very own Nancy Drew."

"Thank you for the tea, Drayton," Theodosia said. She was uncomfortable being the topic of conversation.

"Don't mention it," Drayton said as he strolled back to the front counter.

"If I can help in any way," Sabrina said. "If you have questions, please don't hesitate to call me, okay?"

"Sure."

"In fact, I . . ." Sabrina stopped, lifted a hand, and waved it in front of her face, looking suddenly indecisive.

"What were you about to say?" Theodosia asked.

"This is going to sound super weird," Sabrina said. "But I was actually thinking about consulting a psychic about Celeste's death, someone who has the ability to intuit things. Since the police haven't made any great strides, maybe they could lend some guidance and insight." Sabrina stopped, a stricken look on her face. "Oh dear, that must sound totally idiotic to you. Like I've completely gone off the rails."

"Not at all," Theodosia said. "It's so strange that you should bring this up, because we're having our Victorian Halloween Tea tomorrow and we have a psychic coming in."

Sabrina's mouth dropped open and her eyes got large. "For real?"

"Her name is Madame Aurora and she does tarot card readings as well as intuitive readings on people."

"She sounds perfect!" Sabrina enthused. "Could you . . . I mean, is it possible to arrange for a private session with this psychic *after* your Halloween tea?"

"I'm sure we could make that happen."

"And I'll bring Bettina and Delaine along. Maybe your psychic could give some guidance and insight to all of us."

"You're sure you want to include Delaine?" Theodosia asked. "Last time Delaine had her tarot cards read she completely flipped out. Worried that her boyfriend du jour was going to dump her."

"Okay, maybe not Delaine."

Theodosia thought for a minute. "No, Delaine *should* be part of this. You should all be included. Because . . . you never know what could happen."

Glancing around the tea shop, Theodosia decided she still had time before she had to start decorating for today's luncheon. So she ran into her office and called Riley. She figured Riley might have an update on the investigation, plus she really wanted to tell him about Adam Lynch—about how Lynch had been physically abusive to Bettina.

"Hey," Riley said when he answered the phone. "How are you?"

"Busy," Theodosia said. "But I need to talk to you about a couple of things."

"Why does that not surprise me?"

"Listen, what I have to say *is* going to surprise you." Theodosia took a breath and dove in. "Before Bettina was engaged to Jamie, she was engaged to a guy named Adam Lynch, who's a website designer."

"Bettina was engaged before? I didn't know that."

"It gets better, or should I say worse. Because Adam Lynch was abusive to Bettina."

"What'd he do?"

"When Bettina refused to take him back, Lynch hit her and knocked out one of her teeth."

"Did she call the police? Or get a court order against him?"

"I don't think so," Theodosia said.

"Sounds like she had just cause."

"You'll get no argument from me."

"Adam Lynch is the man's name? Let me look into this," Riley said. "See if maybe a report was filed."

"Did you get the boots I dropped off this morning?" Theodosia asked.

"I got your little bag of tricks and had one of our guys take a look. The Sorel boots were no match to the footprints we found behind the greenhouse." Riley paused. "Where did you find those boots anyway?"

"At Jamie's apartment."

"What!" Riley practically exploded with surprise. "What were you doing there?"

"Just taking a look around," Theodosia said.

"Holy cats, you *are* investigating," he chided.

"Well, not officially."

"What did I say about you being in danger?"

"You said I *might* be in danger. You didn't say it was imminent."

"Theodosia . . ." Riley's voice dripped with disapproval.

That's when Theodosia decided she'd better not tell him about the dark car that had been idling across the street last night. It'd just cause him even more unhappiness.

13

Once their morning customers had cleared out, it was time to kick things into high gear and start decorating for their Under the Tuscan Sun Tea.

"How do you want to do this, honey?" Miss Dimple asked.

Theodosia opened one of her antique cupboards and pulled out a stack of red-and-white checkered tablecloths. "These go on the tables first, then we'll figure out which set of china to use."

"I vote for the Italian Cypress by Oneida," Miss Dimple said. "It's painted with those whimsical orange flowers and green leaves."

"I second the vote," Drayton called out.

"The ayes have it," Theodosia said. "We go with the Italian Cypress."

Theodosia and Miss Dimple set the tables with small plates, teacups and saucers, glasses, silverware, and napkins. Then she added silver trays with decorated sugar cubes and small pitchers of cream.

"What's next?" Miss Dimple asked.

"Haley's got bottles of olive oil and baskets of Italian breadsticks ready to go in the kitchen. So once those are placed on the tables, we can move on to the centerpieces."

Miss Dimple hurried into the kitchen while Theodosia arranged bright yellow sunflowers in antique crocks and piled purple and green grapes into wicker baskets.

"Those are the centerpieces?" Miss Dimple said when she came out. "Lovely." She turned toward Drayton. "Drayton, what do you think? How does it look?"

"Dear lady, I feel as if I stumbled upon the most marvelous bistro in all of Tuscany," Drayton said.

"Let's hope our guests feel the same way," Theodosia said.

Turned out, they did.

When the big hand and the little hand both struck twelve, the floodgates opened and guests began to stream in.

Theodosia greeted everyone at the front door, Drayton administered a fair amount of compliments and air-kisses, and Miss Dimple led the guests to their seats at the tables. Brooke Carter Crockett, owner of Hearts Desire, and Leigh Carroll, owner of the Cabbage Patch Gift Shop, arrived together. Then tea regulars Jill, Kristen, Judi, Linda, and Jessica came bounding in, making for a happy gaggle of tea aficionados. They were followed by a half dozen guests from the Dove Cote Inn, a tea group from Ashleyville, and a handful of women from the Broad Street Flower Club.

As Drayton brewed tea and Theodosia made small talk, another dozen guests straggled in until finally the tea room was packed to the rafters. Which was Theodosia's signal to get the luncheon rolling. She stepped to the center of the room, drew breath, and said, "Welcome, dear guests, to our Under the

Tuscan Sun Tea. For the next hour and a half the Indigo Tea Shop invites you to enjoy the sights, smells, and tastes of Tuscany." Theodosia paused, knowing there'd be a spatter of applause. And there was. Then she continued. "To begin today's luncheon we'll be serving savory rosemary and fontina cheese scones. These will be presented on our three-tiered trays along with baked mozzarella bites and cream cheese and sun-dried tomato tea sandwiches."

Now Theodosia heard murmurs of "Wonderful" and "Delicious" and "Bring it on."

"For your entrée our chef has prepared a homemade sweet sausage lasagna paired with a side salad with rustic Italian dressing. And for dessert you have your choice of tiramisu or cannoli filled with ricotta and cream cheese."

"Or you could have both," Drayton said, stepping forward to join Theodosia. "And because this is a tea shop, it stands to reason we would have a fine repertoire of tea." Now all eyes were focused on Drayton. "For your sipping enjoyment today, I've created a house special that I call *Andiamo.* It's a sublime blend of black tea, orange blossoms, and elderberry. I also have a lovely herbal tea flavored with anise." He smiled, spread his arms open wide, and said, "*Grazie mille* and *mangiamo*!"

That was the cue for Haley and Miss Dimple to carry out large three-tiered trays overflowing with goodies. And as they placed a tea tray on each table, Theodosia and Drayton grabbed teapots and began filling teacups.

Guests eagerly wolfed down the scones, mozzarella bites, and tea sandwiches, and looked downright guilty when they asked for seconds. And when the lasagna entrée was served, it was clear the Tuscan Tea was a roaring success.

"Excuse me," a woman said to Theodosia. "With loose tea leaves, how long can I expect the flavor to last?"

"Give or take a year," Theodosia said. "As long as your tea is stored properly in an airtight container that's kept in a cool dark space."

"And what are the most popular teas?" another woman asked.

"That would be Darjeeling, chai, English breakfast tea, and Earl Grey."

"What country produces the most tea?" another woman asked.

"China, followed by India," Theodosia said.

"We're a hit," Drayton said when Theodosia stopped by the counter for a refill. "Then again, judging from the number of reservations we had, I knew this tea would be a roaring success."

"You did?" Theodosia had hoped they'd sell out and had worried up until this morning when a half dozen reservations came in.

Drayton touched a hand to his bow tie. "I never doubted it for a minute."

By two o'clock the luncheon guests had departed and the afternoon tea sippers had arrived. They were a leisurely bunch, ordering mostly tea and scones, and easy to please.

"I'm thinking of skipping out early," Theodosia told Drayton.

"To go where?" Drayton asked.

"I'd like to talk to that web guy, Adam Lynch, in person."

"Don't get too close to him," Drayton warned. "Or he'll likely knock a tooth out."

Theodosia disappeared behind the celadon curtain and popped into the kitchen. Haley was stacking dishes into the dishwasher while Miss Dimple was nibbling a scone. "Thanks for all the hard work, guys," she said. "You really made our customers happy today."

"Isn't that what we try to do every day?" Haley asked, a Cheshire cat grin lighting up her face. "Give our customers great food? Make 'em feel all warm and fuzzy?"

"Actually, the warm and fuzzy part comes when you look at the week's receipts," Miss Dimple said.

"Spoken like a true bookkeeper," Haley said, then she waved at Theodosia and said, "I know it's a business, but it's *fun*, too."

Theodosia couldn't have agreed more.

Adam Lynch's office was located in the same redbrick building on Broad Street where Carson Crousett, an event planner, also had his office. Theodosia peered in a narrow window to see if Carson was in, but the lights were off. So no dice. A few doors down the hall, she found what she was looking for in the form of a large buzzing yellow neon sign that shrieked THE LYNCH MOB.

When Theodosia walked into their office, the first thing she saw was another neon sign that said WORK SMART and a messy front desk with a young man hunched behind a computer screen.

"Adam Lynch?" she said.

The young man looked up with a startled expression and shook his head. "No, I'm just the intern. Mr. Lynch is back in our work hub."

"Great, would you kindly tell Mr. Lynch that Theodosia Browning is here to see him?"

The young man wrinkled his nose as he stood up slowly. "Are you a client?"

Theodosia gave an enigmatic smile. "You never know."

"Okay. Whatever," the young man said as he slipped through

the door to the so-called work hub. Theodosia heard quiet mumbles for a few moments, then the young man came back out. "Go ahead in, Mr. Lynch is on a phone call, but he's almost finished."

"Thanks."

Adam Lynch had his feet propped up on his desk and was wearing five-hundred-dollar Golden Goose sneakers, ripped blue jeans, and a T-shirt that said IF AT FIRST YOU DON'T SUCCEED, TAKE A TAX LOSS. Long sandy-colored hair was slicked back above a furrowed brow, and he had pale gray eyes and a crooked nose. Lynch's mouth was highly animated since he was in the middle of chewing somebody out.

"Didn't I *tell* you to buy our silver cloud package?" he said in a haranguing tone of voice. "Wouldn't you *think* that would have given you a whole lot more data storage?"

Three other designers who were working on computers threw furtive glances at Lynch. Theodosia figured that a good deal of yelling went on in this office and that employee turnover was fairly high.

When Lynch finally got off the phone, he looked at Theodosia and said, "Did I miss an appointment?" He glanced at his computer screen and said, "I don't think so." Then he swung his feet off his desk and said, "What's up? How can I help you?"

"I understand you designed the website for Cotton Duck."

"My company created it, and we handle all updates and maintenance, yeah. Did they recommend me? Do you need help with a website?"

"Not exactly, but I do have a question for you."

Lynch sat up straight in his bright green ergonomic chair and gave a smile that would warm a shark's heart. "I charge two hundred and twenty-five dollars an hour for my time, whether it's consulting or actual creative work. So, go ahead . . . the meter's running."

"This won't take long. All I want to know is why you hit Bettina West and knocked her tooth out."

"What!" Lynch looked as if he'd been slapped.

"See? Just one quick question," Theodosia said. "Didn't take but a few seconds of your time. Maybe two dollars' worth."

"Who says I hit Bettina?" Lynch asked. His face was starting to turn red, beginning at his collar, then working its way up to his forehead as if he were being dip-dyed in paint.

"Bettina told me you did. She said this incident happened right after she broke up with you and you had the temerity to slash her tires, stalk her, and then spread unflattering lies about her on social media."

The three employees shot quick looks at Lynch. They weren't exactly surprised, more like frightened.

Lynch pursed his lips, fighting to contain his anger. "This is about that wedding disaster, isn't it? I read about it in the newspaper. Saw something on TV, too."

"No, this is about *you*, Mr. Lynch," Theodosia said in a calm voice. "You have a temper that's hot enough to cause a meltdown at a nuclear reactor. A temper you are seemingly unable to control."

"Wait, you think *I'm* the guy who sabotaged that greenhouse? That *I* caused that chick's death?"

"After meeting you I think it's within the realm of possibility."

"No way, I have an airtight alibi," Lynch said.

"That's nice. Maybe when the police drop by to question you—and I know they will—you can regale them with your comings and goings of last Saturday."

"The police? Lady, are you for real?" Lynch grabbed a glass globe that was sitting on his desk and hurled it at Theodosia. It missed her by inches as it whizzed past and smacked into the wall behind her.

"You are an animal," she said.

Now Lynch was on his feet, his chair rocking wildly as his anger reached full fury. He pointed to the door and shouted, "Get out of my office right this minute! Daryl, start earning your keep around here and escort this person to the door!"

The designer who was sitting closest to Lynch scrambled to his feet.

Theodosia held up a hand. "I can find my way out perfectly well, Daryl. As far as Mr. Lynch goes, we're not done yet. Not by a long shot."

"You know what? I'm gonna kick you out myself!" Lynch shouted. "Now scram on out of here and stop bugging me." Lynch dogged Theodosia's footsteps, shouting at her, spitting out his rage, all the way to the front door until she was standing out in the hallway. "And don't ever come back!" was his final outburst.

As the door slammed abruptly in Theodosia's face, she said, "You see, there's that nasty temper again."

14

When Theodosia got back to the Indigo Tea Shop, she was still fuming about her dustup with Adam Lynch. She hadn't actually come right out and *accused* Lynch of sabotaging the greenhouse, but he'd reacted so violently that she now believed he was quite capable of engineering that kind of madness. So he'd definitely solidified his place on her suspect list.

Theodosia looked around for Haley and Miss Dimple, then realized that it was well past four o'clock and they'd undoubtedly gone home for the day—Haley to her apartment above the tea shop with her cat, Teacake, and Miss Dimple to her cottage not far from White Point Garden. Drayton was still at the tea shop, however, languidly pushing a broom across the floor, doing a final cleanup.

When Drayton spotted Theodosia, he said, "So tell me, how'd it go with Adam Lynch?"

"Not very well," Theodosia said. "The man is obnoxious, still angry at Bettina, and a certified maniac."

"If Lynch is that miserable, he might even be miserable enough to sabotage a greenhouse."

"In a heartbeat."

"Really? Well, I hope he didn't try to get physical with you," Drayton said.

"Mostly Lynch just yelled and screamed like a petulant two-year-old and ordered me out of his office. But, Drayton, he knew exactly why I was there. I was barely two words in when he started screeching to high heaven that I was trying to pin the greenhouse collapse on him."

"Seems as if Lynch is not so incapacitated with anger that he can't put two and two together—meaning Bettina's wedding and Celeste dying in the greenhouse collapse. It's been all over the newspapers, so it surely must have caught his eye."

"He said he saw it on TV, too."

"There you go," Drayton said. He leaned his broom against the counter. "So Lynch is a frightening fellow?"

"He's ugly-scary. I can't imagine how Bettina could have dated him in the first place."

"Might I remind you, she didn't just date the man, she was *engaged* to him."

"It boggles the mind," Theodosia said.

"Maybe Bettina likes bad boys."

"Please don't say that. Then I might have to put Jamie on my list, too."

"Seriously?" Drayton said.

"Do you know how many new brides are murdered by new husbands?"

"No, and please don't tell me," Drayton said. "It's too awful to even contemplate."

"Change of subject then. You know we're supposed to attend Celeste's visitation tonight?"

Drayton nodded. "That's why I waited around for you." He glanced at his watch. "But we've still got time. Have you had a chance to eat?"

"Just breakfast and half a scone this afternoon," Theodosia said. "So I am fairly hungry."

"Why don't we mosey into the kitchen and I'll whip up an omelet?"

"You'd dare appropriate one of Haley's precious omelet pans?"

"Along with four of her precious eggs from free-range chickens who probably spend the day doing yoga and listening to new age music."

"Sounds like Haley," Theodosia said.

True to his word, Drayton whipped the eggs into a golden slurry, added salt, pepper, and a dash of cream, then sizzled it all on the stove.

"Perhaps a little cheese, too," he said as he sprinkled shredded cheddar over the eggs.

"I think I'm going to like this," Theodosia said as she watched the eggs bubble and then turn golden when Drayton stuck them under the broiler for thirty seconds.

"No," Drayton said. "You're going to *love* this."

And she did. Every tasty morsel of it.

Forty minutes later, well fed and amped with curiosity, Theodosia and Drayton were on their way to Strait's Funeral Home.

"You know what?" Theodosia said. "Before we hit up Celeste's visitation, I want to make a quick stop."

"At home?" Drayton asked. "To check on your pup?"

"No, Mrs. Barry, his dog nanny, has probably already been

there to feed Earl Grey and walk him. I'm talking about a stop at Greebe's Gym."

"And that would be because . . . ?"

"Because Martin Hunt was an amateur Golden Gloves champion. And apparently still does some boxing."

"And you think the people who run the gym will be able to shed some more light on him?"

"We won't know unless we ask, Drayton."

Greebe's Gym was a storefront operation in a no-nonsense cement block building over on Laurens Street. It was sandwiched between Lundeen's pawn shop (From Dust to Dollars) and Bob Bloomer's locksmith shop (Unlock the Possibilities).

"Look at this," Drayton said. "In one city block you can buy a set of lockpicks, learn how to punch out somebody's lights, and hock stolen merchandise."

"It's the circle of life," Theodosia said.

"Only if it's a life of crime," Drayton replied.

Inside Greebe's Gym, the place smelled like sweat, rubbing oil, and stinky sneakers. Two men were inside a boxing ring, wearing protective headgear and boxing gloves, and about to square off against each other. Other men were working out on Nautilus machines and punching heavy bags. A few men worked speed bags, their fists making sharp *slap-whap* sounds that ricocheted through the overheated room.

A man in gray sweatpants and a Greebe's Gym sweatshirt with the sleeves cut off came over to greet them. "Help you?" he said. Then added, "I'm Frank Greebe, the owner."

"My friend here was interested in a gym membership," Theodosia said.

Drayton's eyes widened in complete surprise, but no more than Greebe's, who was suddenly giving Drayton the once-over.

"You want to get back in fighting shape, huh?" Greebe said.

He seemed particularly fixated on Drayton's tweed jacket and bright pink bow tie.

"Why not," Drayton said in a strangled voice.

"Like I tell my clients, it's never too late," Greebe said, but his voice carried a dubious tone.

"You came highly recommended by a friend of ours," Theodosia said. "Martin Hunt."

"Oh sure," Greebe said. "Hunt hangs out here a bit. Back in the day he was Golden Gloves. Got the talent and the deadly right cross, won a diamond belt and a whole passel of medals."

"And Hunt still boxes here?" Theodosia asked, indicating the boxing ring, where the two fighters wearing boxing shorts and protective headgear were jabbing at each other without much success.

"No, not so much anymore," Greebe said.

"Why not?" Theodosia asked.

"Most people are too afraid to get in the ring with him."

Back in Theodosia's Jeep, Drayton said, "You intentionally blindsided me back there."

"Apologies, because I didn't mean to," Theodosia said. "It's just that once we got inside that gym, I realized all the members were men."

"And I happened to be the handyman." The corners of Drayton's mouth twitched upward at his own joke.

"Well . . . something like that."

"Okay, no harm done," Drayton said. "In fact, in hindsight, it was a rather humorous episode. Did you catch the look of surprise on the owner's face when you said I was interested in joining the gym?"

"You could have knocked Greebe over with a feather,"

Theodosia said as she slowed, braked, then turned into the parking lot for Strait's Funeral Home. "As for your bow tie, he couldn't take his eyes off it."

"I could have been a contender. The Gentleman Boxer."

"You could have. And look, now we go from a boxing gym to this," Theodosia said as she eased into a parking spot.

Drayton gazed at the funeral home, a pile of red bricks that looked none too friendly. "This visitation is going to be just plain sad."

"Don't forget why we're here."

"To ask a few subtle questions?" Drayton said. "Obtain information?"

"If we can, absolutely. And also try to determine if there are any more possible suspects in Celeste's mysterious death. Or maybe see if anyone happens to be giving Bettina and Jamie an extra close inspection."

"They're both going to be here?"

"Jamie got out of the hospital this morning."

They exited the Jeep, walked to the funeral home, and climbed the stone steps. His hand on an old-fashioned brass doorknob, Drayton paused and said, "Someone once told me that killers are known to show up at their own victims' funerals."

"That was me who told you," Theodosia said.

"Why am I not surprised?"

You could tell from the muffled sobs where Celeste's visitation was being held.

"Oh my," Drayton said as they walked through the depressing lobby, with its overstuffed furniture and floral wallpaper, into an even more depressing visitation room. "This is not going to be fun."

There had to be at least sixty people crowded into a room that was designed to hold forty. And most of them were dressed in black and looking mournful. Up in the front of the room, a silver casket rested on a wooden bier, surrounded by dozens of white orchids.

Theodosia wondered if the orchids had been sent compliments of Foxtail Flower Farm, then decided that this detail wasn't important. What was important was who was here.

"Where did Celeste work that she knew so many people?" Drayton whispered as he glanced around the room. There were rows of black metal folding chairs that slightly resembled crouching crows, purple-paisley wallpaper, and a small table in the back where pink punch and sugar cookies were being served. Soft funereal music oozed out of hidden speakers.

"Celeste was a physical therapist, so I think a lot of folks from her clinic are here," Theodosia said. "Plus friends and relatives and maybe even a few of her clients."

The contingent of relatives was huddled up near the casket, so that's the direction Theodosia and Drayton headed. Theodosia approached the casket first, feeling more than a little apprehensive, wondering if it would be open or not. Celeste had sustained serious head and throat injuries, so that could present a problem.

15

But no, it turned out the top half of the casket was wide open, with Celeste lying in quiet repose. Her head rested on a peach-colored silk pillow, and the expression on her face looked for all the world as if she'd simply fallen asleep. Dressed in a high-neck ruffled blouse, with blond hair styled very carefully. No head trauma was visible.

Thank goodness.

Drayton came up alongside Theodosia and said, "She looks beatific, as if she just fell asleep. Like Snow White waiting for her prince to come and kiss her so she can wake up."

"No princes here tonight," Theodosia said. "But it's possible a killer might be lurking."

That caused them both to turn and gaze at the swirl of people.

"I wonder if that's really so," Drayton said.

"Keep your eyes and ears open," Theodosia said. "Watch for anyone who doesn't seem to fit in or is hanging back." Theodosia did a quick scan of the crowd. "But first . . ."

Theodosia and Drayton dutifully extended their condolences to Celeste's family. Sabrina was there to help break the ice and introduce them to her parents and various family members. Once the niceties were out of the way, Sabrina discreetly pulled Theodosia aside and said, "Is there any news?" She blushed slightly, then added, "I don't mean to put you on the spot, but Bettina talked your investigating prowess up to high heaven, so much so that I'm almost expecting miracles."

"No miracles quite yet," Theodosia said, reaching out to pat Sabrina's arm. "But I intend to snoop around tonight, meet a few people, and hopefully ask a few questions."

"You think the killer might be here?" Sabrina looked stricken.

"Not necessarily, but someone here might have seen something or picked up a shred of information. Anyway, that's for me to worry about, not you."

"Bless you," Sabrina whispered.

Bettina and Jamie were at the visitation, of course, Bettina wearing a black dress and looking appropriately sad for her dead maid of honor, while Jamie simply looked tired and hurt. He was dressed casually in jeans and a navy blue sweater and still wore his nose brace. One hand was wrapped in gauze and tape, and he seemed a little bit out of it. Theodosia attributed this to all the painkillers he was taking.

Theodosia went over to talk to them just as Jamie staggered away and headed for the refreshment table.

Good, now I can talk a little more freely.

"Bettina," Theodosia said. "How is Jamie holding up?"

Bettina shrugged. "The doctors say he's healing, and Jamie feels that he's doing better as well. But he seems . . . how should I describe it?" She made a downcast face. "Jamie seems *diminished* to me. Like he's not all there, like he's not quite Jamie."

"He's been through an awful lot, you both have."

"I suppose. At least he's out of the hospital, that's a blessing."

Theodosia looked around. "Did Delaine happen to tag along with you?"

Bettina rolled her eyes. "Aunt Delaine stayed home tonight because she said she was feeling *sick.* But I don't think she really is. More like sick of all the questions from law enforcement and intrusions by the media."

"The media's been hounding you?"

"Some, yeah. Especially that one guy from K-BAM," Bettina said.

"Ken Lotter, I know him. He's not a bad guy, just awfully persistent." Then, "Sabrina talked to you about doing a private session with the psychic tomorrow afternoon, right?"

"Oh yeah."

"How do you feel about that?"

"I think it sounds scary," Bettina said. "And a little bit out of left field. On the other hand, if it helps shed any light on the killer . . . the guy who sabotaged that greenhouse . . . I'm all for it."

"Will Delaine be up for meeting with the psychic?"

Bettina offered a rueful smile. "She's not a fan, so I'll have to work on her some more."

Drayton walked up to them, balancing three cups of punch. "Refreshments," he said. "Although I can't make any promises as to how refreshing this beverage actually is."

Theodosia and Bettina accepted the drinks from Drayton and thanked him.

"I wanted to chat with Jamie," Drayton told Bettina. "Ask him how he's feeling, but he seems to be tied up at the moment."

They all glanced over to where Jamie was leaning against the back wall, talking to a young man dressed in a black leather moto jacket and black jeans. He had curly brown hair, darting eyes, and, judging from the intensity of the conversation, a lot to talk about with Jamie.

"Who's Jamie's friend?" Theodosia asked. At this point she was looking at anyone and everyone who was remotely attached to Jamie.

Bettina frowned. "I don't really know. Although we were at Smedley's Saloon one night having oyster shooters, and I do remember seeing that guy. He waved at Jamie, but when I asked Jamie who he was, Jamie changed the subject. So . . . maybe just an old friend from school?" She shrugged. "Who knows? On the other hand, Jamie's made tons of new acquaintances since he took that broker's job at Hamilton and McLaughlin."

"And that's probably a good thing," Drayton said. "Career-wise."

Theodosia and Drayton wandered about the room then, trying to look incognito but keeping a sharp watch for anyone who seemed out of place.

No one did.

"This isn't working out the way I thought it would," Theodosia said.

"Agreed," Drayton said. "Nobody looks remotely sinister, as if they were trying to replot Jamie's demise. Or go after Bettina."

"Which is kind of a relief."

"I'm going to take another spin over to the refreshment table," Drayton said. "I think one of those cookies has my name on it."

"Go," Theodosia said. She glanced around and her eyes lit

on Jamie again. This time he was talking to a tall woman with short, red, curly hair who was dressed in a gray business suit. Curious, she decided to wander over.

"Shouldn't you be sitting down?" Theodosia said to Jamie. "Didn't you just get out of the hospital?"

"Yes!" the woman cried in agreement. "This guy checked himself out just a few hours ago. Crazy, yes?" She smiled at Theodosia and said, "I'm happy to see someone else is looking out for Jamie's welfare, too." She stuck out her hand and said, "We haven't been introduced. I'm Barbara Campbell. Babs to all my friends."

"Theodosia Browning," Theodosia said, shaking the woman's hand. She noted that the woman wore Ferragamo heels with her business suit and had an expensive-looking leather envelope, really an attaché, tucked under one arm.

Theodosia took a shot in the dark. "You must be one of Celeste's friends?" She gave the woman a commiserating look.

"Actually, no," Babs said, somewhat brightly. "I didn't know Celeste or her family at all. I showed up mainly because I knew Jamie would be here." She paused, a crooked smile on her face as she gazed at Jamie.

"Excuse me?" Theodosia said. She felt as if she'd missed something here. Like, a connection.

"Truth be told, Jamie and I used to be engaged," Babs said to Theodosia.

This filled in the missing piece Theodosia had been wondering about. "I see," she said. And because Theodosia was imbued with a powerfully strong curiosity gene, she asked, "And your engagement was fairly recent?"

"Oh no, it's been over two years since we called it quits," Babs said. Then she broke into a wide grin. "It was the best thing for us. We really weren't *that* compatible—or even madly in love. I think we were mostly good friends who hung around together and figured marriage was the next logical step. Except it wasn't." Babs grinned again and waggled her head comically from side to side as if to say, *What a ditz I was!*

"So no hard feelings?" Theodosia asked.

"None whatsoever," Babs said.

Theodosia looked at Jamie, who said, "Babs and I are lucky that way. We know we'll always remain friends."

"So you were probably an invited guest at the wedding?" Theodosia said.

"The wedding . . ." Babs pinched her lips together and made a sad face. "Yeah, I arrived there and . . . wow, things had already gone ka-pow crazy. The police were all over the place . . . the ambulances . . ." She shook her head. "What a bizarre tragedy, bordering almost on the operatic."

"Babs thinks everything is operatic," Jamie said.

"That's because I was just elected to the Charleston Opera Board," Babs said. "Can you believe it? Little old me? I think it's mostly because I work in PR."

"Do you have your own firm?" Theodosia asked.

"Don't I wish. No, I work at Milne and Kerrison Public Relations," Babs said. "We do work for a bunch of tech and financial companies."

"And I imagine that keeps you busy?" Theodosia said.

Babs lifted her leather envelope and said, "I'm headed home now to work on a press release for Burton Industries." She winked at Theodosia, then said, "But I'm engaged to their CFO, so I'm pretty sure the account is a lock." Then Babs turned a warm smile on Jamie and said, "But I still worry about this big lug. I mean, look at him. Wearing that silly nose splint that covers half his face. Makes him look like the creepy serial killer in that scary movie . . ."

"You mean Hannibal Lecter?" Theodosia asked.

Babs snapped her fingers. "That's the guy. Hey, nice to meet you," she said to Theodosia. Then she turned to Jamie, gave him a chaste kiss on the cheek, and scampered off.

Theodosia decided it was time to round up Drayton and bid goodbye to Sabrina. But when she looked around, Drayton was deep in conversation with an antique dealer friend, and Sabrina was talking to a man she didn't recognize. But wait a minute . . . whoever the guy was, he'd clearly upset Sabrina.

Her antenna tuned up high, Theodosia moved toward Sabrina. And, as she got closer, overheard part of her conversation. Or rather, it sounded more like an angry plea.

"You had no business coming here tonight," Sabrina said in a harsh whisper.

"I have every reason in the world to be here," the man shot back.

"Please leave."

The man crossed his arms over his chest. "Make me."

"Excuse me," Theodosia said. "I don't mean to butt in, but you two seem to be having a problem."

"She's the problem," the man said. He was tall, well over six feet, with bristly dark brows and a scruffy beard that he probably thought made him look like a hip musician. He wore a hoodie and jeans and looked totally out of place. "She doesn't want me here."

Theodosia stared at the man. "And you are . . . ?"

"Karl Rueff."

Celeste's bad-boy ex-boyfriend, Theodosia suddenly remembered. "Of course, I've heard of you."

"Good things, I hope," Rueff said.

"Not exactly. And since Sabrina has politely asked you to leave, I think you should respect her wishes."

"Respect," Rueff snorted. "Fat chance of finding any of that around here."

"Just the same," Theodosia said, "it's probably best that you leave."

"At least I got a last chance to see Celeste," Rueff said as he stomped off.

"Thank you," Sabrina said to Theodosia, once Rueff had left. She waved a hand in front of her face as if to fend off tears.

"Is there a reason you didn't want him here?" Theodosia asked. "Besides the obvious fact that he's ill-mannered and seems to make you upset?"

Sabrina was at a loss for words for a few moments, then finally stammered out, "Karl Rueff is just . . . bad news."

Five minutes later, the killer stood against the back wall, surveying the room full of mourners. And thought, *I did this. I made this happen all by myself.*

The old saying that revenge was sweet was only partially true. Revenge was fine, adequate almost, but a good, bloody death was so much better. That thought, savored with gusto, made the killer feel all warm and tingly inside. Almost brought on a case of the giggles. Top that with the fact that the hick county sheriff and the Charleston police weren't even remotely close to catching the killer, and it became pure poetry. Because—hah—the incompetent fools were looking in an entirely wrong direction.

Now the killer's gaze fell upon the tea shop lady. That one seemed a little too curious, a little too big for her britches. Which meant the killer would have to keep a sharp eye on her. Maybe throw a wrench into things if need be. Or if the snoopy tea lady got *too* close, the killer might have to arrange another accident. Which, in the long run, might prove to be highly amusing.

On the way home, Theodosia told Drayton about meeting Karl Rueff.

"You think he's a problem?" Drayton asked.

"I think Rueff is more than a problem, he's a possible suspect," Theodosia said.

Drayton turned in his seat to study her profile in the dark. "Seriously?"

"Rueff was rude and angry and clearly had a motive for showing up tonight."

"What do you think that motive was?"

"Possibly to gloat."

"You think *he* killed Celeste?"

"It would have been difficult for Rueff to know that Celeste would run into that greenhouse first," Theodosia said. "But we probably shouldn't rule him out."

"It looked like you fraternized with some interesting people tonight," Drayton said. "And who on earth was that curly-haired guy Jamie was having an intense conversation with?"

"I've no idea," Theodosia said as she turned down East Bay Street, then cut over on Chapel. "When I went over to talk to the guy, he saw me coming and basically sprinted out the door."

"That was fairly weird."

"It gave me a strange feeling. As though he really didn't want to talk to me."

"And the woman you were chatting with?"

"An old flame of Jamie's," Theodosia said. "A PR lady by the name of Babs Campbell."

"And I take it that flame has flickered out?"

"Well over two years ago, now they're just friends."

"You're sure about that?"

"Jamie's engaged, Babs is engaged. So I don't think there's a problem."

"There's no chance that Babs . . . ?"

"Could have sabotaged that greenhouse? She was actually an invited guest to the wedding and showed up after the disaster had happened. So no, I don't think so."

"Then who was the maniac who fiddled with those greenhouse gears?" Drayton wondered aloud. "Who's crazy enough to do something like that?"

"I don't know. I simply haven't uncovered enough information yet."

"You mean evidence."

Theodosia gripped the steering wheel a little tighter. "Right. Hard evidence, not just hearsay."

"Still, between Hunt and Lynch and Rueff you've managed to assemble a decent muddle of suspects."

"I have a feeling more will turn up," Theodosia said, "the deeper we dig into this."

"You think that's possible?" Drayton asked as they drove past a large Italianate home on the corner of Tradd and Legare. Orange and green lights lit the front portico, where three life-sized skeletons dangled and danced in the chill October breeze and a diaphanous white ghost with a hollow, deranged-looking face dangled from the upper balustrade.

Theodosia looked over at the strange specter and said, "At this point I think anything's possible."

16

"What I'm still wondering," said Drayton as he sat with Theodosia and sipped his cup of Irish breakfast tea on this Wednesday morning, "is who that curly-haired guy talking to Jamie last night was."

Theodosia looked up from her day planner, where she'd been jotting notes. "You mean the one who sprinted away from me?"

"Precisely."

"I've been thinking about that myself. Whoever he was, it looked as if he was having a relatively friendly conversation with Jamie, so I can't imagine he meant him any harm."

"So that's a good thing? He's not someone who should be on our suspect list?"

"Not unless we run into him again and have just cause," Theodosia said.

"Hey, you guys, look what I got!" Haley called out as she strolled toward them. She was carrying a silver tray heaped with orange and almond scones and had a box of chocolates tucked under one arm.

"Scones for takeout," Theodosia said.

"And do I see a box of chocolates?" Drayton said, his eyes gleaming as he reached out a hand. "Let me see." He had a ferocious sweet tooth and was your basic chocoholic.

Haley handed Drayton the box of candy.

"Mm, this is different from our Church Street Chocolates. Looks like chocolate-covered cherries," Drayton said, studying the label. "Where'd they come from?"

"One of our suppliers left them at the back door," Haley said. "It's like, you know, swag. Like the bunches of fresh herbs my greengrocer leaves, or when Phillipe's Bakery slips in a few extra French baguettes. Hey, are you gonna open that candy?"

"Um . . . maybe." Drayton looked like he was ready to rip the box open with his teeth.

But Theodosia, who was right in the middle of going over plans for today's Victorian Halloween Tea, said, "Perhaps we can sample those cherries later. Seeing as how we still need to finalize a few details."

"I'll stick 'em behind the counter for safekeeping," Haley said, taking the box back from Drayton.

Drayton gazed at it fondly, then turned his focus back to Theodosia. "How many guests today?" he asked.

Theodosia tapped her pen against the side of her day planner. "I just looked at the numbers and we've got forty-nine. In a tea shop that normally seats around forty-two."

"We had two cancellations late yesterday, then four people called this morning, clamoring for reservations. You know me, I couldn't say no," Drayton said. "So now we're oversold."

"It's a problem, but one we can probably deal with. If we set up an additional table—there's an extra one in back—and then wedge seven guests around a table that ordinarily seats six, we should just about make it."

"I can do the setting up if you can do the wedging in."

Theodosia studied her guest list. "Mrs. Conroy is a fairly tiny person. So is Mrs. Maynard. If we stick those two at the same table, we should be fine."

"Done," Drayton said. Then, "You realize we have tickets for the Vampyre Ballet tomorrow night."

"You mentioned that a few days ago."

"And you blew it off."

"Apologies, I didn't mean to. It's because I was all kerfuffled over Bettina's wedding. Or rather, her non-wedding."

"No harm done," Drayton said.

Theodosia rested her elbows on the table and leaned forward, stretching out a kink in her neck. "Refresh my memory, will you?"

"The Wild Dunes Ballet Company is putting on a special torchlight performance at the Heritage Society tomorrow night. On their back patio. I believe it's what they call an interpretive dance."

"Please tell me you didn't volunteer us to serve tea."

"Certainly not," Drayton said. "All we have to do is show up and enjoy ourselves. Nibble some hors d'oeuvres, sip a glass of red wine, and enjoy the program."

"This is a Halloween event?"

"Right. I believe the title of the program is Wilding on All Hallows' Eve."

"Do we have to wear a costume?"

"The invitation said costumes were encouraged but not mandatory."

"Rats, that means we have to wear a costume," Theodosia said. "And I don't have one."

"You've got more clothes than Macy's has inventory."

"Clothing, yes. Costumes, no," Theodosia said.

"Why can't you wear a long black dress, loop a bunch of pearl necklaces around your neck, and go as a sophisticated vampire? Like Catherine Deneuve in *The Hunger*."

"Wait. You watch vampire films?"

Drayton deflected her question. "It'd give you a chance to wear your witchy black boots."

"The expensive black leather lace-up boots that Delaine talked me into buying," Theodosia said, a thoughtful look on her face. "The ones that pinch my toes."

"But they are exceedingly stylish."

"Yoo-hoo," Miss Dimple called out as she pushed open the front door and let in a whoosh of fresh, cool air. "I came in early, just like you asked."

Drayton jumped up from his chair and hurried over to greet her. "And isn't that just the most delightful thing," he said as he helped her off with her coat. "We appreciate your coming in again to help."

"Today's your Victorian Halloween Tea, right?" Miss Dimple said.

"Yup, and we have an extra large group of guests," Theodosia explained.

"I oversold us," Drayton said, looking pleased.

Miss Dimple gave the tea room an appraising look. "Lots of guests," she murmured. "In that case, maybe we should start decorating?"

"I wasn't going to," Theodosia said slowly. "But now that you mention it . . ." She nodded to herself, thinking, then said, "Right, let's do it. It'll make for a fun atmosphere for our morning tea drinkers. And then we'll have that task out of the way."

"Excellent idea," Drayton said. "Especially since you've

already staged the decor in your office." He glanced at his watch. "But is there enough time? We open in twenty minutes."

"There's time," Theodosia said. "If we really shake our tail feathers."

Miss Dimple gave a delighted little wiggle and said, "That I can do."

"Then I'd better hurry up and grab that extra table," Drayton said.

When all the tables were set up and positioned closer together than usual, Theodosia and Miss Dimple covered them with black tablecloths, then added see-through lace tablecloths that Haley had dyed purple. Silver candelabras with tall black candles were placed in the center of the tables, along with crystal balls and white pumpkins.

"It's beginning to look spooky in here," Drayton remarked from his perch behind the front counter.

"Wait until we get the cobwebs up," Theodosia said.

She and Miss Dimple opened packages of fake cobwebs, stretched them out until they looked like delicate spiderwebs, then draped the cobwebs from the chandelier to the cupboards, and then to the tops of all the windows.

"Very nice," Drayton said, admiring their work. "But no spiders?"

"No spiders," Miss Dimple said.

With the cobwebs they had left over, Theodosia and Miss Dimple webbed the front counter, the front door, and a good part of Drayton's floor-to-ceiling tea shelves.

"How am I going to find anything?" Drayton wondered. Then added, "But on the plus side, it does look highly atmospheric. Like taking high tea in Dr. Frankenstein's laboratory."

Morning cream tea was easily handled with just a few local

shopkeepers dropping in for a quick cuppa as well as a few guests from nearby bed and breakfasts.

At ten thirty Lois Chamberlain came in with her little dachshund, Pumpkin, riding in a bookbag she had slung over one shoulder. Lois was a retired librarian who owned Antiquarian Books just down the block and had recently become a tea devotee. Today, Lois was dressed like a grad student, in jeans, an oversized sweater, and clogs, while Pumpkin wore a bright orange bandanna around her neck and sported her usual long-haired, dappled coat.

"I love what you've done to the place!" Lois exclaimed. "*Très* spooky!"

"You like it?" Drayton said.

"It looks like a classy bat cave," Lois chuckled. "Isn't it fun to get into the spirit of the moment—or should I say *spirits* since it's almost Halloween?" She glanced down at Pumpkin, who peeped out of her bag. "Look at this place, Pumpkin, isn't it fun?"

Pumpkin let loose a sharp bark.

"She approves," Lois said.

"Would you and Pumpkin like a table?" Theodosia asked Lois. She'd never balked at the idea of having dogs in the tea shop. Even Earl Grey, as large as he was, sometimes put in an appearance.

"I can only do takeout today," Lois said. "Pumpkin and I are on our way to a book sale over in Summerville. A private collector died, and the heirs called me to come have first look. Of course, they're probably going to overinflate the value of the books."

"You can negotiate a fair price," Drayton said. "I have faith in your business acumen."

"More faith than I do," Lois said. "So, Drayton, whatcha got brewing this morning?"

"I have fresh-brewed pots of spiced plum, lemon verbena, and oolong tea, all ready to go."

"Give me an extra large cup of the oolong."

"And a scone?" Drayton asked.

"Absolutely."

"We have ginger scones right here, and I believe Haley has some white chocolate scones in the kitchen."

Lois pointed to a scone in the glass cake saver. "The ginger scones are fine," she said as Drayton poured her tea, then placed a scone in an indigo blue paper bag. "Can you put it on my tab? 'Cause I really gotta bounce."

"Not a problem," Drayton said. But he didn't, because he never ran a tab for Lois. For her, it was all gratis.

As Lois was running out the door, the psychic was coming in.

"Oh wow," Lois said, when she caught sight of Madame Aurora. "You're wearing an actual cape! Purple with silver moons and stars." And then she was gone.

"Don't mind Lois," Theodosia said as she went over to greet the psychic. "She's one of our crazy neighbors."

"I knew that," Madame Aurora said. Then, when Theodosia looked surprised, said, "Gotcha. It was just a guess."

"Nicely done," Theodosia said. "So . . . we've got you over here at this small table by the fireplace. It's cozy and kind of private for when my guests want to drop by and do a tarot reading with you. Oh, and I draped the table in black velvet. I hope that works for you?"

"It's perfect," Madame Aurora said. She was mid-fifties with dark eyes, heavily penciled brows, and a small rosebud-shaped mouth. Beneath her purple cape she wore a ruffled red blouse and a long black skirt. A half dozen beaded necklaces and silver amulets hung around her neck. A genuine turban was nestled in the crook of one arm, and she wore quaint-looking black velvet slippers that turned up at the toes. Kind of like elf shoes.

With an hour and a half to go before their Victorian Halloween Tea, Theodosia brought out a container of red roses. The tips of the roses had been carefully dipped in black paint, thanks to a little extra work at Flora Dora, the florist down the street. Now all Theodosia had to do was arrange them in crystal vases.

"That's a stunning effect on those roses," Drayton said. "Beautiful, but a little sinister-looking, too." He turned and said, "Miss Dimple, what do you think of . . . Miss Dimple?" His voice rose in sudden concern.

"What?" Miss Dimple croaked. She was swaying slightly as she clutched the back of a chair, hanging on for dear life.

At that exact moment, Haley came speeding out of the kitchen, stopped in her tracks when she spotted Miss Dimple, and said, "Miss Dimple, what's wrong? You look like you're . . . in fact you are . . . turning positively green."

"And my stomach is churning like a broken washing machine," Miss Dimple said in a quavering voice. She gripped the back of the chair tighter. "I don't feel so good."

"Maybe something you ate?" Drayton said.

"That's the problem, I didn't eat anything." Miss Dimple frowned, touched a hand to a flushed pink cheek, and said, "No, I *did* eat something. I had one of those chocolates that were stashed behind the counter. Or maybe I ate two?"

"On an empty stomach?" Drayton asked.

Miss Dimple nodded.

"Maybe too rich for you," Drayton said.

"Or too much sugar?" Haley said. "That can do a number

on an empty stomach." Madame Aurora looked over and gave a concerned nod.

"I'm calling an Uber," Theodosia said. "We need to send you home to bed."

"Good idea," Drayton said.

"But then you'll be left shorthanded," Miss Dimple worried.

"We'll manage," Theodosia said. "It's you I'm worried about."

Once Theodosia had put Miss Dimple in the quickly arriving Uber, she went back into the tea shop, ready to dig in.

"There's a call for you!" Drayton cried from behind the counter.

Theodosia rushed over, grabbed the phone, and said, "Theodosia here."

"Theodosia? This is Isabelle Franklin, the manager at the Dove Cote Inn."

"Yes, Isabelle. What can I do for you?"

"Do you know Bettina West?"

"Sure do."

"Well, she's over here and making quite a scene."

"Bettina's at the Dove Cote Inn right now?" Theodosia was confused. "And she's . . . wait, what is she doing?"

"She's extremely upset. A few minutes ago she crashed a commercial club luncheon we were hosting in one of our meeting rooms and accosted one of our guests."

"Oh boy, do you know which guest it was?"

"A man named Martin Hunt."

The Hunt and Peck guy. "And what's Bettina doing now?"

"I brought her to my office and now she's sitting here crying," Isabelle said.

"Did you call her aunt, Delaine Dish?"

"I did, and Delaine said to call you."

"Ah," Theodosia said. *Thanks a lot, Delaine.* She looked at her watch and sighed. If she took off now, maybe, just maybe, she could squeeze in this weird errand. "Okay, Isabelle. I'll be right over."

17

Bettina was still leaking tears when Theodosia got there.

"I'm sorry about this," Theodosia said to Isabelle Franklin. "Bettina's had to face some soul-crushing problems lately."

Isabelle nodded. "She's been telling me all about it. Her bridesmaid getting killed, her fiancé badly injured . . . I'd say it's enough to drive anyone to distraction."

Isabelle Franklin was a small woman, mid-thirties, with shoulder-length blond hair that she wore held back with her trademark preppy velvet headband. Today she had on a snappy black blazer, a white blouse with a pussycat bow, black slacks, and black patent leather shoes with kitten heels. She was the manager at the Dove Cote Inn and a kind of jack-of-all-trades, handling room reservations, dining, and special events.

"You're very understanding," Theodosia said to Isabelle. Then she turned her gaze on Bettina, who was sitting in a pink leather club chair, looking sad and miserable. "Bettina," she said.

"No real harm was done," Isabelle assured Theodosia.

"Bettina was only in there for ten seconds or so. Gary, our head waiter, came and got me immediately. Then I . . . pulled her out."

"I'm sorry," Bettina blubbered as she blotted her eyes with a tissue. "I didn't think about what I was gonna do . . . well, I actually *did* think about it. Maybe too much. And then I acted impulsively."

Theodosia touched a hand to Bettina's shoulder and said, "If it makes you feel any better, I do that all the time." Which caused Bettina to stutter out a quick laugh, then start crying all over again.

"S-s-sorry," Bettina said. "I know it was stupid."

"We'll get out of your hair now," Theodosia said to Isabelle. "And thank you again for being so understanding."

"Don't mention it," Isabelle said. "And say hi to Drayton for me, will you? Tell him I'm going to stop by soon and pick up some of his famous cranberry-apple blend."

"I will."

Theodosia got Bettina up and onto her feet and led her into the lobby of the Dove Cote Inn. Here was an arrangement of cozy armchairs and sofas done in cream-colored leather and accented with plump pink and green velvet pillows. The Chinese carpet underfoot was an elegant shade of persimmon, brass lamps sparkled on side tables, and a fire crackled in the yellow-brick fireplace. At the front desk, a couple was checking in.

"C'mon, let's sit over here." Theodosia led Bettina to a small love seat that was tucked discreetly behind a potted palm tree. "Tell me what's going on."

"You're not mad at me?" Bettina said.

Theodosia smiled at her. "Should I be?"

"You're too sweet," Bettina said.

"I totally love the flattery, but right now we need to be absolutely straight with each other. Can you do that?"

"I guess."

"So tell me, what possessed you to come storming over here and accost Martin Hunt?"

"Because I started thinking about all the horrible, mean things Hunt said about Jamie!" Bettina cried. "And how Hunt threatened to retaliate against Jamie because he lost all that money—even though it wasn't Jamie's fault at all. Well, not entirely."

"And then?"

Bettina hunched her shoulders. "Then I got ragin'-hot mad and I called Hunt and Peck and the people at the store told me Hunt was over here at a business luncheon. And then I just sort of lost it. My brain flashed code red and I rushed over here."

"What were you going to do?"

"I didn't bring a weapon if that's what you're asking," Bettina said.

"That's not what I was asking."

"I guess I was going to tell Hunt off . . . embarrass him to death. And then I hoped that . . ."

"You hoped he'd confess?" Theodosia asked. "Admit to you that he rigged the greenhouse?"

"Yes!"

"I don't think it works that way in real life."

Bettina pulled a tissue from her purse, wiped at her nose, and said, "No?"

"You were imagining a movie scenario," Theodosia said.

"But Martin Hunt is guilty, I know he is!"

"We don't know that at all. He's only one of several suspects," Theodosia said.

"Really?" Bettina drew a deep breath and then released it in a kind of shudder. "Jeez, I'm sorry. Does this mean you're going to stop investigating?"

"Not if I can help it. You do want me to keep going, don't you?"

"More than ever!" Bettina said.

Theodosia looked at her watch and felt her heart lurch. Time was slipping away. She stood up and said, "Do you need a ride somewhere?"

"I think I'd rather walk," Bettina said.

"Good. Give you a chance to cool off before your visit this afternoon with the psychic."

Theodosia rushed back to the Indigo Tea Shop and surveyed the Halloween special effects. All the morning tea guests had left, tables had been set, candles lit, chairs and tables squished together, and the overhead lighting dimmed.

"Looks good," Theodosia said to Drayton. "Downright spooky."

"Haley went ahead and put sugar cameos at each place setting," Drayton said. "They're meant as favors, right?"

"Right." Theodosia had sourced the candies from a wholesaler in Salem, Massachusetts. They were round sugar cameos, the size of an old-fashioned silver dollar, but instead of a cameo portrait of a lovely lady, they were skeletons in Victorian costumes.

Drayton lifted a single eyebrow. "Did you manage to rein in Bettina before she embarrassed herself?"

"By the time I got there, Bettina was leaking tears and apologizing to Isabelle. The poor girl got a notion in her head that Martin Hunt was the killer, so she decided to accost him."

"Maybe it wasn't such a silly notion. Did you talk to Hunt when you were there?"

"I didn't talk to him, but I can guarantee you he's still on my suspect list. No, all I did was try to impress upon Bettina that accosting someone, getting right up in their face, is not the way to gather evidence or wring out a confession."

"I hope she took your cautionary words to heart."

"We'll have to wait and see." Theodosia looked around the tea room again and murmured, "Something's missing." Then she touched the top of her head, smiled, and said, "I almost forgot my witch's hat!"

That's how they greeted their guests: Theodosia and Haley wearing tall, peaky witches' hats, Drayton in a black Victorian top hat. And wouldn't you know it, some of their guests arrived wearing costumes. There was a Venetian lady, three witches (one with blacked-out teeth!), two fairy princesses, a cowgirl, and a woman wearing head-to-toe leopard print.

With the extra table—and the extra few guests—it was a tight squeeze, but Theodosia finally got everyone situated. After much oohing and aahing over the decorations, Theodosia grabbed a wicker broom, stepped to the center of the room, and tapped the tip of the handle against the floor.

"Welcome to our first-ever Victorian Halloween Tea," Theodosia began. "As many of you probably know, the Victorian era began in 1837 and ran to 1901. This was an exciting time in England when many of the Victorians openly embraced séances, psychics, tarot cards, and crystal balls and even believed in ghost sightings. It was, in a sense, a Victorian death culture, since they also engaged in elaborate funerals, followed strict mourning rules, created postmortem portraits, and built opulent tombs and cemeteries.

"To take you back in time and give you a sense of how immersed the Victorians were in communing with the spirits, I'd like to introduce Madame Aurora, our visiting psychic." She waved a hand in her direction. "Madame Aurora?"

Madame Aurora stood up to acknowledge the applause, gave a friendly wave, and bobbed her turbaned head.

"Please feel free to wander over and converse with Madame Aurora anytime you want, and be sure to have your tarot cards read," Theodosia said. "And now, I'm sure you'd all like to hear about our Victorian Halloween menu. For starters, you have your choice of cranberry scones with clotted cream or English crumpets with rose petal jam. Your second course will be a bowl of pureed pumpkin soup with a side of deviled eggs. And thanks to our very own Earl of Sandwich over there"—Theodosia gestured at Drayton—"we'll be serving Hampshire chicken salad on crostini and sliced apple and cheddar cheese on sourdough bread. And of course there's tea. Drayton, if you would?"

Drayton removed his top hat and bowed. "I have three special teas for your sipping enjoyment," he said. "One is a salty caramel pumpkin black tea from Simpson and Vail, the second is a bewitching house brew that I call Haunted Hibiscus. This one's a blend of white tea and hibiscus with a bit of lemon thrown in. And my third brew is called Ghostly Green, it's a Japanese green tea flavored with bits of orange and papaya."

First courses were served then and teacups filled. Once everyone was nibbling and sipping, Theodosia made the rounds, talking to her guests, encouraging them to visit Madame Aurora's table. And by the time the tea sandwiches had come out, the guests had started to do exactly that. More than a few wandered over to Madame Aurora for private conversations and tarot card readings.

One of the guests, who was dressed as a witch herself,

turned in her seat to speak with Theodosia. "I was just wondering," she said. "Do *you* believe in tarot card reading?"

"I believe that it's a fun thing to experiment with," Theodosia said. "But do I believe that it can predict the future—or put me in touch with my dead grandmother? Then, no, I don't think that's going to happen. But really, you should have a go at it yourself. Talk to Madame Aurora, see what the cards might indicate for you. It could be fun."

When it was time for dessert, Theodosia once again tapped her broom on the floor, bringing lunchtime conversation down to a low buzz. "I realize I haven't warned you about dessert," she said.

Now there was a smattering of applause. The regulars all knew that Haley was an excellent pastry chef.

"To satisfy your sweet tooth, we'll be serving Victorian-style petits fours as well as generous slices of devil's food cake," Theodosia told them.

"And more tea," Drayton said from the counter. "Lots more tea for whoever wants it."

A steady stream of guests continued to find their way to Madame Aurora's table, while other guests wandered around the tea room, shopping Theodosia's well-stocked highboys for tea towels, trivets, jars of honey, tins of tea, and her proprietary T-Bath products.

"They're practically clearing our shelves," Theodosia confided to Drayton. "Which means I'd better get my Christmas orders in fast."

"I couldn't agree more," Drayton said as he sped off, clutching a teapot in each hand.

Bettina and Delaine arrived just as the luncheon had worn down and the last guests were leaving.

"Perfect timing," Theodosia said as she greeted them at the door.

"Is it really?" Delaine said as the few remaining guests slipped past her. "Because I for one have been busy as the proverbial one-armed paperhanger. My shipment of cruise clothes arrived this morning, and I'm frantic to get everything unpacked, steamed, and onto the racks. My customers need to *plan* their wardrobes. They surely can't be expected to show up in St. Martens or St. Lucia wearing just any old skirt and T-shirt."

"I think your assistant, Janine, can manage just fine," Bettina said.

"We'll see," Delaine said. She reached into her bag, pulled out a small bottle of perfume, and proceeded to spritz herself.

"Are you layering scents again?" Bettina asked.

Delaine shook her head. "Layering is out, now zoning is in."

Theodosia decided to ignore Delaine and focus on Bettina. "Are you feeling any better?" Theodosia asked.

"I feel silly, is what I feel," Bettina admitted with a rueful smile. "That was just plain dumb of me, to go rushing over to the Dove Cote Inn like that. I let my anger get the best of me."

"There, there," Delaine said. "Never apologize for your emotions. They're yours to own."

"That's very deep," Bettina said. "Who said that?"

Delaine looked puzzled. "I just did."

"Oh, I thought maybe you were quoting the Dalai Lama or somebody famous," Bettina said.

"You don't think I'm quotable?" Delaine said in a sharp tone.

"We know you are," Theodosia said. *No debate there.*

Delaine was about to say something else when Sabrina came flying through the front door.

"Is everyone here? You haven't started without me, have you?" Sabrina asked in a rush.

"You're right on time," Theodosia said. "We were just about to start." She led everyone over to Madame Aurora's table, where candles flickered all around her, then sat them down and made introductions.

"And you're trying to make contact with a dear departed spirit?" Madame Aurora asked in a gentle tone. Theodosia had briefed her earlier about Celeste's murder, so she pretty much knew what to expect.

"*Departed* sounds like Celeste hopped a plane to Miami," Delaine said. "When in actuality the poor girl is dead." Then she looked around the tea shop and gave a mock shiver. "Why does this place have to look so darn *spooky*? With the lights dimmed and cobwebs draped everywhere, I feel like I'm trapped in a haunted house. And this weird music . . ."

"It's Halloween," Bettina said. "Get over it."

"I think it sets a perfect mood," Sabrina said. "Kind of sad and soulful."

Delaine folded her hands in her lap. "Whatever."

"Perhaps we could begin with some energy cleansing," Madame Aurora suggested. She made a point of looking directly at Delaine.

"Why are you staring at me?" Delaine cried. "My energy is squeaky-clean."

Madame Aurora dropped her gaze to her stack of tarot cards with a *What did I do to deserve this?* look. Then she said, in a soft voice, "Tell me what answers you've come to seek."

"Best-case scenario," Sabrina said, "would be finding out who killed my sister, Celeste."

"Because we know for sure it wasn't an accident," Bettina added.

Theodosia could feel the energy coming off Sabrina and

Bettina, and it felt like despair without much hope. Though she wasn't a believer in psychic readings or tarot cards, she did believe there was something more out there. Call it an afterlife, heaven, or just some kind of great continuum; it felt as if there had to be some otherworldly realm where good souls went once they'd left their earthly bonds.

Madame Aurora shuffled her tarot cards, then laid them out in the pattern of a cross. Turning one card over slowly, she revealed the Tower card. "This card indicates the past, in this case a loss or painful process."

"Yes!" Bettina said. "That's it exactly. We've lost our dear, dear Celeste." She gazed at Madame Aurora with anxious eyes. "What else do you see in the cards?"

Madame Aurora turned over a second card. "This indicates the future," she said.

"The Six of Wands card?" Delaine said. "What's that weird imagery supposed to mean?"

"It's an indication of destiny and reaching a significant goal," Madame Aurora said. "It means energy aligning with spirit guides and angels."

"Oh my gosh," Sabrina said. "That feels so right on!"

"But where is Celeste now?" Bettina asked. "Is there any way to know?"

Madame Aurora turned over a third card to reveal the Wheel of Fortune card. "This card means your dear departed is taking a step into the great unknown. That she is between worlds right now."

"That doesn't sound like a very comfortable situation," Delaine said.

"Many souls take a good deal of time to find their way," Madame Aurora murmured.

"If you say so," Delaine said.

"But will her killer be brought to justice?" Sabrina asked with a worried look. "That's what's really on our minds."

Madame Aurora turned over the card at the very top of the cross. It was the Hanged Man card.

"That looks awful," Delaine cried, just as all the lights in the tea shop winked out.

"Help!" Bettina cried. "What just happened?"

"This is too scary for words!" Delaine stuttered out.

"It's simply a blown fuse," Drayton called out in a loud but calming voice.

"Really?" Theodosia said. "Now we've got a blown fuse?"

"Give me thirty seconds and I'll have it fixed," Drayton promised. He grabbed a flashlight from under the counter, snapped it on, and headed for the fuse box in the back of the shop.

They all sat there in the dark for thirty seconds, then forty seconds, then a full minute, feeling more and more uncomfortable. And just when Delaine stood up and cried, "I need to get out of here!" the lights came back on.

"Everybody okay?" Drayton called from the back hallway.

"We're good," Theodosia said.

"That remains to be seen," Delaine said. Then she sat down and turned her focus back to the Hanged Man card. "What did you say this indicates?"

"The Hanged Man doesn't necessarily mean danger or death," Madame Aurora said. "It only indicates that an answer still hangs in the balance."

"So we don't really know anything about Celeste," Bettina sighed.

"Here I was hoping the cards would help *point* to the killer," Sabrina said, sounding disappointed. "Reveal some sort of clue."

Madame Aurora gently waved her hands above the cards, as if to intuit a message from them. Then, with eyebrows raised, said, "This is a fairly interesting turn of events."

"What is?" asked Delaine.

"I'm getting a message that someone in this room *knows* the killer," Madame Aurora said. At which point everyone turned to look at Theodosia.

"Me?" Theodosia squeaked. This was an unexpected twist. "Trust me when I say I *don't* know the identity of the killer."

"But it's possible you may have exchanged words with this person," Madame Aurora said. "Which means you need to take great care, because this person is hiding a dangerously dark nature."

"Wow," Bettina said. "Theo, you must be hot on the trail."

"If I am, I'm not aware of it," Theodosia said.

"Be patient," Madame Aurora counseled. "Remain persistent in your investigation."

"I'm getting chills," Delaine said. "This sounds like . . . good news?"

"I'll say," Bettina said.

Everyone seemed to relax then and sit back in their chairs to ponder Madame Aurora's words. Turned out she wasn't finished. Staring directly at Sabrina, the psychic reached out and grasped the girl's right hand.

"You also figure in the cards," Madame Aurora said. "Because of your close, personal loss."

Tears sparkled in Sabrina's eyes. "My dear sister," she choked out.

"But this loss has led to something extremely beneficial," Madame Aurora continued.

Sabrina looked completely befuddled. "I'm sorry." She shook her head. "No. I don't understand what you're talking about."

"Finances," said Madame Aurora.

"Oh, I don't think so," Sabrina murmured.

This time the medium was almost defiant. "No, no, I can feel it, the vibrations are quite distinct." She picked up her deck, dealt two more cards, and then a final card. It was the Nine of Cups. "You see? This tells me you are about to profit from a great tragedy."

Sabrina's eyes widened in surprise, her shoulders tensed, and she stood up abruptly, practically knocking her chair over backward. "This isn't working for me," she gasped. "I . . . I don't believe a word of what this woman is saying."

Delaine, green eyes glittering, turned to stare at Sabrina and said, "Why not?"

18

Tears clouding her eyes, Sabrina staggered away from the table, heading for the front door. Stumbling in her haste to escape the tea shop, she was tripped up by a chair leg, faltered, and was immediately intercepted by Theodosia, who'd also leaped from her chair.

"Please don't run off like this," Theodosia said to Sabrina.

"Let me by," Sabrina hissed. Her face glowed red, her breathing was shallow, and she looked horribly upset.

But Theodosia continued to block Sabrina's way and remained insistent. "I really think we need to talk."

"No, we don't," Sabrina protested.

Bettina, Delaine, and Madame Aurora watched the two women closely, wondering who was going to come out on top. Drayton was also following the action, a look of bewilderment on his face.

"I'm sorry, but I'm sure we have some unfinished business here," Theodosia said. She kept her voice even but insistent.

"This situation is making me very nervous," Bettina said.

"Like Sabrina has something to hide," Delaine said in a strident voice.

"I wonder what it could be," Bettina said.

That was the last straw for Sabrina. Her head dropped, her shoulders began to shake, and she stood there in abject misery.

"Drayton, could you bring us some tea?" Theodosia asked.

Drayton nodded sharply as Theodosia put her arm around Sabrina and said, "Come on, let's go back to my office and talk about this."

Theodosia got Sabrina seated in the big cozy chair she called the tuffet, then knelt down beside her.

"Why are you so upset?" she asked. "What caused you to run off like that when Madame Aurora said you were about to profit?"

Sabrina waved a hand in front of her face. "It's nothing, really. I'm . . . I'm mostly embarrassed."

"You needn't be. But I do think there's something you want to tell me. That might have to do with . . . finances?"

Sabrina took a deep breath, blew it out, and said, "It's just something our grandfather set up for us a while back."

Theodosia studied Sabrina. Her stiff posture and tight body language indicated that she was clearly hiding something. But what could it possibly be? Theodosia's mind quickly stuttered over a few ideas.

Something about Jamie? Or Celeste? No, it has to be about money.

Then, like a piece of a puzzle clicking into place, Theodosia figured out the answer. "Wait. You say your grandfather set it up? You're talking about a trust fund, aren't you?"

Sabrina looked like a captured animal, as if she wanted to chew off her foot to escape a trap. "Yes, I suppose that's what the lawyers call it," she snapped.

"So you're in line to inherit some money?"

"Celeste and I both are. Were."

"When?" Theodosia asked.

"This year. Next month."

"But Celeste is deceased." Theodosia flinched at the word. It sounded so final—probably because it *was* final. "So what happens with Celeste's share of the inheritance?"

"Really, it's no concern to you . . ."

"It goes to you, doesn't it?" Theodosia said, probing gently. "In the event of Celeste's death, you receive all the money."

"I guess," Sabrina said. It was almost a whisper.

"How much? How much total?"

"Ten."

"Ten thousand?" Theodosia asked.

Sabrina twisted in her chair uncomfortably. "Ten million."

"Dear Lord," Theodosia said. Ten million dollars was an absolute fortune. Invested carefully, she knew that amount could easily double within a decade. Or, even dismissing the investing part, ten million dollars was enough to retire on, and live life in a rather grand fashion.

On the other hand, it was also ten million reasons to kill someone.

"Knock knock." It was Drayton outside the office with a tray of tea.

"Come in," Theodosia said.

Drayton bustled in, set the tea tray on Theodosia's desk, then poured out two steaming cups. "There you go," he said, leaving as unobtrusively as he'd come in.

Theodosia handed a cup of tea to Sabrina. "Here, sip a little tea. It'll make you feel better."

"No, it won't," Sabrina said. "Nothing's going to make me feel better now. You and your stupid psychic just made me look like murder suspect number one!" More tears trickled down her cheek. "You know darn well that Bettina and Delaine will arrive at the conclusion that *I* killed Celeste. That *I'm* the killer."

"They won't think that at all."

"Yes, they will. Because that's exactly what *you're* thinking!"

"I'm not," Theodosia said, even though she had to admit the idea was buzzing around in her brain.

Sabrina shook her head. "It was such a bad idea to talk to a psychic. Stupid me, what was I thinking?" She ran a hand through her hair, mussing it up.

"You were thinking about your sister, whom you loved and cared for very much," Theodosia said in what she hoped was a commiserating tone.

Sabrina's lips twisted in a sneer as she said, "Is that what you *really* think? Now that I'm set to inherit all that money?"

Theodosia didn't have an easy answer.

"Yeah," Sabrina spat out. "That's what I thought." She stood up, gave Theodosia a withering glance, and left.

Bettina, Delaine, and Madame Aurora were gone by the time Theodosia emerged from her office carrying the untouched tea tray.

"The tea was not good?" Drayton asked, worry creasing his face.

"It was fine, Sabrina didn't want any."

"But you had a heart-to-heart talk with her? Before she went flying out the door?"

"Not exactly," Theodosia said.

"Then what?"

"You're not going to believe this."

"Try me," Drayton said.

"I need a cup of strong tea first. Then I'll tell you everything."

Drayton ducked behind the counter, poured a cup of Plum Deluxe's blackberry mojito tea, and handed her the teacup. "Now tell me."

Theodosia took a fortifying sip, then said, "Okay, I'm just going to come right out and say this . . . ask this. Do you think Sabrina could have murdered her own sister?"

"What!" Drayton cried. "Of course not. I can't believe that poor distressed woman could ever contemplate murdering her sister. No, absolutely not. Besides, there's no way Sabrina could have known Celeste would walk into that greenhouse first."

"Except for the fact that Sabrina knew Celeste was the snoopy one. Always wanting to be first, no matter what."

"Wait a minute. Are you implying that Sabrina had a motive of some sort? That she would somehow profit from Celeste's death?" Drayton asked.

"I'm afraid so. Turns out there's a ten-million-dollar trust fund that was supposed to be split equally between the two sisters. But in the event of one sister's death, the other sister inherits it all."

"Holy snack crackers!" Drayton cried. "Sabrina told you this?"

"She just now admitted it."

"Ten million dollars? That's a bloody fortune."

"It surely is," Theodosia said.

"Wait, do you really think Sabrina would murder her own sister over that kind of inheritance money? Or hire someone to do it for her?" He gave a quick shake of his head as if to toss off that idea. "No, that would be too cold and calculating for words."

"It would," Theodosia agreed.

"Gracious," Drayton said, giving it a second thought and looking nonplussed. "Could she? Would she?"

"I don't know. I hope not."

Drayton wasn't often at a loss for words, but he was floundering now. "Well, now that the handle's come off the wagon, what do we do?"

"I've got to inform the police, for one thing," Theodosia said. Then she glanced at her watch. "As for right now, I'm afraid we have to switch gears and start getting ready for the cemetery crawl tonight. We need to help Haley assemble tea sandwiches, then pack everything up and transport it. As far as Sabrina and the money goes, we need to set that situation on the back burner."

"I agree, let it percolate for now, because we don't have a lot of time to figure it out," Dayton said. "Gracious, I still have to select and brew my teas, then give Haley an assist."

"One of us should call Miss Dimple and make sure she's okay."

"I already did," Drayton said. "She said she's mostly just tired and hopes to be in soon."

"Do you think . . . ," Theodosia began, just as the front door rattled in its frame. She turned as Riley poked his head in and said, "Well, hello there," in a cheery tone of voice.

"Hi," Theodosia said back to him.

Riley tiptoed over, gave Theodosia a hug and a kiss on the forehead, then looked around the tea room. "I love what you've done with the place. Cozy, snug, a little bat cave moderne, but without all the endless knickknacks that professional decorators seem to love."

Theodosia placed a hand on his chest and gave a playful shove. "You know it's for Halloween."

"One of my least favorite holidays," Riley said as Theodosia reached over to pick up a teapot that had been left on one of the tables. "It's when all the crazies come spilling out into the real world. It's hard enough to keep our streets safe *without* a bunch of devils and vampires running wild. People see a guy in a costume, they think it's all fun and hilarious. They don't know that Mr. Devil or Vlad the Vampire might hijack their car at gunpoint."

"That really happens?" Drayton asked as he placed a large silver tea urn on the counter.

"Believe it," Riley said, stepping over to talk to him.

"I had no idea things could get that crazy," Drayton said. He nodded to Riley, then carried his tea urn into the kitchen.

"So how was your fancy luncheon?" Riley asked. He wandered behind the front counter, idly running his hands over the scatter of tea tins Drayton had left sitting there.

"Good. Great. But I have to tell you something," Theodosia said.

"Oh yeah?"

Theodosia quickly told Riley about the tarot reading and the ten-million-dollar trust fund that Sabrina was set to inherit. Riley listened eagerly to the first part of her story, then his face changed to a solemn expression when she got to the money part.

Once she'd finished, Riley let loose a low whistle and said, "Ten million?"

"What do you think? Does that put Sabrina in the category of suspect?"

"There's no actual hard evidence that she murdered her sister, but it does elevate her to a person of interest." Riley slapped a hand down on the counter and said, "This is fairly key information. I need to talk to my boss and also notify Sheriff Ambourn."

"I was hoping you'd talk to Sabrina first."

"Why?" he asked.

"As a favor to me. And I guess to Sabrina, too. Before this thing gets too big and takes on a life of its own."

"I suppose I could do that," Riley said. "Talk to her and get a few more details. Maybe talk to her lawyer or whoever's handling the trust."

"Thank you," Theodosia said as Riley reached over and flipped the lid off the box of chocolate-covered cherries that was sitting there. He fished one out and was about to pop it in his mouth when Theodosia yelled, "Stop!"

Riley stopped, the chocolate-covered cherry just inches from his mouth. "What?" he asked.

"Miss Dimple ate two of those chocolates this morning and went home sick," Theodosia said.

"They made her sick?" Riley squinted at his piece of candy. "Naw. Couldn't have."

"Give it up, please." Theodosia grabbed a small trash can and held it up to him. "I'm serious."

Riley dutifully dropped his candy into the trash. "What's the real reason?" he asked as he grinned at her. "You worried I'll spoil my appetite?"

"No, I'm worried you're going to get sick and die," Theodosia said.

"You really think there's something wrong with that candy?"

"It wouldn't be the first case of sabotage this week," Theodosia said.

Riley frowned. "In that case, maybe I should . . . you want me to take the candy with me and have our lab look at it?"

"It would settle my mind if you did that, yes."

"Our lab rats are going to think I've gone absolutely cuckoo.

First I bring them a plastic skull, then a pair of boots, now a box of chocolates. They'll think I'm on some weird scavenger hunt."

"About that skull," Theodosia said, glad he'd reminded her. "Did they find any prints on it?"

"Funny you should ask," Riley said. "My guys said it looked like it'd been wiped clean."

"Why am I not surprised?" Theodosia said. Then, "Please, please talk to Sabrina."

"I will do that."

Five minutes after Riley had left and Theodosia had locked the front door, there was a *scritch-scratching* at the window.

Like the raven in Poe's poem? Theodosia wondered. Then shook her head to dismiss that weird thought.

But the scratching continued, so Theodosia walked to the front of the shop, peered out the window, and found Ken Lotter smiling in at her.

Oh dear.

Unlocking the door, she opened it wide and said, "Lotter? What do you want? We're closed, you know." Ken Lotter was the slick-looking, gelled-haired, up-and-coming features reporter for K-BAM TV. He was youngish, maybe mid-thirties, with big teeth and an even bigger smile.

"What do I want?" Lotter said. "I think you know what I want. I want a little inside information, thank you very much."

"You and everyone else."

"I know you catered that flower farm wedding and I know all about your heroics. I also know you were poking around that collapsed greenhouse."

"So what?"

"So I think you found something. Or are in the process of trying to figure something out."

Theodosia sighed. "I think we'd all like to know what happened that day."

Lotter gave her a dazzling smile. "Everyone already knows that a criminal act took place. The police are probably calling it murder by now. But here's the thing. You, you adorable little auburn-haired beauty, have a knack for solving crimes. This I know."

"Mr. Lotter, right now I have a knack for making tea sandwiches for tonight's cemetery crawl. So if you don't mind . . ." Theodosia began to close the door.

"All right," Lotter said. "Have it your way, but if you see me shadowing you, don't be surprised."

This time Theodosia closed the door all the way. And made sure it was locked.

Twenty seconds later—maybe less than that, maybe *ten* seconds later—there was an insistent knock at the door.

"What!" Theodosia shouted through the door.

"Open up, it's me!"

"Who's 'me'?"

"Bill Glass."

Theodosia opened the door and peered out at the scruffy-looking publisher. "What do *you* want?"

"What was that cock of the walk Lotter doing here?" Glass asked, looking thoroughly incensed. "Here I thought I was your one and only when it came to talking to reporters."

"There is no one and only. There is no news. I have nothing to tell you," Theodosia said.

"But you're still looking into that bridesmaid's death," Glass said, shaking a finger at her. "Which the police are now calling a murder."

"Glass," Theodosia said, "if I knew something, I'd tell you. Just to get you off my case."

Glass clapped a hand to his heart and said, "You would? Really? That's more than I could ever hope for."

"You are so full of it, Glass." This time Theodosia shut the door hard, locked it, and vowed not to open it again.

19

Forty minutes later, with most of the tea sandwiches assembled and Drayton readying all their wicker picnic baskets, Theodosia slipped away on a small investigative mission. She didn't hold out a lot of hope that she'd be successful, but Teener's Costumes and Tricks was only a few blocks away, so that's where she ended up. Browsing the aisles and looking at endless racks of garish Halloween costumes as well as noisemakers, spooky masks, rubber bats, orange wigs, plastic pumpkins, and . . . yes, plastic skulls. Interestingly, the shop sold skulls exactly like the ones that had been placed on Jamie's hospital tray and that she'd found in his apartment.

Theodosia lifted one of the skulls off the shelf and carried it to the checkout counter, where a teenage boy wearing a clown costume, yellow fright wig, and a name tag that said RICKY had just finished ringing up a customer.

"Did you sell any skulls like this recently?" Theodosia asked him.

Ricky stared at her, his eyes large and limpid under his

scruffy wig. "Are you kidding me? We've sold a million of them."

"Probably not a million," Theodosia said. "More like, what, a couple of dozen?"

Ricky shrugged. "I guess."

Theodosia took out her iPhone, went to the Hunt and Peck website, found a photo of Martin Hunt, and showed it to Ricky. "Did this guy buy one of your skulls?"

"I dunno."

"Take a closer look, would you?"

Ricky gave a cursory glance. "Sorry, but we've been super busy all week. And I don't pay much attention to customers."

"This is a pretty stressful job, huh?" Theodosia asked.

"Are you kidding?" Ricky said. "A four-hour shift standing on my feet, answering questions and ringing up purchases? You try it sometime."

"I hear you."

"It's darn near killing me!" Ricky cried.

"I'll bet it is," Theodosia said, trying hard not to laugh out loud.

On an ordinary night St. Philips Cemetery was a spooky place. Tilting tombstones loomed like rows of jagged teeth, ancient moss-covered graves carried faint inscriptions, and headless marble statues stood guard. Now add in green and purple lighting, candles sputtering atop gravestones, and tendrils of fog ghosting in from the Atlantic Ocean and you had yourself a spooky, highly atmospheric setting.

"How many people should we expect tonight?" Drayton asked Theodosia. He and Haley had set up two tables under one of the cemetery's gigantic live oaks. One table held an array of scones, tea sandwiches, and brownie bites; the other held two large silver tea urns and stacks of paper cups. "And I must say, these paper cups are less than optimal." His eyes flicked up. "As is that umbrella of Spanish moss dripping down above us."

"Think of them both as biodegradable," Theodosia said. "As for the number of guests tonight, best guess is we'll attract the most visitors just because St. Philips is smack-dab in the heart of the Historic District. So we have to be ready. Julie Braun, who heads the marketing committee, thought we might get between two hundred and three hundred guests."

"And they'll all want tea and goodies?" Haley asked.

"I think . . . yes," Theodosia said. "In fact, I see some early cemetery crawl folks now."

A group of five teenage girls fluttered up to their table. They all wore black pussycat ears and had small black spots adorning their noses.

"Tea?" one of them asked.

"And brownies?" another asked.

"Right," Drayton said, snapping to. "Help yourself to the brownies and scones while I pour you all cups of tea."

St. Philips Cemetery was situated directly behind St. Philip's Church and was one of the features on Charleston's famed Gateway Walk. The walk itself ran from the Unitarian Church on Archdale Street, meandered across King Street, and went behind the Gibbes Museum of Art. When it crossed Meeting Street, things really got interesting. Lots of statuary, gardens, pattering fountains, stands of palmettos, and tall, sculpted hedges. A cryptic inscription on a plaque attached to the Governor Aiken Gates proclaimed, THROUGH HANDWROUGHT GATES, ALLURING PATHS LEAD ON TO PLEASANT PLACES. WHERE GHOSTS OF LONG-FORGOTTEN THINGS HAVE LEFT ELUSIVE TRACES.

Elusive traces were haunting Theodosia right now as she greeted guests, handed out cups of tea, and, in the back of her mind—always in the back of her mind—wondered who could have had a hand in killing Celeste.

She was deep in thought when a familiar voice said, "Theodosia? Earth to Theodosia?"

Theodosia shook her head to help get rid of her thought cobwebs and saw Lois Chamberlain standing there. Naturally, Lois's little dachshund, Pumpkin, was snuggled in her bookbag.

"Oh my gosh, Lois, I was so lost in thought that I almost didn't see you. Apologies."

"No apologies needed," Lois said, chuckling as she held up a hand. "I take the liberty of spacing out all the time."

Theodosia snapped her fingers. "You were on your way to a book sale this morning. Did you buy any books?"

"Excuse me, have we met? Of course I ended up buying the entire collection. You should see my poor old Ford Bronco. The springs are sagging from carrying so many kilotons."

"But I bet you'll sell every one of those books and turn a nice, juicy profit," Theodosia said.

Lois winked at her. "That's the name of the game, isn't it? Don't just make a living, make a profit."

"Words to live by," Theodosia said.

Five minutes later, Babs Campbell drifted by, looking adorable in a black cashmere sweater and tartan plaid skirt.

"Burberry, right?" Theodosia said, nodding at her skirt.

"Yes, but it's *ancient*," Babs said. "I'm one of those crazy people who hangs on to every stitch of clothing from, like, decades ago. I never feel the urge to purge, so I don't throw anything away."

"And when it comes back in style, you're all set."

"Exactly," Babs laughed.

"Okay, now I have to ask," Theodosia said. "What is that delightful scent you're wearing?" Maybe because Delaine was always spritzing on perfume, "zoning it" as she called it, Theodosia was becoming more aware of what fragrances people were wearing.

"It's called Hidden Hearts, orange blossoms with a top note of vanilla."

Theodosia talked to Babs for another few minutes. Then, when she figured they were sufficiently cool with each other, laid a big question on her.

"Babs, do you have any idea as to who might have fiddled with the greenhouse gears and pulleys?"

"You're a curious lady, aren't you?" Babs said. But she said it with a warm, understanding look on her face. "Do you freelance for the police or something? Or are you writing a true crime book?"

"No, I'm just an interested party working on my own. I actually own a tea shop." Theodosia lifted a hand to indicate the tea table, where Haley was passing out scones and Drayton was pouring tea.

"Wait!" Babs cried. "Not the Indigo Tea Shop?"

"That's me."

"I *adore* that place. You don't know this—I mean, how could you?—but you're kind of an inspiration to me. I've been thinking about chucking my PR job at Milne and Kerrison in favor of opening a coffee shop. Except my coffee shop would be super contemporary with a name like Live Wire or Hot Shots. And instead of just coffee, lattes, and macchiatos, we'd serve creatively flavored brews. You know, like almond brittle, berry, and gingerbread coffee."

"Similar to our flavored teas," Theodosia said.

"Exactly. Fun, huh?" Then Babs turned serious. "Other than the fact that you were catering the wedding, why *are* you asking questions about that greenhouse collapse?"

"Because I promised Bettina that I'd look into things."

"You mean track down whoever might have caused it?"

"If it comes to that, sure."

"Now I'm really impressed."

"Don't be. I'm just snooping around, listening to rumors and asking questions."

"But an actual murder is nothing to fool with," Babs said in a serious tone of voice. "You've got to be careful you don't get too close to what really happened. You don't want to put yourself in danger."

"I'm trying not to do that, believe me," Theodosia said, even as she remembered Madame Aurora's chilling words about the killer having a dangerously dark nature.

"Wow, I wish I could help," Babs said. "I still think the world of Jamie, and it makes me heartsick that he was injured so badly. And that poor woman . . ."

"Celeste," Theodosia said.

"Tragic. You're showing such care and concern for her family that I wish I could help figure something out."

"Maybe you can," Theodosia said. "Since you know Jamie so well . . ."

"Yes?"

"If you think of anything, anything that's relevant, maybe something in Jamie's past—a problem with a former girlfriend or someone in business—will you let me know?"

"Cross my heart, I promise I will think long and hard about that," Babs said.

"Thank you."

Babs melted into the crowd then, and Theodosia walked back to their tea table, only to find Adam Lynch, of the Lynch Mob fame, yukking it up with Haley.

"So I told them social media was the only way to go with this thing," Lynch was telling her. "More and more events are advertised successfully via websites—Instagram, TikTok, or Facebook—even if the announcement only runs for a couple weeks."

"You certainly drew a good crowd," Haley said.

Lynch leaned in and favored her with a wolfish smile. "Say now, what time do you get off tonight?"

"Adam Lynch," Theodosia said as she approached him. "Come to crow about what a great job you did?"

Lynch turned toward Theodosia, his pupils practically constricting at the sight of her. "I *did* do a good job," he snarled. "Look at this throng of people."

"Do you think maybe some of the folks are here because the event was featured on Channel Eight's *Good Morning Charleston*?"

"Ah, whatever," Lynch said with a disdainful wave of his hand.

"And the fact that local businesses all put up posters?" Theodosia said.

"You think you're tough, don't you?" Lynch said, as his lips pulled into a sneer.

"No, but I like to think I'm smart and reasonable enough that I don't have to intimidate people by hitting them and knocking out teeth," Theodosia said.

"That never happened!" Lynch shouted as he turned and stalked off.

"Whoa, *that's* the guy who knocked out Bettina's tooth?" Haley said. "The one she was engaged to way back when?"

"Yes, so please try to avoid him at all costs."

"He's a real creeper, huh?" Haley said.

"The worst," Theodosia said.

"Thanks for watching out for me. Lynch was coming on pretty strong."

"No problem," Theodosia said. She got busy then, setting out more brownie bites and unstacking some of Drayton's dreaded paper cups.

Until a familiar voice called out, "Got a cup of tea for me?"

20

Theodosia glanced up to find Riley standing there, a smile lighting his face. She touched a hand to her heart and said, "You surprised me. Caught me completely off guard."

"Good. That's the way I like it," Riley said. "Keeps you on your toes."

"I thought you were tied up tonight. Something about meeting with local politicians about crime in their neighborhoods?"

"I was, and I am still doing that. But I took a break so I could swing by here and say hello."

"What do you think?" Theodosia asked, sweeping a hand to indicate their tea table set among flaming torches and flickering candles.

"I'd say the whole setup looks pretty cool. A bit of spookiness tempered by a smidge of history."

"Lots of history here. Signers of the Declaration of Independence and the US Constitution are buried here, along with a vice president of the United States and several local fat cats."

"I stand corrected," Riley said. "So . . . I take it you've been busy?"

"Getting there. The larger crowds are just starting to make their way down Gateway Walk." Theodosia came out from behind her table, hooked Riley's arm, and led him a few steps away. In a quiet voice, she said, "Did you by any chance follow up with Sabrina like I asked?"

"I spoke to Sabrina by phone and quizzed her briefly. She was reticent, as would be expected, and, boy, is she ever mad at *you*."

"I can't help that I uncovered a possible motive for killing her sister."

"No, you can't. And it's a decent motive at that. Probably seventy-five percent of crimes in America have money as the root cause."

"What did Sabrina have to say for herself?"

"That she was embarrassed at overreacting to the tarot card reading. That she would never, ever think about harming her sister. And thank you for calling and would I please try to solve Celeste's murder?"

"And she acted fairly calm and rational?"

"I'd say so," Riley said.

"So maybe Sabrina's completely innocent."

"Maybe."

"Did you call Sheriff Ambourn and mention Sabrina's inheritance?"

"I called the good sheriff, and he intends to question Sabrina in person. But she's off to Chicago first thing tomorrow with her parents. They're doing a proper funeral and then a cemetery service."

"What if we find evidence against her?"

"If we uncover actual hard evidence, then we take it to a

judge and get an arrest warrant," Riley said. "Next step would be calling Chicago PD and having her extradited."

"That sounds kind of extreme."

"Because it is," Riley said. "Look, we still have to play it by the book, okay? And chances are good that Sabrina's completely innocent. I mean, the money was always there, always coming to the sisters. I think you just got a little hyped up because of what that fortune teller said about you possibly knowing the killer and Sabrina profiting from a great tragedy."

"You're probably right. And Madame Aurora might have been laying it on a little thick as well. Okay. What about that box of chocolates I gave you? Or is it too soon to know anything?"

"Tell me who brought you those chocolates again?" Riley said.

Theodosia shrugged. "I don't know exactly. They were dropped off at the back door this morning. Haley thought by one of her suppliers. Why? Why are you looking at me like that?"

"Because your hunch proved correct. That candy contained small traces of strychnine."

"What!" Theodosia cried. "Then it's no wonder Miss Dimple went home sick."

"It's a good thing *you* didn't go home sick. Sweetheart, somebody is targeting you."

Theodosia sighed. "Because I've been asking questions."

"Asking the *wrong* questions," Riley said. "Questions that are making someone very nervous. Which means I need to issue yet another stern warning."

"I know, you're going to tell me to drop this investigation because I'm getting too close for my own good. That I pinged a trip wire somewhere and now I'm the one who's in danger."

"I couldn't have said it better myself."

"But you know I can't stop," Theodosia said.

"Sure you can. You just say to yourself, 'Theodosia, that's it. I gave it a good shot, now it's up to the police and sheriff's department.'"

"But I'm the one who uncovered most of the clues," Theodosia said.

"Which means you're the one who's going to pay the biggest price."

"I'm sorry," Theodosia said. "I just don't see it that way."

"Try harder."

Theodosia knew that Riley would continue to harangue her unless she shut him down. Luckily, a large contingent of cemetery crawlers was heading in their direction . . .

"Can we talk about this later?" Theodosia said. "Right now I need to get back to my table and help Drayton pour tea. Because he's, um . . ." Theodosia fumbled her words, suddenly losing her train of thought. Because she'd just seen someone she recognized. It was the elusive curly-haired guy that had been at Celeste's visitation last night. The one who'd been talking to Jamie. "Um," Theodosia said again.

Riley frowned at seeing Theodosia's unease, then followed her gaze. When he saw who'd caught her eye, he said, "Please tell me you don't know that guy?" Drawing closer to her, he looked both anxious and concerned.

"I don't know him, but I recognize him. He showed up at Celeste's visitation last night. Why are you asking? Do *you* know him?"

"Yes, but not in a good way. That's Jimmy Simonton, one of Charleston's big-time drug dealers. His street name is Slide and he deals mostly in high-end cocaine and hashish with maybe a little meth thrown in for up-and-coming tweakers."

"If you know so much about him, why isn't he in jail?" Theodosia asked.

"Long story short, because his old man's a hotshot criminal attorney over in Goose Creek. So anytime Slide has a brush with the law, he manages to slither off the hook."

"You're saying he's a professional criminal?"

"Of the worst kind," Riley said, giving Theodosia a peck on the cheek. "So please . . . stay away from him."

"I intend to," Theodosia said as she waved goodbye and hurried back to her tea table.

"What was Riley doing here?" Drayton asked as he poured cups of tea.

"Just taking a break. Checking out the cemetery crawl."

"I'd say it's a smashing success. I mean, look at these crowds, they just keep coming."

"I wonder if the other cemeteries are this crowded."

"Probably are," Drayton said. "But we see it more here because Gateway Walk serves as a perfect funnel. No matter where you step onto the walk, it brings you out right here." He looked up, smiled at three women who'd just come to the table with curious looks on their faces, and said, "Let me pour you a cup of Indian spice, you'll like it, a mild black tea with hints of cardamom and clove."

"Hey," Haley said to Theodosia as she was plating more brownie bites. "Jamie and Bettina were just here, did you see them?"

Theodosia shook her head. "No. But I'm surprised Jamie's out and about tonight. You'd think with this crowd of people he'd be worried about getting jostled. And with his injured hand . . ."

"Jamie's taking it slow and easy. In fact, he's sitting right over there, chilling out on one of the gravestones." Haley waved a hand in his general direction. "That old gravestone with the lamb on top?"

"Oh sure. Did Jamie get a cup of tea or a scone? Should I take something over to him?"

"That'd be nice," Haley said. "Since Bettina is flitting around like the little social butterfly she is."

"Probably telling everyone when her wedding will be rescheduled," Theodosia said. She glanced over, saw Jamie sitting on a tomb in the dark and looking a little glum. So she grabbed a cup of tea and two brownie bites and hurried over to him. Just as she got there, Jamie ducked his head forward and sniffed something off the back of his good hand. Then he straightened up, a loopy smile on his face.

"Jamie!" Theodosia shouted. "What are you doing?"

Jamie's head whipped left, then right, and spotted Theodosia bearing down upon him. He still wore a stupid grin and had a faint trace of white powder under his left nostril. "What?" he said. He sounded dumb; he sounded stoned.

"You *know* what. You're doing cocaine! Are you crazy? You just got out of the hospital!"

Jamie thrust his hands out in a placating gesture. "You have no idea how much pain I'm in. I feel so rotten I gotta do something to take the edge off."

"Not cocaine!"

"Look, I hardly ever do this, okay? This is like a total one-off for me."

"Oh my gosh, Jamie." Theodosia didn't know what to say. She was dumbfounded. This wasn't the sweet-natured, clean-cut, Southern-mannered Jamie she thought she knew. Or had that all been a sham?

"Please don't be mad at me," Jamie begged. "And for gosh sakes please don't tell Bettina about this. Or Delaine. Jeez, if

Delaine found out I did a line, she'd probably give herself a spontaneous aneurysm."

"Where'd you get the coke?" Theodosia asked.

"A guy I know," Jamie said.

"A guy named Slide?"

Jamie looked shocked when Theodosia tossed out that name. "Maybe," he stammered.

"You have to promise not to do this again. Or I *will* tell Bettina."

"Like I said, it was a one-off. Something to help me deal with the pain," Jamie said hurriedly. He held up his bandaged hand and winced again, as if to reinforce his words.

"I'll drop it for now," Theodosia said. "If you promise not to . . ."

"I *won't*," Jamie protested. "I promise. I'll stay clean, okay?"

"Okay," Theodosia said. She exhaled slowly, then looked around. The cemetery was thronged with people now, many of them stepping off the walkway to examine the ancient graves. One man was down on his hands and knees with charcoal and some tissue paper, making a rubbing of an old inscription.

"You drew a good crowd here tonight," Jamie said, as he accepted the tea and brownie bites from Theodosia.

"Adam Lynch walked by earlier," Theodosia said. "Did you happen to see him?"

"Nope. And I hope Bettina didn't, either," Jamie said. "You know, she really despises that guy."

"She told you that?"

"Oh sure, Bettina and I are completely open with each other. We've promised to never keep secrets," Jamie said.

Except your secret about snorting coke, Theodosia thought to herself.

"But that was a bad relationship," Jamie said. "Toxic. She was lucky to break up when she did."

"What else do you know about Adam Lynch?"

"Just that he's a dangerous guy. A hothead."

"Is Lynch crazy enough to kill?" Theodosia asked.

Jamie screwed up his face as if he was deep in thought. Finally, he said, "I think so. I didn't before, but now I do."

Theodosia, Drayton, and Haley served tea and scones until nine thirty, at which point the crowds had pretty much dwindled down to nothing. Then Drayton and Haley packed up the leftovers while Theodosia backed her Jeep into the St. Philips parking lot. Once they'd loaded up their tables and baskets, Theodosia drove back to the Indigo Tea Shop, where they opened the back door and shoved everything inside.

"We'll sort it out tomorrow," Theodosia said. Haley nodded tiredly, then climbed the back stairs to her apartment. Theodosia drove Drayton home, bid him good night, and drove home to her own cottage.

Parking her Jeep in the back alley, Theodosia glanced over at the enormous house next door to her, a turn-of-the-century pile of stone known as the Granville Mansion. All the windows were dark, nobody living there as yet. Maybe the owner had it up for sale, she thought as she walked into her backyard, though there wasn't a FOR SALE sign out front. As she passed the small fishpond, where tiny goldfish swam lazily, a bright spark of orange suddenly caught her eye.

What?

But Theodosia knew what it was before she even got to her back door. Sitting on her doorstep was a squat orange candle, its single flame writhing and dancing in the wind. Next to it sat a white skull. The same kind of skull that had been gifted to Jamie.

What is this, a warning? Somebody's sending me a warning?

She walked back to the alley, the tiny hairs on the back of her neck prickling like crazy. She scanned one way, then the other; the alley seemed deserted. Nothing moving, nobody there. She walked back to her back door, looking over her shoulder a few times.

The notion that someone had come to her house, where she lived, where her dog was probably sleeping, made her blood boil.

Well, to hell with them.

Theodosia licked her thumb and forefinger, leaned down, and snuffed out the candle. She ignored the prickle of heat between her fingertips and the momentary sizzling sound. Then, with a disdainful glance downward, she kicked the skull out of her way and went inside.

21

"You're not going to believe this," Theodosia said.

"Try me," Drayton said.

It was Thursday morning at the Indigo Tea Shop, and Theodosia and Drayton were sipping their morning cuppas. Haley was rattling around in the kitchen, baking butterscotch scones and pumpkin muffins, singing to herself. Something about "Wake up and smell the breakup."

"Remember the box of candy that turned up here yesterday?"

"The yummy-looking chocolate-covered cherries?" Drayton said. "The ones you wouldn't let me eat?"

"And a smart thing that was. Riley had them tested at the police lab and found they contained traces of strychnine."

Drayton practically choked on his tea. "Strychnine? As in rat poison? No wonder Miss Dimple went home sick!"

"It's a miracle she didn't drop dead," Theodosia said. "And you, you were all set to *snarf* down the entire box."

"Because I thought it *was* candy," Drayton cried. "Not some kind of death sentence."

"You see the true meaning behind those chocolates, don't you?"

"Tainted?"

"Yes, but more than that—it's part of a pattern. The chocolates were the second thing this week to be sabotaged."

"Jeepers, you're right." Drayton shook his head. "Lucky I didn't waltz myself into an early grave." He thought for a few moments. "So someone, maybe even Celeste's killer . . ."

"Probably Celeste's killer," Theodosia said.

". . . knows we've been investigating her murder," Drayton finished.

"That's my read as well."

"Gracious."

"You know that Charleston PD is definitely referring to it as a murder now," Theodosia said. "I caught a short clip on the news this morning. K-BAM was yapping about the ongoing investigation."

"Was it that Lotter guy who's been bugging you?"

"Who else? Oh, and I have a little weirdness to share with you."

"What's that?"

"I caught Jamie using drugs last night."

"At the cemetery crawl?" Drayton said. "What do you mean, like prescription pain pills?"

"Pain pills are what I attributed to Jamie acting spacey. And he probably is taking those. But last night I caught Jamie doing a line."

"A line," Drayton repeated.

"Of cocaine."

Understanding dawned on Drayton's face. "Oh my! *That* kind of line. How awful. Are you going to tell Bettina?"

"Jamie begged me not to. But, I don't know, it's kind of a big thing."

"It is if they're still planning to get married," Drayton said. "You don't want Bettina marrying somebody who's saddled with a drug problem."

"Jamie doesn't see it that way. He told me it was a one-off, something to help dull the pain."

"You think that's true?"

"I doubt this was the first time Jamie used coke, and I doubt it'll be the last time," Theodosia said.

"Then you've got to tell Bettina the truth." Drayton took a sip of tea, contemplated the Chinese design on his teacup, and said, "Where would Jamie purchase cocaine anyway?"

"You remember me mentioning the curly-haired guy who showed up at Celeste's visitation?"

"No. Well, maybe."

"Turns out his name is Slide and he's Charleston's friendly dope dealer."

"How do you know this?" Drayton asked.

"Riley told me when he dropped by last night."

"He told you just out of the blue like that?"

"No, he told me because Slide was right there," Theodosia said.

"Slide was at the cemetery crawl?"

"Kind of hanging out. I'm guessing Jamie probably set it up, told Slide to meet him there so he could make the buy." Theodosia stopped, then pursed her lips as if she was about to say something more.

"What?" Drayton said. He waggled his fingers. "You were going to say something else. What's whirring in that clever brain of yours?"

"I was thinking about Slide. What if Jamie owed him money for drugs and couldn't pay?"

"So you're thinking . . . what?"

"What if Slide rigged the greenhouse to make a point? Pay up or face dire consequences?"

"Are drug dealers that nefarious?" Drayton asked.

"What do you think?"

"I suppose they probably are."

The door from the kitchen whapped open and Haley yelled out, "Hey, you guys, it's almost nine! We open in five minutes!"

"I guess we're not going to solve any murders sitting here," Drayton said as he got up from the table.

"And we've still got all that stuff from last night to sort through," Haley added, clearly in martinet mode.

"Got it," Theodosia called back to her. She was going to tell Drayton about the skull she found on her doorstep last night, then decided, *No, I'll let it go until later. He's got enough to digest as it is.*

The Indigo Tea Shop was busy with customers this morning. Theodosia did her graceful ballet of dipping, pouring, and spinning back to the counter to grab more pots of tea. Drayton happily brewed pots of Puerh and chamomile tea, as well as a special request for vanilla chai.

At ten o'clock Delaine and Bettina walked through the front door, looked around, saw Theodosia, and gave friendly little finger waves. Theodosia hurried over to greet them and seated them at a small table near the front door. She glanced back at the tea room, decided she could spare a few minutes, and plopped down alongside them.

"Did you see the segment on the news this morning?" Delaine asked.

Theodosia nodded. "I did."

"The police are calling it a murder now," Delaine said. "Even though we've known that all along."

"That's for sure," Bettina said.

"I have a question for Bettina," Theodosia said. "Do you remember the curly-haired guy who was ghosting through the crowd at Celeste's visitation?"

Bettina ticked a finger in Theodosia's direction. "You mean the same guy I saw at Smedley's Saloon? That Jamie didn't introduce me to?"

"That's the one," Theodosia said. "His name is Jimmy Simonton but his street name is Slide."

"This man is a musician?" Delaine asked.

"Not quite," Theodosia said. "Slide happens to be our friendly local drug dealer."

"What!" Delaine cried.

Theodosia ignored Delaine and focused only on Bettina. "Jamie used to hang around with him, right?"

"I *think* so." Now Bettina looked seriously flustered. "But he doesn't anymore."

"But he did," Theodosia said.

"Maybe. For a while," Bettina said.

Theodosia decided to just spit it out. "Was Jamie buying drugs from Simonton? *Is* Jamie buying drugs from Simonton?"

Bettina's eyes widened and her lashes fluttered like frightened butterflies. "Not that I know of."

"Jamie doesn't do drugs," Delaine scoffed. "He's a straight arrow."

"You're sure about that?" Theodosia asked.

Delaine lifted her chin and said, "I happen to be an excellent judge of character."

Theodosia knew that Delaine was a terrible judge of character. She'd hooked up with more dingbats, drifters, and con artists than you could shake a stick at. But this wasn't the time to bring up her relationship shortcomings.

"I think you need to have a serious talk with Jamie," Theodosia said to Bettina. "A real heart-to-heart. If you truly care for him . . ."

"Of course I do!" Bettina cried.

"Then you'd better hash out his relationship with Slide."

"I will," Bettina said. "For sure." She ducked her head, embarrassed. "I do hear what you're saying."

"Good," Theodosia said.

"It feels as if you two are talking in riddles," Delaine said.

"No," Bettina said. "We're clearing the air."

"If the air is sufficiently cleared, do you think we could order?" Delaine asked. "Some of us have actual businesses to run."

Theodosia smiled and took their orders.

Ten minutes later, Theodosia was at the counter, asking Drayton if they had a tin of Mufi Cha, a traditional Japanese barley tea.

"We did at one time," Drayton said, studying his shelves. "But I'm not sure . . ." He turned, looked past Theodosia as the front door snicked open, and said, in a low voice, "We have a guest."

Theodosia whirled around and registered a tall man who'd just entered the tea shop. He was standing just inside the front door, looking all buttoned up in what was probably a thousand-dollar three-piece suit and carrying a Gucci briefcase. She hurried over to him, offered a warm smile, and said, "May I help you? Would you like a table or are you meeting someone?"

"More like trying to connect with a particular individual," the man said. He had a square jaw, dark brown eyes, and reddish-brown hair that was a tad over collar length. His eyes roved about the tea room until they finally settled on Delaine. "I think I might have found her."

"You're looking for Delaine?" Theodosia asked.

"You can confirm that's Delaine Dish?" the man asked. "Excellent. Her assistant at Cotton Duck said I might find her here."

"Is there a problem?" Theodosia asked. She was getting strange vibes from this man.

"Shouldn't be," the man said as he brushed past Theodosia and went over to Delaine's table. "Excuse me, Miss Delaine Dish?"

Delaine looked up at him. "Yes?" Then, deciding she rather liked what she saw—a good-looking man, three-piece suit, Gucci briefcase—she smiled, cocked her head, and purred, "What can I do for you?"

"My name is Howard Pinzer and I'm a lawyer with Collins, Druid, and Dunn. Our firm happens to represent Celeste Haynes's family in a wrongful death suit."

"What!" Delaine screeched.

Howard Pinzer twiddled a business card between his fingers, then handed it to a stunned Delaine. "We'll be in touch."

Delaine dropped the card like it was covered in rat poop. "Be in touch!" she screamed. "Be in touch about what?"

But the lawyer had already spun away from her.

Delaine stood up, her face flushed bright pink and her arms beating the air. "I'm *talking* to you!"

The front door slammed shut and Mr. Pinzer was gone—poof—like Beetlejuice disappearing into the Netherworld.

"Delaine," Theodosia said, in a commiserating tone. "What in the world . . . ?"

"Did you see that?" Delaine sputtered. "The nerve of that guy. Some uppity lawyer isn't going to pin a wrongful death suit on me! I had nothing to do with Celeste's accident. I only *planned* the wedding, I didn't *sabotage* that stupid greenhouse."

Bettina tugged at Delaine's sleeve. "Sit down, please. You're embarrassing me."

Delaine sat down as Theodosia tried to soothe her.

"It's probably nothing," Theodosia said. "An opening salvo, very pro forma. I'm sure nothing will come of it."

Delaine settled back in her chair. "That lawyer seemed awfully pleased with himself."

"They learn that in lawyer school," Bettina said. "How to manufacture bluster at the drop of a hat."

"And he wants to bring a lawsuit? Against me?" Delaine pressed the heels of her hands into her eye sockets and screamed, "YOU HAVE TO FIX THIS!"

Bettina nudged her again. "You're still embarrassing me."

Delaine took her hands away and stared at Theodosia. One of her false eyelashes had come loose and now it trembled with every blink. "Theo, you see what kind of trouble I could be in? Now I'm *begging* you to kick your investigation into high gear and find the killer!"

"I've been giving it my best shot, Delaine. But I'm afraid I haven't turned up all that much," Theodosia said.

"Not so. You've been more proactive than the sheriff's department and the police put together," Delaine said. "You had Martin Hunt's name the day after the greenhouse collapse. And Adam Lynch's name the day after that."

"You two really should have told me about Lynch," Theodosia said.

"We never thought it was important," Delaine said, waving a hand. "Lynch was in the past, and the past is the past."

"That's not always true," Theodosia said.

"And now we've got crazy Sabrina, who's all whipped up over Madame Aurora mentioning her finances," Delaine said. "What was *that* about?"

"It turns out Sabrina stands to inherit a pile of money," Theodosia said.

"How big a pile?" Delaine tapped a fire-engine red nail against the table. "How much money?"

"Ten million dollars," Theodosia said.

Delaine's eyes popped wide open. "What!" she screeched. "Did you say ten m-m-million?"

Theodosia nodded. "Sabrina and Celeste each stood to inherit five million."

Delaine was no slouch at putting two and two together. "So with Celeste out of the way, Sabrina inherits it all?"

"Correct," Theodosia said.

"So that's why Sabrina was so upset at yesterday's tarot reading," Bettina said. "She thought we'd suspect *her.* Which . . . now that we have this information . . . we kind of do."

But Delaine's anxiety was so maxed out she was ready to burst. She whapped the palm of her hand against the table, making the teacups jump and clatter in their saucers. "There you go," she spat out. "Sabrina *has* to be the killer! It's like on those TV detective shows when they talk about following the money!"

"Exactly," Bettina said. "When you know who profits, you find the killer!"

Theodosia sighed. If only it were that simple.

"Excuse me," Drayton said as he walked up to their table. "Are you staying for tea?"

"No!" Delaine cried. "Not after what's come to light. Come on, Bettina, let's get out of here so Theodosia can get to work."

Drayton stared after them as they fled the tea shop, then turned to Theodosia and said, "Did I miss something?"

"Now they're convinced that Sabrina is the killer."

Drayton nodded sagely. "Of course."

The killer was feeling another hint of unease, another nip of uncertainty that plans might not work out perfectly. First, that tea shop woman had stuck her nose into things. And now she was running around, questioning people, looking for suspects, and making trouble.

Was she smart enough to figure things out? Would she eventually come to the conclusion that Jamie had been the intended target? Would she figure out why?

There were, of course, ways to send her careening off course. Or if it came right down to it, to get rid of the tea shop lady altogether.

Yes, a new plan would have to be implemented. Spook her, tease her, then reel her in for a final showdown.

This wouldn't be easy, but it would make for an exciting challenge.

22

Today's tea luncheon hadn't been billed as a special event. But Haley managed to make it special when it came to her menu.

"This is spectacular," Theodosia said as she perused the recipe card where Haley had scrawled her luncheon offerings. "Carrot cake scones, she-crab soup, Cobb salad, prawn salad tea sandwiches, cucumber and cream cheese pinwheels, and turkey, Brie cheese, and apple tea sandwiches."

"Oh gosh, I forgot to write down the rest of it," Haley said. "There are also three dozen cream scones in the oven. And for dessert we have cheesecake with strawberry topping."

"As far as that cheesecake goes . . ."

"Yes?"

"You need to save a couple pieces for Drayton and me."

"Will do."

Lunch was easy today, with all the guests loving Haley's menu. Theodosia took orders, ran them into the kitchen, then poured tea, and served the food as it was ready.

"You holding up okay?" Drayton asked after she'd made six quick trips into the kitchen.

"If you mean do I miss having Miss Dimple here to help, then yes. She does take some of the pressure off."

"By the way, you were going to check on her again?"

"I called her first thing this morning."

"And she's still not dying from strychnine poisoning?" Drayton asked.

"She said she felt fine."

"Maybe she's one of those rare humans who are immune to poisons and such things."

"One of the lucky ones," Theodosia said. "Maybe. Thank goodness she's coming in tomorrow."

"But you seem to be handling things well."

"Only because I'm not too aerobically challenged," Theodosia said. "But if I didn't have Earl Grey to pull me out of the house most every night and pace for a couple of miles, I'd probably be gasping for air."

"Funny," Drayton said, his mouth twitching slightly.

By early afternoon, the lunch rush had let up. And thank goodness for that, because that's when Babs Campbell came wandering in.

"Hi, how are ya?" Babs cried, giving Theodosia a ginormous hug.

"Great, nice to see you, too." Theodosia was amused by Babs's energy level. She wondered if the girl was constantly sipping the kind of high-octane coffee she had talked about serving in her soon-to-be coffee shop.

"I need to have a confab with Drayton," Babs said.

"Drayton's right here," Drayton said. Babs turned slightly and found that she was standing two feet from him.

"Drayton!" Babs exclaimed. "Ooh, I have a few questions

for you. Mostly about coffee. Do you know anything about coffee?"

"Tea is my expertise, but I'm fairly well-versed on coffee as well," Drayton said. "What do you want to know?"

"Everything!" Babs cried. "Like I was telling Theodosia, I want to open a coffee shop in the university neighborhood and serve a bunch of different flavored coffees. You know, like you guys serve flavored tea."

"Interesting idea," Drayton said.

"Babs mentioned she might want to do almond-brittle-, berry-, and gingerbread-flavored coffees," Theodosia said.

"I can see her serving orange blossom, blackberry, and chocolate coffee as well," Drayton said.

"See, that's exactly what I need," Babs said. "Smart ideas and some gentle guidance. There's a small shop—actually a former donut shop—off University Avenue that's come up for rent, so I . . ." She stopped abruptly, dug in her purse, and pulled out a sheaf of papers. "I went ahead and wrote a business plan. I cribbed the template off the Internet and I know my ideas are pie-in-the-sky stuff, but is there any chance you guys would take a look at it and give me a few pointers?"

"I can go over it with you right now," Drayton said. He glanced at Theodosia. "Theo, can you also . . . ?"

"Afraid not. Against my better judgment I've got to run and do a podcast," Theodosia said. "But, Babs, if you leave me a copy of your business plan, I'll be sure to look at it when I get back."

Babs gave a fist pump. "Super!"

Air Supply was a sound studio over on Bogard Street, a small brick building tucked between Lyle's Laundromat and Chrysalis Lamps and Chandeliers. Theodosia walked in the front door and was greeted by a young man wearing a Cheap Trick T-shirt who was stuffing CDs into envelopes. He looked at her and said, "Are you Theodosia? You look like a Theodosia. Charlie's already set up in studio B, go right in."

"Great," Theodosia said, her heart suddenly picking up in cadence. Could she do this? Should she do this? Well, she'd come this far; she may as well jump in with both feet.

Charlie Skipstead was sitting behind a microphone in a dimly lit studio, fiddling with dials when Theodosia walked in. She was young, late twenties, with long dark hair, green eyes, a gold nose ring, and an enigmatic smile. Today she wore a Mötley Crüe T-shirt and shredded (not torn, but shredded) jeans with trendy black ballet slippers.

When Charlie saw Theodosia, she jumped up from her chair and cried, "You found us! Thrilled to have you!"

"Gulp," Theodosia said.

"No, no," Charlie laughed as they hugged. "This is going to be super easy. Heck, you worked in marketing, dealt with the media, you're probably a pro at this."

"Not exactly."

"You will be by the time we're done. Here, sit down and I'll adjust your microphone."

Theodosia took the chair next to Charlie's and looked around the studio. It was small, maybe eight by twelve feet, with a soundboard and two microphones. The carpeting was thick and lush, and all four walls were covered in some kind of gray foam rubber that looked like egg cartons. She figured it helped enhance sound as well as cancel any outside noise.

"Your mike's good to go, so now you can slip on these headphones," Charlie said, handing Theodosia a pair of fat headphones. "That's if you can get them over your hair. Gosh, you have great hair."

"Thank you," Theodosia said, giving her hair a self-conscious pat. She drew a deep breath and said, "What now?"

"Now we get to play around. I'm going to adjust sound levels and values . . ." Charlie fussed with a few lighted dials. "And I'm also going to record this to my laptop as well."

"And you're going to ask me questions?"

Charlie nodded. "That's how it works."

"About Celeste's death last Saturday?"

"It's been in the news, so it's super, super timely. My listeners should be extremely interested." Charlie held up a finger. "I'm going to start my theme music now, then do a quick intro. Once I introduce you and ask my first question, you jump in and we'll go from there."

"And we're doing this live?"

"Right."

"What if I flub something?"

"You won't. But since I'm also recording this, I can go back in later and edit out any ahs, ums, or strange pauses for the archived version."

Theodosia sat there expectantly as Charlie's opening music filled her ears. It was an upbeat but slightly mysterious tune that seemed to promise a dose of the unexpected. Then Charlie cut in with, "This is Charlie Skipstead, host of *Charleston Shivers*." Her voice was low and melodic as she said, "My special guest today is amateur detective Theodosia Browning, the proprietor of Charleston's Indigo Tea Shop. Theodosia, I understand you're hot on the trail of a vicious killer, someone who sabotaged a greenhouse where a wedding reception was about to take place. And—either on purpose or inadvertently—murdered the maid of honor."

"I'm not exactly hot on their trail," Theodosia began.

"But you have uncovered suspects?"

"Actually, yes. There are three—no, four—people who had motive."

"And those motives would be what?" Charlie asked.

"I'd have to say revenge, anger, and financial gain."

"Those are all powerful motives. And much to the surprise of the investigating officers, I understand you've uncovered an actual clue. Tell us about that."

"It was kind of a slam dunk," Theodosia said. "In trying to figure out how the killer approached the greenhouse, I checked out a nearby park where I figured he might have parked his car."

"And did you find his car? Or talk to a witness? Or find tire treads?"

"Better than that," Theodosia said. "There was a woodsy trail that led in the direction of the flower farm, and along the way I spotted a motion-activated trail cam."

"That's quite a lucky break. So you have an actual photo of the killer?"

"Of his shoes anyway. The camera was aimed quite low to catch images of the park's wildlife. Foxes and mink and creatures like that."

"That's amazing," Charlie said. "And I know our listeners are on the edge of their seats right about now. So let's go to our mystery hotline. Listeners, if you'd like to ask Theodosia a question, just phone us at 1-800-MYSTERY."

As if by magic, the phone rang. Charlie punched a button and said, "This is *Charleston Shivers* and you're on the air. What's your question please?"

There was a hollow clunk on the line, like a phone being dropped, then a gravelly voice said, "I want to know if Theodosia enjoyed her special present last night?"

"Her present?" Charlie gave Theodosia a questioning look.

Theodosia was taken aback . . . was this the person who'd left the skull? Her hands suddenly felt cold, and a shiver literally ran down her spine. Then she pulled it together and said, "Some joker left a plastic skull on my doorstep last night." Her mouth was cottony and her heart thumped like a timpani drum, but she fought to sound outwardly calm. And disdainful. "I guess they wanted to scare me, but the funny thing was, I wasn't one bit scared. I kicked the skull aside and never thought about it again."

"You hear that?" Charlie said to the caller. "Your stupid Halloween prank backfired. Theodosia's too smart to be scared by a cheap plastic skull. Hah! What I'd call a cheap trick."

"Call it anything you want," said the strange voice, "but I figured she'd want to get the *buzz* firsthand." The voice paused. "That's a clue in case you missed it."

"A clue to what?" Theodosia asked. She was still struggling to remain calm, to keep her wits about her.

"You'll find out soon enough," the caller said.

"Okay, thanks for . . . ," Charlie began.

Theodosia made a chopping motion with her hand and Charlie immediately pushed a button to cut off the call and stop recording. "Honey, are you okay?" she asked as she peered at Theodosia.

"Not really," Theodosia said.

"You sounded fine to me, calm and in control."

"My knees are shaking and I feel like there's an unexploded depth charge sitting in the pit of my stomach. Because I . . . I think that really might have been the killer. I didn't tell a soul about that plastic skull. But his voice . . . it's like nothing I've ever heard before."

"I've hit this a few times," Charlie said. "Crazy anonymous callers who try to disrupt the podcast. You can download voice-changing programs off the Internet or buy a handheld device for thirty bucks. And I think that's what your caller—or killer—was using." She furrowed her brow. "You think it was the person who sabotaged the greenhouse and killed Celeste?"

"I do."

"They said the word *buzz* was a clue. Any ideas on that?"

Theodosia shook her head. "Not really. It felt like a non sequitur."

Charlie touched a hand to Theodosia's arm, as if to steady her. "Are you okay to keep going?"

Theodosia swallowed hard. "I am if we don't go too long."

Charlie asked a few more questions, then Theodosia steered Charlie away from the greenhouse incident and talked about a mystery she'd been involved in a couple of months ago—a murder at an old grist mill.

Afterward, when the session was over, Theodosia still felt spooked. Which was why, sitting in her Jeep outside the studio, she immediately called Riley and told him what had happened.

"How very nonlinear," he said. "Not what I'd expect at all."

"Ditto that. Do you think you could try to trace the call?"

"What's Charlie's studio number?" Riley asked.

Theodosia gave it to him.

"I'll jump right on it. Now you take care. You're going right back to the tea shop?"

"I am."

"Good."

Theodosia hung up and looked around. Was anyone watching her, looking to get a reaction? There was a dark car—a sedan—parked down the street from her, maybe a figure sitting inside. Could that be the caller? The killer?

Theodosia sat there for a full five minutes, wondering what

to do. Then she turned on the ignition and slowly pulled away. Looking into her rearview mirror, she didn't see anyone following her. Thank goodness.

Back at the Indigo Tea Shop Theodosia told Drayton about the podcast and the weird person who'd called in.

Drayton listened carefully as he poured Theodosia a cup of tea, then said, "You didn't tell anyone about the skull at your back door?" He pushed the tea across the counter to her.

"Nope. I was going to tell you, but I didn't want to worry you."

"That's great because now I'm beyond worried, edging into full-blown hysteria. Theo, I think the killer has their eye on you."

Theodosia took a sip of tea, swallowed, and said, "That's what I'm afraid of, too."

Drayton peered at her. "Are you really? Afraid, I mean?"

"I was when they called. Now . . . now I'm feeling some better. Probably more angry than fearful."

"And you didn't recognize the voice?"

"Like I said, they must have used some kind of voice-changing machine."

"I'm glad you called Riley and that he agreed to try and trace the call. Maybe he'll luck out and this will wrap up quickly. Riley will locate the killer and all will be revealed." Drayton clapped his hands together. "Bing, bang, boom, case closed."

Theodosia's cell phone tinkled in her bag. "That could be Riley now." Checking her screen, she said, "Yup," and clicked on. "What did you find out?"

"We've got the number, but it's a cell phone on one of those cheap-ass fly-by-night carriers," Riley said. "Legal is working right now to get a subpoena to the carrier so they can hopefully provide more information."

"That's good."

"That's not good. It's a cell phone—probably a burner bought at one of those big-box stores—and whoever owns it could pull the SIM card or toss the phone in a ditch, and we'd never find it in a million years."

"But we have to pin down that caller!" Theodosia cried.

"But probably not via their phone."

"Disappointing," Theodosia said.

"That's life in the big bad world of law enforcement," Riley said. "We'll keep battering away at this, but in the meantime . . ."

"I know what you're going to say. Stop investigating and keep my nose clean."

"What? There's an echo in here? Yes, step away from the investigation and chill out. What are your plans for tonight? Stay home and read a book, I hope. A romance rather than a mystery."

"I was going to go to the Heritage Society with Drayton. Some Halloween-themed dance thing."

"Okay, that sounds fairly safe. But call me later, okay?"

"I promise," Theodosia said. She hung up, turned to Drayton, and said, "I'm not exactly in the mood for this Vampyre Ballet tonight."

"So what? Go home, get glammed up, and come anyway. It'll help take your mind off things for a while."

23

Theodosia did go home and get glammed up. She dug around in her walk-in closet and found a midlength black, gauzy skirt, a faux-leather black bustier to go with it, and her way-too-expensive witchy black boots. If she added a few strands of pearls like Drayton had suggested, she'd be rocking a Coco-Chanel-meets-spooky-ballerina look. So . . . almost perfect for tonight's Vampyre Ballet.

Once Theodosia had figured out her costume, makeup was easy. A dab of brow gel, some tinted moisturizer, and loads of black mascara. *Well, maybe a touch of lipstick, too.* She looked in the drawer of the vanity she'd inherited from her mother and found the perfect dark lipstick, one called Burnt Suede by Yves Saint Laurent. She sat down on the vanity's low padded bench and gazed in the mirror as she applied her lipstick. *Nice.* A subdued pop of color rather than a slash of outrageous color that so many women (like Delaine) thought was the height of glamour.

Styling her hair was another matter. First she tried twirling it into a chignon and piling it on top of her head. But that seemed to yield an almost unwieldy mass of hair. She took a brush, stroked her hair until it crackled, then pulled it to one side and held it in place with a silver barrette. Better. Now add the pearls and a few glittery rings and she'd be good to go. Oh, and maybe a spritz of Chanel No. 5 behind her ears and a half spritz of Miss Dior, since perfume zoning seemed to be the latest thing.

Theodosia called Drayton from the back patio, where Earl Grey was snuffling around, hoping to flush out a rogue rabbit or squirrel.

"I'm going to pick you up in ten minutes, okay?" she said.

"I'm not only ready, I'll be outside waiting for you," Drayton said. "Honey Bee has been walked and fed, while I have been walked but *not* fed. Hopefully, the Heritage Society will have heaping platters of delightful hors d'oeuvres for us to feast on."

"Okay, see you soon."

As Theodosia turned and walked back toward the house with her dog, her eyes caught sight of the skull from last night. She stared at it, then walked over and gave it a good, swift kick, like Inter Miami's Lionel Messi booting a soccer ball down the pitch. The skull flipped into the air, arced for a good ten feet, then—CRASH—smashed hard against the brick chimney, cracking into a dozen pieces.

Score!

True to his word, Drayton was waiting for her on the curb outside his house. He looked dapper in a black tuxedo, purple bow tie and cummerbund, and full-length cape.

"Good Lord," Theodosia exclaimed as he climbed into the passenger seat. "You look like the Phantom of the Opera."

"And I even have the mask," Drayton said.

"No you don't."

He responded by holding up a white half-mask that looked remarkably similar to the one the Phantom had worn. "Do you want me to hum a few bars from the musical?"

"No need. And I actually think you look dashing without it."

"My thought exactly," Drayton said, tossing his mask to the floor. Then, "Will Riley be joining us? I have an extra ticket."

"Not likely. There's something about the word *ballet* that sends ordinary men scrambling toward a bucket of greasy chicken wings, a recliner, and a big-screen TV."

"Are you saying I'm not ordinary?"

"You're extraordinary," Theodosia said as she cruised down Tradd Street for a few blocks, then turned on Meeting Street and started looking for a parking spot. "Speaking of which, why don't you use your X-ray vision to find us . . . ah, never mind, I see a spot. Hope I can squeeze in."

Theodosia parked (gingerly) between a BMW i5 and a Lexus RX 350. As they exited her Jeep and crossed the street, she said, "Looks like a tony crowd here tonight."

"You know how it is," Drayton said. "There are lots of what stockbrokers like to call high-net-worth individuals living in this area. They're not your run-of-the-mill Halloween partyers or trick-or-treat types, so they find a nice hoity-toity event like a Vampyre Ballet at the Heritage Society rather appealing." He grinned. "Must bring out the devil in them."

The Heritage Society was Drayton's pride and joy because he'd served on the board of directors of this cherished museum for over a dozen years. Historians, genealogists, authors, and scholars flocked to the Heritage Society to use their well-stocked library and to study many of its exhibits.

The Heritage Society was also one of Theodosia's favorite places but for a different reason—it stirred the romance and fantasy within her. Tucked inside this marble edifice was a library filled with leather chairs, cases of floor-to-ceiling leather-bound books, and brass lamps with emerald green shades. A half dozen period rooms were furnished with English and French furniture, priceless silver, and faded (but still glorious) oil paintings. There were also collections of drawings, old pottery, sculptures, antique linens, and even antique firearms. With its high ceilings, manor house interior, and tucked-away rooms, the place reminded Theodosia of a castle, where tapestries dampened sounds, contented hounds could stretch out in front of an oversized fireplace, and a girl could curl up and read to her heart's content.

Theodosia and Drayton made their way through the large rotunda that served as the entryway, rubbing shoulders with several dozen guests and greeting friends. Many of the men were in black tie; most of the women wore some sort of costume that entailed a long dress, gobs of jewelry, and a feathered mask.

"Lots of sparkle and bling here tonight," Theodosia remarked.

"Everyone looks like they're off to a Mardi Gras party in the Garden District," Drayton said.

"Have you ever attended one of those parties?"

"Once, years ago. A delightful woman by the name of Baby Fontaine invited me to her home for a private Mardi Gras party. It was splendid. An ambrosia of French antiques, Louisiana cuisine, and quirky New Orleans characters. Almost as strange as the folks we have here in Charleston." He looked around. "I say, everyone seems to be headed for the Great Room, where the drinks and hors d'oeuvres are being served. Shall we amble that way as well?"

"Lead on," Theodosia said.

The Great Room was exactly that. Great in size and in spirit. It had high ceilings, tall clerestory windows, and carved walnut paneling. Hanging high above the center of the room was a recent installation—a Dale Chihuly chandelier of frosted green-and-amber glass formed into unique twists and squiggles.

In honor of the Vampyre Ballet, the caterers had set a table laden with delightful tidbits and local favorites. There were plump Carolina oysters on the half shell, jumbo steamed shrimp, bruschetta with a mixture of goat cheese, serrano peppers, and honey, as well as mini crab cakes and fig and prosciutto flatbread.

"Delightful," Drayton proclaimed as he took a small plate and headed straight for the oysters.

"And there's champagne," Theodosia said as she heard the telltale POP of a cork.

"Trust Timothy Neville to put on a delightful spread for his guests."

"Did I happen to hear my name mentioned?" came a voice from behind them.

Theodosia and Drayton both whirled around to find Timothy Neville, the executive director of the Heritage Society, grinning at them.

"Timothy!" Theodosia cried. And promptly enveloped him in a big hug.

Drayton, who saw Timothy on a weekly basis, extended a hearty handshake.

"Come to see the vampires flit among the flickering torches on our back patio?" Timothy asked with a twinkle in his eye. He was a small man, impeccably turned out in a bespoke tuxedo. What little hair Timothy had left was slicked back, emphasizing his prominent cheekbones, dark eyes, and small, agile mouth. Board members loved Timothy, donors fawned over him, and curators feared him since his knowledge of art, antiques, and architecture was encyclopedic. He lived nearby in a spectacular mansion on Archdale Street with a full-time staff and a Siamese cat named Chairman Meow.

"We could hardly miss a spectacle featuring vampires," Drayton said.

Timothy rocked back on his heels. "The fact of the matter is, one of our most generous donors also sits on the board of the Wild Dunes Ballet Company, so an arrangement was struck." He shrugged. "Why not? It's practically Halloween, so it's all in good fun."

"Props for going with such a quirky idea," Theodosia said. "A Vampyre Ballet is completely opposite from your usual scholarly programs on Charleston architecture and low-country plantations."

Timothy nodded. "Shakes up people's expectations, doesn't it?"

"Which is always a good thing," Theodosia said.

Timothy moved off to greet more guests while Theodosia and Drayton walked the buffet line, grabbed glasses of champagne, and greeted a few more friends. Brooke Carter Crockett, owner of Hearts Desire, was there, wearing a short black sequin shift along with a jangle of silver necklaces and bracelets that she'd created herself. Leigh Carroll, from the Cabbage Patch Gift Shop, was also there with her boyfriend, Darien Brown, and his sister, Kenesha Taylor.

Finally, Drayton tapped his watch and said, "It's almost time for the ballet to begin. We should probably stroll out to the patio and take our seats."

"Can we take our champagne with us?" Theodosia asked.

"I've got a better idea. Let's finish what we have and grab a fresh glass."

Standing in line at the bar, Theodosia decided she *was* having a good time after all. It had been a good idea to come here tonight. After a hectic few days, this was proving to be a welcome interlude. She didn't have to think about murderers, suspects, or plastic skulls. She could let her brain relax and . . .

"Theodosia?"

Theodosia was suddenly aware of Babs Campbell elbowing her way through the crowd. She was wearing a short pink tweed dress and black boots. A pair of black velvet cat ears were perched adorably atop her head.

"Babs," Theodosia said. "I had no idea I'd see you here tonight."

"I had no idea I'd be coming," Babs said. "But my friend over there . . ." She squinted, shrugged, and said, "Well, Helen *was* over there. Anyway, she had tickets and called at the last minute." Babs turned, glanced over her shoulder at Theodosia, and said, "Have oodles of fun, see you later."

"I was just saying hi to Babs," Theodosia said to Drayton as he spun around and handed her a fresh glass of champagne.

"She's here?"

"She came with a friend," Theodosia said.

"Babs and I had a good meeting today," Drayton said. "She's a smart girl."

"You think? How'd her business plan look?"

"There are a few bugs to work out, like how she's going to bite off her fair share of customers in an already-crowded coffee shop market. But her operating numbers made sense and her enthusiasm is off the charts."

"Sometimes a gung ho attitude is the most important thing for a new entrepreneur," Theodosia said. She could remember her own excitement when she'd finally decided to kick marketing to the curb and open the Indigo Tea Shop. She'd been steadfast in her vision and had ignored any and all naysayers. It was also why she felt strongly about helping Babs as well as other young women find their way in business. If they needed a mentor, a cheerleader, or just a hard nudge, she felt it was her duty to pitch in and help. In fact, she'd already helped one young woman start a housecleaning business and another to start a jewelry pop-up shop.

They strolled down the hall with the rest of the crowd and walked outside to the Heritage Society's rather expansive garden. On any other day you'd find the patio set with casual tables and chairs, planters overflowing with flowers, a reflecting pool, and a rotating display of sculpture pieces. Tonight, the back patio had been turned into a dance theater. The reflecting pool had been covered over by a large platform that gave the ballet dancers much more room to move about, the tables and chairs had been replaced by multiple rows of black folding chairs, and large flaming torches sprouted from all the planters. A purple backdrop had been strung up along with a crisscross of overhead twinkle lights.

"I wonder which ring of Dante's hell this is supposed to be," Drayton joked as they strolled into the makeshift outdoor theater.

"Hopefully an entertaining one," Theodosia said.

Drayton pulled out his tickets, studied them, and located their seats in the sixth row.

Theodosia looked around, nodded to a few friends, and noticed that Adam Lynch, owner of the Lynch Mob, was talking to guests a few rows over. Lynch was wearing a black leather jacket and dark green slacks, and his hair looked wet, as if he'd managed to squeeze in a workout, then taken a shower and hurried over here. But the real killer was that he was passing out business cards.

"There's Adam Lynch," Theodosia said, gently nudging Drayton.

"Mmn, the web graphics guy you told me about." Drayton barely gave Lynch a second glance.

"And there's . . . oh my."

"What? Who?"

"Jimmy Simonton, aka Slide, is here. Looks like he's cruising around, talking to people."

Drayton leaned forward to get a better look at Slide. "He's the infamous dope dealer? I daresay he doesn't look the part. That fellow is wearing a Brioni tuxedo."

"Okay, so he's a high-net-worth dope dealer."

"You mentioned that Mr. Slide has a well-to-do father. Maybe Slide senior is one of the Heritage Society's donors."

"Which would account for Slide junior having tickets."

"Does he appear to be with someone?" Drayton asked as people suddenly filled the rows next to them and in front of them. "Did he bring a date?"

Theodosia cocked her head to watch Slide. "Doesn't look like it. Maybe he's here to do business."

"That would be heresy. Selling drugs on Heritage Society property."

"There's not much we can do about it unless we catch Slide in the act. And I have a feeling Slide's honed his act to perfection."

At that precise moment, the lights dimmed and an announcer's voice came over the sound system. It said, "Ladies and gentlemen, kindly take your seats. Our program will begin in exactly three minutes." As guests scrambled to find their seats, the announcer continued: "As Halloween approaches, we want to welcome you to the terrifying yet hauntingly beautiful domain of the vampire as the talented members of the Wild

Dunes Ballet Company perform their interpretive and highly original Vampyre Ballet, conceived, written, and choreographed by renowned ballet master Ignatius Pollatino."

"Who?" Drayton said under his breath. "I've never heard of him."

Theodosia smiled to herself, knowing this wasn't exactly a production at the Met. She reached over, patted Drayton's hand, and said, "He's probably new."

A minute later, the ballet started for real. With a fog machine pumping out streams of fog, the dancers burst onto the stage. The women wore pointe shoes, the men were barefoot, and all wore full-length unitards with filmy capes that swirled around their bodies. Theodosia wasn't sure if they were all supposed to be vampires—that wasn't quite clear—but their pirouettes, dancing, and high-flying leaps all commanded—in fact, demanded—the audience's attention. There were projections on the back screen of crumbling castles and gnarled trees, and the sound engineer had done a spooky mash-up of pieces by Tchaikovsky, Franz Liszt, and Marilyn Manson.

"This is certainly different," Drayton whispered to Theodosia.

"Are you kidding?" Theodosia said. "It's completely off the chain."

The ballet was quirky, daring, and divided into two "chapters," the first one called "Shadows" and the second called "Surrender." Halfway through "Surrender," pyrotechnics reminiscent of a rock concert were ignited. As golden sparks burst all around the dancers and guests, the music and dance grew more frenzied, and a dancer in a red cape leaped onto the stage.

Theodosia was totally engrossed until she noticed Slide rise from his chair, ghost his way down the dark center aisle, and head back inside the Heritage Society. A minute later, two other men got up and headed in the same direction, all of which caught Theodosia's attention.

What's going on? A dope deal? Only one way to know for sure.

Theodosia whispered "Excuse me" to Drayton, ducked her head as she eased her way down the row of seats, and hurried into the Heritage Society.

24

It was dark inside the building, with just a few lights glowing down the long corridor. Which meant Theodosia was unable to see exactly where the three men had disappeared to.

Maybe to the men's room? Or . . . where else could they be?

She tiptoed down the hallway, past an exhibit featuring black-and-white photos of an old low-country rice plantation, then stopped. Some twenty feet on, a narrow shaft of light spilled from one of the smaller meeting rooms.

Is that where Slide is? And the other two men?

Slowly, carefully, Theodosia worked her way down the corridor until she was standing outside the Palmetto Room. She put her ear to the crack of the door and tried to listen in. No luck. She could hear low murmurs but not a darn bit of actual conversation.

While she was trying to figure out what to do—call the police? Notify Timothy Neville?—the door suddenly opened and one of the men strolled out. He glanced at her with very little curiosity, slicked back his hair with both hands, then headed back out to the patio.

Great. But what about the other guy?

Ever so carefully, Theodosia grasped the brass doorknob and turned it slowly. Once she had the door open a good five inches, she tried to calm her breathing and listen in. And heard . . .

An argument.

Slide was haranguing the man, threatening him.

"Do you know what happened to the last lowlife who tried to rip me off?" Slide snarled.

"Take it easy, okay? I told you I'd get the money. I'm good for it!" the man said.

"You better, because the last guy who stiffed me ended up with cracked ribs and a broken nose to match," Slide said.

Theodosia couldn't help but wonder if Slide was referring to Jamie. But no, Jamie hadn't cracked any ribs, had he?

There was a scuffle and a shuffle of footsteps from inside the room, the two men obviously going at it. But it ended as fast as it had started, and the door where Theodosia was standing began to slowly creak open. Quick as a flash, Theodosia jumped back. She glanced around frantically and dove behind a nearby potted plant. Thank goodness it was a bird-of-paradise with a huge array of foliage, because when the two men cruised past her, they didn't have a clue that she'd been snooping on them.

Rushing back outside, Theodosia took her chair on the patio and tried to calm her beating heart. The dancers were spinning wildly, and the program looked as if it was coming to a conclusion.

Drayton leaned toward her and whispered, "Where were you? What were you doing?"

"I was following Slide," she whispered back.

"Bad idea."

"No, I almost caught him in the act."

Drayton's head jerked back. "Of dealing drugs?"

"I *think* so."

"Lord have mercy," Drayton said. "You realize you missed the most exciting portion of the dance program? It's about to . . ." He glanced up at the stage. "Well, looks like this *is* the conclusion."

The music rose to a loud crescendo as dancers executed jaw-dropping leaps and fiery spins, then the dancers all bent low and formed a circle. Around and around they whirled as applause started up, then they all sprang into the air in one final, dazzling leap. Seconds later, the show was over and the dancers all stood together, facing the audience, hands joined as they took a collective bow. The audience was on its feet, applauding heartily as patio lights flashed on.

"We've got to do something," Theodosia said.

"You mean like call the police?" Drayton said. "Difficult to get them to make an arrest when there's little or no proof." They sat there, debating what to do, as all around them the audience filed back inside the Heritage Society.

Then Theodosia said, "When I said *do something*, I was thinking about something a bit more clandestine."

Drayton stared at her, then said, "No. Not again. Not ever. You know how terrified I am when you pull me into one of your unauthorized explorations."

"You mean when I do a hot prowl?"

"You make it sound like an innocent bit of fun, like telling ghost stories around a campfire, when it's actually breaking and entering. I know we've done this before, but this time I want no part of it."

"Even if it means solving a crime? Figuring out who murdered Celeste? Or getting a dangerous drug dealer off the street?" Theodosia asked.

"Now you're rationalizing."

"And you're putting your head in the sand when we could be doing something important."

"How do you know Slide's not on his way home right now?"

"Because he was all jacked up. Come on, he's a young guy brimming with ego and swagger. He's going to hit a few clubs, do some shots, probably make a few sales."

"You don't even know where Slide lives," Drayton said.

"Actually, I do." Theodosia pulled out her phone and read off the address.

"How do you know this?"

Theodosia shrugged. "Internet."

"What's the address again?"

"Six seven two Cannon Street."

"That sounds familiar," Drayton said. "In fact, we know someone who lives there."

"We do?"

"Remember when we interviewed that woman from the Westside Theater? The one with the faux-British stage name?"

"Lucinda Harrington, who's really Lucy Harris? That's right. She lives in that rehabbed apartment building."

"The Vanderhorst Square Apartments," Drayton said.

"Let's call Lucy and ask her if she'll let us through the security door."

"That's fairly presumptuous," Drayton said. "Do you even have her number?"

"Let me check my phone. Um . . . yes, I still do. In fact, I'm going to call her right now."

Theodosia punched in the number and waited. Lucy

Harris's phone rang six, seven, eight times, then clicked over to voicemail.

"Rats," Theodosia said as she hung up. "She's not answering."

"Good. It was a bad idea anyway."

Theodosia slid her phone back into her purse. "Maybe by the time we get there, she'll be home."

Drayton frowned. "And if she's not?"

Theodosia grabbed Drayton's arm and pulled him to his feet. "Then we'll come up with a different idea."

They drove to Slide's apartment, Theodosia bubbling with excitement and nervous energy, Drayton feeling a sense of dread.

"This is so not a good idea," Drayton said.

"Come on, this is a great idea," Theodosia said. "We'll slip in and out like a wisp of fog. It'll be a matter of minutes. No big deal."

"Actually, it *is* a big deal." Drayton gazed at Theodosia in the darkness and noticed that she was glancing repeatedly in her rearview mirror. "What? Something wrong?"

"I know it sounds crazy, but I think someone's following us."

"It's a busy night with lots of cars on the road."

"This car I've had my eye on has a wonky left front headlight," Theodosia said. "It's sort of canted sideways. I noticed it a few blocks back, and every turn we've made it's followed us."

"Not much you can do about it," Drayton said. He looked back at the car and said, "I doubt it's anything to be concerned about."

"Oh no?" Without hitting her brakes, Theodosia cranked the steering wheel hard right at the next intersection, spinning them into a fast turn. Then she pulled to the curb, slammed on the brakes, and flipped off her lights.

"What kind of stunt is that?" Drayton cried. "You almost clipped the bumper on that Prius."

"Wait one."

They watched as the car with the wonky headlight sailed through the intersection, the driver never looking left or right.

"Now we're going to see who that is!" Theodosia cried. She flipped a U-turn and accelerated hard, speeding after the mysterious car. She caught up with it almost immediately and tailed it for two blocks, then three blocks, all the while noticing that the driver seemed to be slowing down and looking for something. Looking for them? For her Jeep?

"Now what?" Drayton asked. "You're going to run them off the road?"

"Not exactly, but we're going to find out who that jerk is," Theodosia said. "And what they're up to." She hit the gas, pulled up alongside the car, edged the nose of her Jeep in front of the car, basically forcing it to the curb.

When the mysterious car rocked to a full stop, Theodosia put the right-side window down so she could see exactly who'd been following her.

It was Bill Glass.

"Glass!" Theodosia shouted. "That was you? What do you think you're *doing*?"

Bill Glass looked only slightly sheepish. "Following you. I figured you were hot on some suspect's tail. You know, because of the greenhouse thing. I thought I could get a story out of it. You can't blame me for trying."

"You scared the crabgrass out of me!" Theodosia shouted.

"Sorry," Glass said, but he didn't sound one bit remorseful.

"Go away, go home," Theodosia shouted, in the same

manner you'd scold a wayward dog who'd ventured outside his yard. "Go home!"

She pulled away fast, leaving Glass to eat her exhaust.

At one time the Vanderhorst Square Apartments had been a two-story dirty yellow-brick building that housed a bar, food market, and plumbing supplies shop. An enterprising developer had bought the building, stone-blasted the exterior, knocked out all the interior walls, and completely rehabbed the massive interior space with help from a Charleston Housing Authority grant. Now the entire structure had been turned into stylish one-of-a-kind apartments.

When they arrived at the charming building on Cannon Street, Theodosia pulled over and said, "What do you think?"

"I think this is madness," Drayton said.

"I get that. What I mean is, what do you *really* think?" When Drayton remained silent, Theodosia shut off the engine and said, "Let's try to keep an open mind."

"What's that supposed to mean?"

"It means we should go take a look-see." When Drayton didn't reply, she said, "Tell you what, I'll go in by myself. Because I really don't want to force you into doing something that's against your principles."

"Well . . ."

Against his better judgment, Drayton followed Theodosia up the walk to the main entry of the apartment complex. A black wrought iron fence surrounded the entire building with an elaborate curlicued archway over the front walk. Enormous plantings of bougainvillea and palmettos added a patina of richness to the exterior.

"This place is really adorable," Theodosia said. "Look how

some of the lower-level apartments have their own patios and a few of the upper-level units have little wrought iron balconies, Juliet balconies. The developer managed to keep the funkiness of the old building and refresh it at the same time."

Drayton crossed his arms in front of himself. "I bet we won't even get in the front door."

Theodosia grabbed the door handle, pulled it open, and said, "This way to the lobby." They stepped inside an almost Victorian-looking lobby replete with crown molding, a chandelier, two brocade chairs, and a wall of mailboxes.

"And look here," Theodosia said. "They've installed a nice new buzzer system. One buzzer to contact each resident."

"Do you see Slide's name there?"

"I see his given name, yes, and I'm pushing his buzzer right now."

"He'll be home," Drayton predicted.

Slide was not at home. Theodosia made sure of it, pressing his buzzer thirty or forty times, enough to drive any sane person bonkers.

"See? Nobody home," she said.

"Do you intend to pick the lock?" Drayton asked. "To get inside the complex?"

"No need," Theodosia said as she hastily jabbed five or six other buzzers. When a man answered, "What?" in a tinny voice, she said, "Delivery." And the main door was buzzed open, just like that.

"I can't," Drayton said. "I shouldn't."

"But you're curious. Admit it."

Drayton lifted a shoulder as Theodosia pulled him through the security door.

Fairly bouncing on the balls of her feet as she looked around, Theodosia said, "This place is really lovely. This wasn't just a developer's dream, they also hired a seriously talented decorator." The hallway carpet was a muted floral design, the wallpaper was a rich cream and pale yellow stripe, and old-fashioned lamps with glass globes glowed next to each apartment's recessed doorway.

"Not bad," Drayton allowed as he looked around.

"We're looking for apartment 210. Which would be . . . upstairs," Theodosia said.

They found the stairway halfway down the first-floor hallway, a staircase that took them up eight steps to a landing where a table with a vase of silk flowers stood, then up another short stairway to the second floor.

"Since you're still following me, is this a tacit agreement to take a look in Slide's apartment?" Theodosia asked.

Drayton's lips twitched. "Maybe."

Theodosia fished a credit card out of her wallet—an old Visa card that had long since expired—and slid it between the lock and the doorjamb. Poked it this way and that.

Drayton watched her carefully. "Are you sure that's going to . . ."

"Work?" Theodosia said. "It already has." She pushed the door open, leaned in to turn on a light, and stepped all the way inside. When Drayton hesitated, she reached back, grabbed his sleeve, and pulled him inside as well.

Slide's apartment wasn't exactly a decorator's dream. He had a beige sectional sofa, an innocuous brown wooden coffee table, a contemporary rug with an interlocking circle design, and a big-screen (really big-screen) TV.

"Except for the TV, this doesn't look like the den of a dope dealer," Drayton said. "It's more like a conservative little old lady who attends church on Sunday and watches a lot of Turner Classic Movies."

"Hold that thought while we have a look around," Theodosia said.

She rummaged around in the living room—which didn't have a lot of places to hide anything—then checked out the kitchen. She opened cupboards, pulled out drawers, and checked under the sink. Strangely enough, Slide came across as a neatnik.

"Huh," Theodosia said when she looked inside the freezer. "Not much here except frozen vegetables. Some green beans, three packages of broccoli."

"A vegetarian dope dealer?" Drayton said.

"Don't know." Theodosia tiptoed into the bedroom, did a quiet ransack of the dresser drawers, looked under the bed, and checked out the closet. After twenty minutes of searching, even looking at floor vents and electrical outlets, all she found was more bland decor.

"Maybe Slide's not a genuine dope dealer at all," Drayton said. "Maybe he's a fraud who gets off on having a shady reputation."

"No, Riley said Slide was a dealer." Theodosia looked around. "And I'd have to say he's a clever one at that."

"Why do you think that?"

"Because Slide doesn't keep his merchandise here."

"Then where?"

"Maybe he's got a storage locker somewhere, another apartment, or he uses his parents' house. I don't know. But this place is spick-and-span clean. You could bring a dope-sniffing dog in here and the poor mutt would fall asleep from boredom. So I think . . ."

BRINNNG!

"Dear Lord, what's that?" Drayton cried as he lurched for the door, almost tripping over his own feet.

"Just my phone," Theodosia said, pulling it out of her

pocket and silencing it immediately. "Sorry about that ringtone, I'll change it to a chime."

"Never mind that, someone must know we're here!" Drayton cried. His nerves jangled as he envisioned being placed under arrest, having an unflattering mug shot taken, and spending a torturous night in jail.

Theodosia put the phone to her ear and said, as calmly as possible, "Hello?"

That's when Bettina started screaming at the top of her lungs. "Help! Oh, Theodosia, I need you! Please come quick! Pleeeeease!"

"What's wrong?" Theodosia asked. "What's happened?" Bettina was sobbing so hard Theodosia could barely understand her. "Calm down, take a deep breath, and tell me what's going on."

"What's happened?" Drayton was suddenly at Theodosia's elbow.

She shook her head. "I don't know." To Bettina she said, "You're going to have to calm down and speak a little more slowly. Tell me what's wrong, honey."

"I'm hurt bad," came Bettina's wet blubber. "And—you're not going to believe this—but, oh jeez, Jamie's been kidnapped!"

25

"Kidnapped?" Theodosia said.

"Who's kidnapped?" Drayton asked, but Theodosia held up a finger to silence him. Had she heard Bettina correctly? The girl was injured and Jamie was kidnapped? Was this yet another bizarre chapter in her terrible wedding saga?

Bettina uttered a series of high-pitched yelps, then quavered, "It's unbelievably crazy! Jamie and I had just finished eating dinner at Gaulart and Maliclet on Broad Street. Then, when the valet brought Jamie's SUV around, I asked him to help Jamie get into the passenger seat—which he did. But when I came around to the driver's side, this ninja-type person jumped out of nowhere and attacked me!"

"Attacked you how? Did you fight back?" Theodosia asked.

Crying even more heavily, slurring her words, Bettina blubbered, "I couldn't do *anything*! The guy hit me with a Taser! It felt like lightning exploding inside my entire body—my arms and legs started shaking and my heart felt like it was going to burst out of my ribs. And then . . . then my legs turned to jelly and I collapsed on the pavement and hit my head!" Her voice rose again, shrill and raw. "The last thing I remember was the car driving away! With Jamie in it!"

"Did anyone help you? The valet? A passerby?"

"Yes, yes, the valet guys called 911 right away, and the police are on their way, but Jamie's gone!" Now her emotions were completely out of control. "Jamie's gone!" she howled. "He's been kidnapped!"

"Stay where you are," Theodosia cried. "I'll be there in five minutes."

When Theodosia and Drayton arrived at Gaulart & Maliclet, the street out front was an open-air calamity. Uniformed officers were running around interviewing witnesses, red-jacketed valets were trying to maneuver departing customers' cars around police cars, and tourists with puzzled faces stood gaping, suddenly worried about crime in what was supposedly a genteel neighborhood.

An ambulance from CCEMS, Charleston Country Emergency Medical Services, was on the scene, its blue lights spinning lazily. Bettina was sitting on the back of the ambulance, legs dangling, as an EMT put a series of Steri-Strip bandages on her temple.

Theodosia jammed her Jeep into a No Parking spot, and she and Drayton hurried over to Bettina.

"Are you hurt?" Theodosia asked in a rush.

"Dear girl, what happened?" Drayton asked.

"I *think* I'm gonna be okay," Bettina said between hiccups.

The EMT nodded and said, "She's doing fairly well. Her blood pressure's coming back down to normal, and her respiration is good. She has a nasty abrasion on her right temple that needs a couple of stitches. So we'll run her over to the ER and get that taken care of."

Bettina clamped desperate eyes on Theodosia and said, "But Jamie's *gone.*" She hiccupped again. "Kidnapped, I think."

"You think?" Theodosia asked.

"No, I *know* he was. I saw it with my own eyes," Bettina said.

"Did you see who did it?" Theodosia asked.

Bettina shook her head. "Nuh-uh. It happened too fast. Somebody came up behind me, kind of smacked me on the head, then tasered me. The pain was so bad that I totally blanked out."

"But you saw Jamie's SUV drive away? With Jamie in it?" Drayton asked.

"I saw that much, yes," Bettina said. She touched a hand to her chest and looked at the EMT. "I think I'm having a heart attack."

"Probably not, but let's slip that blood pressure cuff on you again," the EMT said.

Theodosia patted Bettina's knee and said, "I'll be right back. I want to talk to the police."

Theodosia turned away from the ambulance and studied the scene. There were two police cruisers blocking Broad Street with four harried-looking uniformed officers pushing back lookie-loos even as they tried to question witnesses and take statements. Worried murmurs rippled through a crowd of bystanders . . .

"What happened?"

"Somebody got killed?"

"We better get out of here."

"Maybe we should . . . ," Drayton began, just as a shiny black Suburban with smoked windows threaded its way through the crowd. The Suburban had a large push bar on front, and set just above the bar were red and blue pulsing lights.

"Uh-oh," Theodosia said.

Drayton glanced at her. "What?"

"Looks like this got kicked upstairs."

They both watched as one of the back doors flew open and Pete Riley stepped out. Then the back door on the other side opened and Detective Burt Tidwell, head of Charleston PD's Robbery and Homicide Division, eased out.

Tidwell was a bear of a man, bulky, imposing, and quick with his temper. Most of the people in city government feared him, while the detectives and officers that worked under him admired him unconditionally. Theodosia had had several run-ins with Tidwell before—mostly when she was looking into local crimes that had stirred her imagination and caused her to don her Sherlock Holmes cap and launch her own brand of investigation. Suffice it to say, Detective Tidwell mostly frowned on this course of action.

"Miss Browning," Tidwell said, his hangdog face clouded with anger as he came striding up to her with his trademark beady-eyed stare, "I should have known you'd be mixed up in this." His eyes skidded across to Drayton as well.

"I'm not mixed up in this," Theodosia said. She tried to keep her voice even and not let Tidwell fluster her. Forced herself to focus on the soup stain on his horrible green tie, which was a total mismatch for his liver-colored jacket. "Drayton and I are only here because Bettina called and asked for our help."

"Bettina of the unfortunate, unrealized wedding," Tidwell said. "With the collapsed greenhouse and dead bridesmaid."

"Well, yes."

"And you've been investigating that death ever since,"

Tidwell said. He raised his shoulders and dropped them, his belly puffing out in a sigh.

"Actually, I—"

"No," Tidwell said, waving an index finger at her. "That was not a question."

Theodosia switched her gaze to Riley. "You told him."

"No question," Riley said. "I had to now that Celeste's death has mushroomed out of control and spilled over into Charleston proper."

"Where *we* have complete jurisdiction," Tidwell said.

"Great," Theodosia said. "So what are *you* going to do about it?"

"We've already put out a BOLO on Jamie's stolen SUV," Tidwell said.

"A *Be on the Lookout*," Riley explained.

"I know what it means," Theodosia said. "And that's a good first step. But what else are you guys going to actually do?"

"We are going to investigate and apprehend," Tidwell said, enunciating each word carefully. "While you two are going to leave well alone." With that, he spun away from them, a light-footed maneuver for such a large man.

Riley shrugged. "You heard the man."

Theodosia let out an exasperated sigh as she backed away from Riley, unhappy that he wasn't going to give her any help. Just the same, she kept a watchful eye on Tidwell and Riley as one of the uniformed officers hurried up to them.

"We've got an eyewitness here," the uniformed officer said, gesturing at a young man who was standing on the sidewalk, fidgeting with his car keys. "Saw the whole thing."

"I'll talk to him," Tidwell said. "Meanwhile, let's string some tape and get this entire street blocked off."

"Yes, sir."

Tidwell turned to Riley. "You go talk to the girl."

"Now what do we do?" Drayton asked as Tidwell and Riley both got busy.

"Go back to the drawing board?" Theodosia said. "Try to figure out who on earth would want to kidnap Jamie—and hurt Bettina as well?"

"That sounds like a tall order."

"Probably because it is."

"Theodosia!" A shrill voice rose above the din of the crowd and the honking of horns from frustrated drivers who'd just found their street blocked off.

"Hold on to your hat," Drayton muttered under his breath. "Delaine just arrived."

Delaine came spinning toward them like an F3 tornado. Her face was twisted into a mask of fear, her hair was a flyaway mess, and her red fingernails seemed to claw at the air, propelling her forward. Only her clothes were impeccable—a tight black long-sleeved silk T-shirt tucked into a short black leather skirt and her trademark four-inch stilettos.

Delaine threw her arms around Theodosia and started to sob. Then she pulled away and threw her arms around Drayton. "My poor, dear Bettina!" she wailed. "How could anyone possibly want to hurt her?"

"Or kidnap Jamie," Drayton said.

Delaine straightened up and brushed at her tears. "Yes, Jamie," she said, as if it was an afterthought. Then, head up, chin out, Delaine was striding down the street, headed for the ambulance, where Bettina was still being tended to.

"Now Delaine's really going to put the screws to you," Drayton said to Theodosia. "She doesn't trust the police, but she loves to put her faith in you." He turned and gazed at the restaurant, a white building, very French-looking with its touches of brass and its black wrought iron balcony above the front door. "Great coq au vin," he said.

But Theodosia's mind was still in a whirl. She felt terrible that she hadn't been able to figure out Celeste's murder. And now this. Jamie kidnapped, Bettina tasered and beaten up. What was going on? She just couldn't see a clear answer. Was she letting people down, people who were dear to her? It sure felt that way.

"I've been trying to figure this whole thing out," Theodosia said to Drayton, "but haven't come up with much. And now this . . ." She waved a hand at the chaos around them. "I never anticipated anything like this happening. What a complete and total mess."

"It could get messier," Drayton said. "You know, if Jamie . . ."

"What?" Theodosia spun toward him. "What are you saying, Drayton? If Jamie is murdered?" She shook her head. "If someone wanted Jamie dead, then why bother to *kidnap* him? Why not just engineer a nice clean drive-by shooting?"

"I don't know," Drayton said. "Maybe there'll be a ransom demand. Are Jamie's parents well-off?"

"I think so," Theodosia said. "On the other hand . . ."

"What?"

An idea—an ugly idea—had slithered into Theodosia's brain. She glanced around to make sure no one was listening. "You don't, um, suppose that Jamie arranged to kidnap himself, do you?"

"Sweet Fanny Adams, why would Jamie do a thing like that?" Drayton cried.

"What if he wanted to get out of marrying Bettina?"

Drayton was dumbfounded. "*What?* Explain please."

"The thing is, you hear about runaway brides all the time.

But I have a sneaking suspicion there are plenty of runaway grooms, too."

"I thought that was an urban myth, stories that were spread on the Internet."

"Not exactly," Theodosia said. "Remember what we talked about before?"

"Dead brides and grooms?"

"Yes. And I know this sounds really weird, but I did some more research on it. Newly minted brides—and newly minted grooms, too—have a strange tendency to die on their honeymoon."

"They do?"

"Think of all those poor young people you hear about on the news who fall overboard on cruise ships . . ."

"You do hear about that," Drayton said. "And it's more than a once-in-a-blue-moon thing."

"And might I remind you, when new brides or grooms *are* killed, it's more often than not done at the hands of their spouse."

"That's terrifying," Drayton said.

They stood there and gazed at each other, unsure what to do now.

"An alternate explanation," Drayton said, "and I pray this is true, is that maybe Jamie's kidnapping was a Halloween prank, something Jamie's friends cooked up."

"A boys-will-be-boys thing," Theodosia said slowly. "It's possible. Except for the fact that Bettina was tasered so hard she collapsed and split open her head. That goes beyond the boundaries of a Halloween prank."

Drayton looked around at the chaos and shrugged. "I guess all we can do is keep our fingers crossed and hope that Jamie turns up tomorrow."

26

But Friday arrived and Jamie didn't turn up. He didn't call, he didn't text, he didn't show up at the front door of Bettina's apartment claiming amnesia. He also didn't wander into the Indigo Tea Shop. Jamie was gone. Kidnapped. With a half dozen witnesses to attest to it.

That was the heartbreaking news as of Friday morning. And Haley was eating it up.

"Kidnapped?" she said. "I didn't know that kind of thing still happened. I thought it was only in old movies from the sixties."

"Oh, it happens," Drayton said. "And, for your information, movies from the sixties aren't *that* old."

"They are if you were born at the tail end of the nineties," Haley said.

"The thing we need to focus on," Theodosia said, "is *who* would mastermind this kind of plot? And why?"

"Aren't the police working on it?" Haley asked.

"Yes," Drayton said. "As are we."

"Oh. Okay," Haley said.

"What about that fellow Martin Hunt, who owns Hunt and Peck?" Drayton said. "He hated Jamie for making bad stock picks."

"And what about that angry guy, Adam Lynch, who tried to hit on me?" Haley said. "You told me he was Bettina's former boyfriend. You think he's still carrying a torch for her?"

"It's possible," Theodosia said. "Though he trash-talks Bettina every chance he gets."

"Maybe his trash talk is all an act and Lynch still loves Bettina. Maybe he kidnapped Jamie so they couldn't get married," Haley said.

"Maybe," Theodosia said as her brain pulsed with worry. She'd had wild dreams about this all last night, but they hadn't spun out an answer to this madness.

"I don't think Sabrina could have managed a kidnapping, since she's in Chicago for Celeste's funeral and burial," Drayton said.

"Unless Sabrina jobbed it out to someone. Went and hired herself a hit man," Theodosia said.

"That seems unlikely," Drayton said.

"You never know," Theodosia said. "She's got the money for it. Or, as an alternate thought, Sabrina could have come back and done this herself. Remember, there's ten million dollars in play."

"But why would she want to kidnap Jamie?" Drayton asked.

"I don't know. Maybe because she blames him for her sister's death?" Theodosia said.

"Wait, back up a minute," Haley said. She touched a hand to her forehead, then waved it in the air. "You're saying Sabrina might actually have tasered Jamie?"

"You can buy a Taser online just like you can buy a voice-changing apparatus," Theodosia said. She thought for a minute.

"We also can't rule out Karl Rueff, Celeste's old boyfriend. We barely know anything about him, so he's kind of a wild card in all this."

"Lots of possibilities," Haley said.

"Lots of suspects," Drayton said. "Seems like any one of them could have had a psychotic break."

"If that were true, wouldn't last night's scene have been all helter-skelter?" Haley asked.

"It *was* all helter-skelter," Theodosia said. Then she stopped to consider her words. "No, I'm wrong, because last night's kidnapping was planned. It was *orchestrated* right down to the last detail. Someone knew exactly where Jamie and Bettina would be eating dinner and figured out the best way to catch them in a trap."

"A kind of pincer move," Drayton said. "Using their car, an unsuspecting valet, and a Taser shot."

"Who could hate them that much?" Haley asked.

"Remember that weirdo who called yesterday?" Drayton said to Theodosia. "When you were on Charlie's podcast?"

"Oh, you told me about that," Haley said.

Theodosia gave a little shiver. "I still have a sick feeling that caller might have been Celeste's killer."

"They could also be the person responsible for Jamie's disappearance," Drayton said.

"But investigating that phone call is a dead end," Theodosia said. "Because the phone . . ."

"Was a burner," Drayton said. "So forget the phone and concentrate on what that person said to you about a clue. They hinted that you'd eventually figure out what it meant."

Theodosia blinked. "They did?"

"Yes. In fact, you were fairly emphatic about it," Drayton said. "You told me the caller said *buzz*."

Theodosia reached up and scratched her head. "You're right, the caller said the word *buzz* was a clue. But I can't for the life of me figure out what *buzz* means or how it connects to Jamie."

"We need to think about this some more," Drayton said. "See what we can come up with."

"*Buzz?*" Haley said. She looked confused as well.

At seeing their frustrated faces, Theodosia said, "Okay, the person who called in might have been talking gibberish, but I guess it wouldn't hurt to focus on it some more. But first . . ."

"I know," Haley said. "We have work to do."

At ten o'clock, with four tables of guests served and sipping tea, Miss Dimple arrived to help with today's Harvest Tea.

"How are you feeling?" Theodosia asked. She was still worried about possible aftereffects from the tainted candy.

"Right as rain," Miss Dimple said with a big grin as she hung her pink cardigan sweater on the coatrack. "After I went home this past Wednesday, I crawled into bed with my cats and slept for something like ten hours. It feels like I stockpiled enough sleepy time to last me a week." She looked around the tea shop. "Not too busy today."

"Wait until noon, we will be."

Miss Dimple reached for an apron and said, "Fine by me."

They waited on customers, bagged scones for takeout, and took a few late reservations. When eleven thirty finally rolled around, and their morning tea customers had pretty much cleared out, Theodosia went to the cupboard and pulled out her Fall Harvest by Dansk plates, soup bowls, and matching cups and saucers. She loved the grape, pear, and vine motif and figured it was in perfect keeping with today's Harvest Tea theme.

Miss Dimple picked up one of the plates, studied it, and said, "Such a lovely pattern, almost as if it were painted in watercolors. What do you want to use for tablecloths?"

"Let's use the sunny yellow ones," Theodosia said.

"Works for me."

"And if you ransack my office, you'll find a crate full of apples, pumpkins, gourds, and Indian corn to put on the tables."

"Already checked it out," Miss Dimple said. "And should I grab that bucket of black-eyed Susans and put them in vases? Wait, no, maybe the stoneware crocks would look more earthy?"

"Looks like you're one step ahead of me," Theodosia said. She wandered over to the front counter where Drayton was hard at work and said, "Judging by all those enticing aromas, it seems you've selected your teas and are ready to start brewing them."

"Indeed, yes," Drayton said. "Two black teas and one green tea, with flavors all in keeping with our harvest theme."

"Great."

Drayton looked up from where he was measuring rich black tea into a yellow floral teapot. "You don't sound all that enthusiastic."

"Probably because I'm not. I have to confess . . . my heart's just not in this tea luncheon."

"I'm glad to hear you say that because neither is mine," Drayton said.

"Until this Celeste business is cleared up—and we get Jamie safely back home—everything feels fuzzy and muddled."

"Like slogging through molasses," Drayton said.

"Walking on eggshells."

"Treading through treacle."

"Treacle? That sounds *awful*," Theodosia said. Still, such an amusing word made her crack a smile. "What on earth is treacle?"

"A British word for something heavy and syrupy. A lot like molasses," Drayton said.

Theodosia made a face. "Treacle. Odd word. Promise me you'll never use it in front of our guests."

And Drayton did not. Rather, he helped greet all the guests who arrived at noon, reciprocated a few hugs, exchanged air-kisses, and handed the guests off to Miss Dimple, who promptly seated them at the various tables. When the arrival of guests slowed to a trickle, Drayton left Theodosia at the front door and ducked behind the front counter to tend to his tea.

Theodosia greeted a few guests that Neela Carter from the Tangled Rose B and B had sent over, then was stunned when Babs Campbell wandered in accompanied by two friends.

Theodosia pulled Babs in close for a hug and said in her ear, "I didn't expect to see you here today."

"I didn't expect to be here," Babs whispered back. "After that mess last night."

A few minutes after Miss Dimple had seated Babs and her two friends, Babs got up from her table and hurried over to talk to Theodosia.

"Can you believe that Jamie was kidnapped?" Babs said, keeping her voice purposefully low. "Once I heard the news, I was so upset I didn't even want to leave my apartment . . ." Babs glanced back at her table. "But my friends basically ordered me to come to tea with them. You know, because I told them how much encouragement you and Drayton have given me about opening a coffee shop."

"Because we care about you and want you to do well," Theodosia said.

"So . . . have you heard anything at all about Jamie?"

"Unfortunately, not a thing," Theodosia said.

"Jamie's kidnapping has completely thrown me for a loop—do you know it's been spread all over the news? This morning's paper even did a story connecting it to the death at the wedding. Or, I guess I should say, the would-be wedding."

"Do you have any idea what could have happened to Jamie? Because I'm fresh out," Theodosia said.

"Believe me, if I had an inkling of who might have engineered Jamie's kidnapping, I'd be sitting down with the police right now," Babs said. "That guy's friendship means a lot to me."

"Drayton and I think the kidnapper was the same person who sabotaged the greenhouse," Theodosia said.

Babs frowned, bit her lower lip, and thought for a moment. "You're probably on the right track, though I can't say I've thought about it in those terms." Tears glistened in her eyes. "Gosh, I feel awful about this."

"The police are doing all they can. Drayton and I are trying to figure things out as well."

"Well, I've been praying," Babs said. "*That* couldn't hurt."

Theodosia touched a hand to Babs's shoulder and squeezed gently. "Good for you. Sometimes praying is the best thing anyone can do. Now, please, try to enjoy your luncheon."

Babs nodded. "I will."

Just when Theodosia was ready to abandon her post at the front door and go welcome her seated guests, Angie Congdon arrived with a good-looking, silver-haired gentleman in tow. Angie was a forty-something bubbly blonde who was the owner of the nearby Featherbed House B and B. Today she wore a red cashmere crew neck sweater with a denim pencil skirt.

"Angie!" Theodosia exclaimed. "How delightful to see you!" Angie had been engaged for a number of years to a man named Harold but had recently broken it off. Maybe she'd gotten tired of waiting? For whatever reason, Angie had wasted no time in finding herself a brand-new boyfriend.

"Theodosia," Angie said, pink color rising in her cheeks, "I'd like you to meet Gordon Twombley."

"Your name sounds about as British as a tin of Duncan's of Deeside shortbread," Theodosia said as she shook hands with him.

"Probably because I am British," Twombley said. "But after living in London's Mayfair for almost twenty years, I had the wild idea to fly across the pond and take up residence here."

"Then welcome to Charleston," Theodosia said as she studied Twombley. He had an open broad face, pale blue eyes, and a nose that looked like it might have been broken once or twice. On the other hand, he could have been a rugby player in his younger days. A well-cut powder blue blazer, a pink shirt, and pressed khaki slacks concealed his somewhat stocky physique.

"Gordon is an antique dealer," Angie said.

"Oh my, then you really have come to the right place," Theodosia said to him. "Charleston is basically awash in antiques and antique lovers." She smiled at Twombley. "So you'll be opening a shop?"

"Already have," Twombley said. "I found a dandy sublease over on King Street. A charming little brick building with a small flat directly above it."

"He named the shop Mayfair Antiques," Angie said. "To remind him of his London roots."

"So you'll be selling British antiques," Theodosia said as she led them to a table and got them seated.

"British and French," Twombley said. "Thanks to a recent trip to the Paris flea markets."

"Those *are* fun," Theodosia said, remembering a day once spent at Saint-Ouen-sur-Seine.

After seating Angie and her guest, Theodosia glanced around the tea room and decided it was time to introduce the menu. As she strode to the center of the room, one of her guests, Harriet Jones from the French Quarter Tea Club, saw her coming and clinked her knife against her water glass. That settled the chattering crowd down so Theodosia could speak.

"Welcome, dear guests, to the Indigo Tea Shop's Harvest Tea," Theodosia said. "You'll be happy to know that our chef has been busy traversing the low country, shopping local markets and country stands so we could bring you the freshest and finest produce in season."

That announcement brought a smattering of applause.

"For our luncheon today, we'll begin with artisanal cheddar cheese scones, the cheese having been sourced from Ashe County Cheese in the Blue Ridge Mountains. The scones will be served with honey butter as well as our homemade Devonshire cream. Second course will be butternut squash bisque topped with crème fraiche. And for your main course, we're hoping to delight you with three savories: turkey, apple, and goat cheese tea sandwiches, chicken and bacon tea sandwiches, and prosciutto and artichoke crostini. Our dessert, because our tea shop is famous for desserts, will be blackberry cobbler drenched in fresh cream, as well as cake mix cookies. As for our teas today . . . I'll have Drayton Conneley, our tea sommelier, tell you all about them."

Drayton stepped to the center of the room, a pink and floral teapot tucked in the crook of his arm, and said, "Today we have three fresh-brewed teas for your sipping pleasure. Fujian silver, orange pekoe tea, and, for our green tea lovers, a lovely Chinese Lung Ching."

After a quick question from a guest about tea bags versus tea leaves, Miss Dimple and Haley brought out platters heaped with scones, and the luncheon was off and running.

Twenty minutes later, with only crumbs left to hint at the demise of four dozen scones, Theodosia helped serve the soup course. Then she chatted with guests, cleared a few dishes, and promised one woman that she'd for sure give her the recipe for the butternut squash bisque.

Halfway through the savories course, Babs grabbed Theodosia's arm and said, "I need to talk to you. I have some . . . key information you might be interested in."

27

"Let's talk over by the front counter," Theodosia said. She didn't know what Babs had in mind but decided she didn't want her guests to overhear their conversation.

Babs followed Theodosia to the counter and said, "I just now remembered something that may or may not be related to Jamie's disappearance. It concerns Karl Rueff."

"Celeste's ex-boyfriend," Theodosia said. She didn't know much about Rueff except that, in the back of her mind, she'd always thought of him as a long-shot suspect.

"It occurred to me that I kind of know Rueff," Babs said. "Well, not personally, but I'm familiar with him."

"Because he showed up at Celeste's visitation?"

"No, there's something else."

"Okay." Theodosia was interested because . . . well, you never know.

"I just remembered that our firm, Milne and Kerrison, did some damage control for Karl Rueff a year or so ago."

Theodosia gave an encouraging nod. She knew that, besides

placing newsworthy stories about people and products with select media, PR firms also helped shut down unflattering stories. Since PR firms enjoyed hotlines to senior writers, editors, and management, exerting pressure to dump a story wasn't unheard of. In fact, it was referred to as a kill shot.

"What did Karl Rueff want killed?" Theodosia asked.

"I don't recall the exact details, but it had to do with Bluestone, the tech company Rueff works for. He's a VP there and they'd developed some AI product that had been hailed as a major breakthrough for being super user-friendly, but then it turned out to be a dud. Rueff was suddenly all over us and wanted any and all stories and rumors killed before the media, major investors, and tech magazines got wind of their problem."

"And this relates how?" Theodosia asked.

"Because Karl Rueff was basically a hard-ass about it, really difficult and unpleasant to work with." Babs paused. "And I know that Rueff is Celeste's ex-boyfriend, so I was wondering if maybe he was somehow involved? In her death or . . ."

"Or with Jamie's kidnapping?" Theodosia said.

Babs nodded. "And I heard that you had an in with a police detective, so I thought . . ."

"That I might want to mention this to him. That Rueff has a prickly, tough-guy personality."

"Right."

Theodosia thought for a few moments, then said, "Your inside story on Rueff is interesting. And even though it doesn't offer anything concrete, it still could be relevant."

"Good," Babs said. "I was hoping you'd say that. And I'll keep offering up a few more prayers for Jamie's safe return."

Theodosia gave her a quick hug. "Do that."

* * *

While the guests were digging into their blackberry cobbler, Theodosia called Riley on his mobile phone, knowing that phone was permanently glued to his ear. Which is why he answered on the first ring.

"Riley here."

"Hi, it's me," Theodosia said. "Any news?"

"Afraid not. Your boy Jamie is still MIA."

"Are the police taking his kidnapping seriously?" For some reason, Theodosia was afraid they weren't.

"We've got everybody out looking for Jamie and that jacked SUV. We even assigned a squirrel cop."

"What does that mean?"

"Guy was pulled off park patrol."

"Oh. Okay. Listen, there's a guy by the name of Karl Rueff," Theodosia said. "He's an ex-boyfriend of Celeste and supposedly a fairly nasty guy."

"And, let me guess, you think he's involved in Jamie's kidnapping?" Riley asked. "I don't see the connection."

"I know it's circuitous, but it's there. This Rueff character might be worth looking into."

"Maybe," Riley said, but he didn't sound all that convinced.

"Okay, forget I mentioned it. At the very least, will you call me if you hear anything?"

"Will do."

Theodosia went back to circulating among her guests. She helped one woman choose a couple of tins of tea—"starter teas," the woman called them, since she was just getting into tea drinking. And she helped two more women select teapots and tea strainers from displays on her highboy. The teapots were wrapped in Bubble Wrap and indigo blue tissue paper and sent off with a wave and a hearty thank-you. After that, it was time to clear tables and get set up for afternoon tea.

By midafternoon, fretting that nothing had broken yet, that nothing was getting done, Theodosia decided to call Karl Rueff herself and ask a few gently probing questions. She went online, looked up Bluestone Software, and called their main number.

"Bluestone Software," a cultured woman's voice said. "How may I direct your call?"

"I'd like to speak with Karl Rueff," Theodosia said.

"I'm sorry, Mr. Rueff left early today, he had a plane to catch."

"Is there any chance of getting a message to him?"

"If he calls in, sure," the woman said. "I'll be at the front desk until five."

"You can't give me his personal number?" Theodosia asked.

"I'm afraid not."

"Okay then." Theodosia gave the woman her name and number and said, "Just ask Mr. Rueff to call me. Tell him it's important."

"If he calls, I'll tell him."

"That went well," Drayton said as he carefully aligned his armada of steeping teapots.

"The luncheon? Yes, it did," Theodosia said. "Even though my mind was only halfway in the game."

"I know the feeling. And now we've got afternoon tea to deal with." Drayton furrowed his brow as he added water to a teapot and said, "The word that's supposed to be a clue . . . *buzz*. Do you think it relates to beehives?"

"You're thinking about the community beehive project over in Petigru Park?"

Drayton shrugged. "That comes to mind. Although *buzz* could also relate to gossip."

"You mean like the morning buzz?" Theodosia said. "But that's kind of . . . generic. Don't you think?"

"What about *buzz saw*?" Drayton asked.

"I don't like where your mind is going with that."

Drayton's face reflected a fair amount of intensity. "Still . . . we can't discount it as a possibility."

"What are you saying?" Theodosia asked, her voice suddenly sounding strained. "That Jamie's being kept prisoner in a sawmill? Do sawmills even exist anymore?"

"I suppose it wouldn't have to be a working sawmill."

"You mean, like, a defunct sawmill?" She grabbed the edge of her apron and twisted it.

"It's just a thought," Drayton said.

"It's a terrible thought," Theodosia said. Drayton's sawmill idea conjured up images of spinning blades with high-pitched whines. She shook her head to clear it and pointed to a pink-and-green teapot. "Is that my tea for table four? The vanilla orange jasmine blend?"

"That's it."

Theodosia grabbed the teapot and carried it to a table of six women who'd driven over from Goose Creek. They'd requested what they laughingly called "the full monty." That meant scones with Devonshire cream, two flavored teas, an assortment of tea sandwiches on three-tiered trays, and an array of petite desserts also served on three-tiered trays. A large party always warranted a little extra time and care, so Theodosia fussed over them, brought seconds on Devonshire cream, and answered questions. She also let Drayton's idea of a sawmill ruminate in her brain.

When her table of six finally left, when there were only two tables remaining in the entire tea shop, Theodosia grabbed a take-out cup of Dimbula tea, asked Drayton to hold down the fort, and ran down Church Street to Antiquarian Books.

Lois's shop was a jewel of a bookshop. A small white building with yellow awnings set between two redbrick buildings. Hand-lettered gold script on the front window announced ANTIQUARIAN BOOKS. And this week's window display was a collection of mystery books. Theodosia saw a pair of old Nancy Drew books from the thirties that she'd kill to have, along with vintage books by Edgar Allan Poe, Agatha Christie, Dorothy L. Sayers, and Erle Stanley Gardner.

Pumpkin's sharp bark rang out the minute Theodosia stepped through the front door.

"Hello there, baby Pumpkin," Theodosia said. She knelt down to pet Lois's adorable little dachshund and said, "I think I might have . . ." Theodosia dug in her pocket as Pumpkin's bright eyes followed her every move. "Yes, I *do* have a treat. Would you like it?" Pumpkin wagged her tail and immediately sat down, an expectant look on her furry face. "Here you go, sweetie."

"Is that you, Theodosia?" Lois called from behind a row of bookshelves.

"It's me," Theodosia said. "And I brought you a cup of tea."

"Wonderful," Lois said as she suddenly appeared, dressed in a yellow sweater, blue jeans, and her trademark scuffed brown clogs. "Nothing like hot tea on a cool day. And I see Pumpkin got a goody as well."

"My jacket pockets basically sag with dog treats," Theodosia said. "It's the one thing that keeps Earl Grey on his toes. Such as they are."

She looked around the bookshop and smiled as she took in its quaint laid-back atmosphere. Tiffany-style lamps hung from raw wooden ceiling beams, faded Oriental carpets covered the floor, unpainted wooden bookshelves that still smelled like fresh-sawn wood were stocked floor to ceiling with books and carried labels that read FICTION, HISTORY, LOCAL LORE, COOKING, ROMANCE, MUSIC, ART, BUSINESS, and RELIGION. Upstairs in the loft were the MYSTERY and CHILDREN'S sections.

"This tea is delish," Lois said as she took a sip. "One of Drayton's concoctions?"

"It's his favorite Ceylonese Dimbula tea, rich with a hint of sweetness."

"Tell Drayton I'm in love."

"I'll do that," Theodosia said. "Now I have a weird question for you."

"As an ex-librarian I thrive on weird questions," Lois said.

"Are there any old sawmills in the area?"

"Well, that came zinging out of left field, didn't it?" Lois said. "Sawmills, old sawmills," she murmured to herself. "Off the top of my head I don't know of any that exist, but I probably have a reference book or two that we could check." She took another sip of tea, then spun toward the large oak library table that served as her desk. "Now where are my glasses?" Lois surveyed the scatter of papers and invoices, then looked down and found her glasses dangling around her neck on a multicolored Croakie. "Here they are. Okay, let's have a look-see."

Lois led Theodosia to the section marked LOCAL LORE, knelt down, and pawed through a shelf of books. "Maybe this one . . . no, that's written by Sidney Malcolm, far too pompous and scholarly. I think we're better off with something a little more commercial." She plucked a book off the shelf, stood up, and showed it to Theodosia. The title was *Low-Country*

Shadows. "This book has lots of historical information on old churches, rice and indigo plantations, heart pine logging, and oystermen. Good photos, too." Lois turned to the index at the back of the book. "Okay, now we're getting somewhere." She turned a few pages and said, "Take a look. Here's a photo of an old sawmill."

Theodosia took the book from Lois and gazed at the photo. It was an old-timey black-and-white photo, almost like an old daguerreotype, with a caption under it that said SAWMILL WORKERS TAKING A BREAK. It was dated 1936 and showed a half dozen men, all wearing rough work clothes, clustered around an enormous round blade with jagged edges. It was terrifying to think that a blade like that could chew its way through large tree trunks. The men in the photo were all thin and had hollow eyes, like soldiers you'd see in old Civil War photos. A carved sign hung on the sawmill's back wall said WHISKEY CREEK SAWMILL.

"Do we know where this is?" Theodosia murmured to herself. Then saw an inscription carved under the sawmill's name. CAT ISLAND. "Cat Island, I've been there." She studied the picture again. "Do you think this sawmill is still in existence?"

"No idea," Lois said. Then, "Tell me why you're so interested in sawmills."

Theodosia drew a deep breath and told Lois. Started with the murder of Celeste at the greenhouse, the possible suspects she'd uncovered, and the taunting voice-changed person who'd called in during her podcast with Charlie Skipstead.

"This is all because of a mysterious caller?" Lois said.

"No, there's more," Theodosia said. She told Lois about what had happened last night—Bettina's frantic call about being tasered and Jamie being kidnapped. Lois listened without asking a single question. Pumpkin listened as well, cocking her head a few times as if to make sure she was hearing Theodosia correctly.

By the end of the story, Lois had a hand pressed to her chest, and her mouth was wide open in amazement. "And you think the word *buzz* is a genuine clue? And that it might refer to a sawmill?"

"I don't know that at all. It's really just a guess."

"One thing I know about you is that you're mighty smart when it comes to educated guesses," Lois said. "And connecting the dots."

"But is *buzz*—a possible sawmill reference—one of those dots? The story I just told you is weird and discombobulated, the facts are all true, but . . ."

"True crime," Lois said.

"Sure, but I don't know where to go from there."

Lois nibbled her upper teeth against her lower lip, then said, "I know of another possible reference."

"What do you mean?"

"You know how there are all these crazy pop-up haunted houses around town? People pay to go through them and scream and get scared out of their wits when phony ghosts and goblins jump out at them?"

"Sure, there are at least a dozen haunted houses this year. I saw a list in the paper. A lot of them are sponsored by clubs and charities as fundraisers. I think some animal rescue group even had one last year."

"Right," Lois said. "So there's a haunted sawmill over on Ashley Avenue, just down from the Medical University."

"You're kidding." Theodosia felt her heart skip a beat.

"I know it's probably a long shot," Lois said. "But all the same, if *buzz* is your *clue* . . ."

"It's not a bad idea, maybe worth checking out," Theodosia

said. She tapped the book with a fingertip. "Lois, do you mind if I borrow this book from you, just in case . . ."

"In case of what?" Lois asked.

"I don't know."

"Take the book," Lois said. "But please be careful."

28

"How's Lois?" Drayton asked when Theodosia returned to the tea shop.

"She's good," Theodosia said. "Actually, she's pretty darn smart. I told her about that clue, the *buzz* clue, and she suggested we look at a kind of haunted house—a haunted sawmill—that an organization is putting on over near the Medical University."

"You've got to be kidding. A haunted sawmill? That's what it's called?"

"No, it's actually called the Haunted Mill of Death and it's being sponsored by a group of dental students. They're raising money to buy braces for kids in need. I looked it up on my phone as I was walking back here."

"And you think what? That Jamie somehow offended a dental student, so they kidnapped him and are holding him there?"

"That does sound pretty weird."

"Still, you think we should drop by and take a look?"

"It's a long shot, I know. But what else do we have? And maybe it's worth checking out. Their website says it opens at five." Theodosia looked at her watch. "If we leave now, we can probably beat the Halloween rush."

"If you say so," Drayton said. He spun on his heels and called out, "Haley!"

Seconds later, Haley's head popped out from behind the swinging door. "You screamed?"

"Can you finish up here? Theo and I are going to check out a haunted sawmill."

Haley looked puzzled. "A what?" Then comprehension dawned on her face. "Because of the clue?" she said. "*Buzz*? You think that's what it refers to?"

"I have no idea," Theodosia said.

"Well, good luck," Haley said. "Don't get caught in parade traffic."

"There's a parade?" Drayton said. "Tonight?"

"Tonight and tomorrow," Haley said.

"Why?"

"Duh. Because it's Halloween."

Drayton pursed his lips. "Drat."

The killer watched Theodosia and Drayton from the back alley. They exited the tea shop and climbed into Theodosia's Jeep with a minimum of fanfare and drove away. The killer followed, a few car lengths behind them, until it was apparent where they were headed. The haunted sawmill. Well, that wouldn't score them any answers, but it was good for a chuckle. Maybe it was time to start playing a more serious game of cat and mouse. The killer smiled. Better yet, maybe it was time to draw them into the trap.

* * *

Haley had been right about traffic. Driving was bonkers and the blocks around the Medical University were all parked up. Theodosia figured it had to be people touring the haunted sawmill, some looking for a good spot to view the parade, and other folks heading for the Medical University. Probably in that exact order.

"What if we turned down one of these alleys?" Drayton finally said after they'd circled the block three times. The sun was beginning to set, and twilight was coming on.

"Park behind someone's garage?" Theodosia said.

"Not *behind* behind, I don't want to be rude and block somebody in. But maybe tuck in behind their trash can or something. We're only going to be ten minutes, right? Fifteen at the most?"

"Worth a try, I guess."

"There, right there!" Drayton cried as they bumped down a darkened alley past mostly small single-car garages. "On that spot of gravel next to the garage."

"I guess," Theodosia said as she eased her Jeep in. "We won't be parked here very long."

"Just a quick in and out of that sawmill," Drayton said.

Except it wasn't quite that easy. First they had to stand in line to buy tickets, then they had to stand in another line to enter the Haunted Mill of Death.

"Why are we doing this again?" Drayton asked.

"We're exploring all options," Theodosia said as they shuffled along, stuck in a crowd of mostly youthful hoodie wearers. "*Buzz* might not refer to this particular place, but you never know."

Drayton stood on tiptoes and peered at the entrance. It was an ominous-looking black door gouged with deep scratches. Above the doorway, a tilting wooden sign with droopy red letters said HAUNTED MILL OF DEATH, ABANDON ALL HOPE YE WHO ENTER.

"Dante Alighieri must be spinning in his grave," Drayton muttered as they handed their tickets to a plaid-shirted ogre with a painted green face, orange wig, and enormous axe held over his shoulder. Then, he added, "Here goes nothing," as they stepped into darkness.

They found themselves wandering a narrow path of wood chips through a dark room that had been made to look like a haunted forest. Owls hooted, bat wings fluttered, and curious eyes shone from a virtual forest of trees.

"These are real trees," Theodosia said as she reached a hand out and touched rough bark.

"Don't touch my tree!" a man screeched as he popped out from behind the tree. He wore a white hockey mask, blood-soaked (hopefully, fake-blood-soaked) denim jacket, and saggy jeans.

"Holy Hannah!" Drayton exclaimed as he and Theodosia jumped back instantly.

Then they were shuffling ahead into a narrow chute where people dressed as zombie lumberjacks threatened them with saws, awls, and long pikes.

"Should I begin to faint, kindly make an attempt to catch me," Drayton said, as behind them a gaggle of teenage girls screamed with happiness.

"Take it easy," Theodosia said. "It's all playacting."

"These characters might be, but I'm dead serious," Drayton said.

The next room they entered was even worse. Chicken wire

on each side of the pathway kept a bunch of lumberjack lunatics from assaulting them. Still, the crazed lumberjacks, dressed in plaid shirts, straitjackets, torn overalls, and heavy boots, clawed at the chicken wire, screamed at them, and shook the wire with all their might.

Theodosia studied the setup directly behind the chicken wire fence. There was a large circular saw and a wooden table with a man lashed to it, the implication being that the man was about to be run through the buzz saw and cut in half.

"Jamie?" she called out. Then a little louder, "Jamie?"

"You think that's him?" Drayton asked.

"I don't know, it's so dark in here it's hard to tell."

Suddenly, one of the lumberjacks stuck his face right up to the chicken wire and said, "You looking for somebody? Maybe a hot date?" He stuck his tongue out and waggled it at Theodosia, causing her to step back.

Rude, Theodosia thought. *So rude.*

On the other hand, she'd come all this way, so she wasn't about to run away with her tail between her legs. She moved closer to the chicken wire and, in a no-nonsense tone of voice, said, "Jamie?"

Mr. Rude was back again. "Whatcha want, lady?"

"I'm looking for Jamie Wilkes," Theodosia said. "I heard he might be here and there's kind of a family emergency."

"Seriously?" Now Mr. Rude sounded almost human.

"Is Jamie here?" she asked. "I mean, he's not the guy lying on the table back there, is he?"

Mr. Rude shook his head. "That's a dummy." He rolled his eyes and turned to one of his fellow lumberjacks. "But they shoulda tied up Bucky here. He's the real dummy of the group." At which point all the men behind the chicken wire started cracking up and slapping one another on the backs.

"This is awful. What could be in store for us next?" Drayton asked as a stooped man carrying an old-fashioned lantern met them on the path and led them into the sawmill proper. Here, giant saws whirred and screamed, a rumbling wall of logs threatened to topple down upon them, and crazed lumberjacks moaned and leered at them. The floor was covered with sawdust, and bits of sawdust flew about in the air as well.

"I'm getting bubkes from this," Drayton shouted over the whine of the saws and screeching music. "No link to Jamie. Nothing." He brushed sawdust off his jacket lapels. "What about you?"

"Nothing," Theodosia said. "Let's get out of here." They hurried toward the exit, pushed through a heavy door, and emerged into cool night air and blessed silence.

"That was both tasteless and terrifying," Drayton said as they walked the length of the building. Then, turning the corner, he was astonished at the number of people who were milling around, waiting in line. "Look at this mob. You wouldn't think a haunted sawmill would be that big a draw."

"The university's only a couple blocks away," Theodosia said. "And this area's jammed with apartments, dorms, coffee shops, and bars, so it's already a big draw."

They cut through the line of ticket buyers, then tried to ease their way through another throng of teens and twenty-somethings. Most were on their phones, hanging out, texting, and checking in with friends.

"Excuse me," Theodosia said as she shouldered past a gaggle of girls who were arguing about where the best party was. And that's when she spotted a familiar face. Or, rather, a familiar cap of hair.

"Drayton," Theodosia said, stopping so fast he literally bumped into her. "I think that's Jimmy Simonton over there."

"Who?"

"You know, Slide."

"Who? Oh! You mean . . ."

"The drug guy, yes." Theodosia was already on her phone and calling Riley.

"You think Slide is here for the haunted sawmill?" Drayton asked.

"No, I think Slide's here to do business."

"Were we supposed to go to dinner tonight?" Riley asked when he answered the phone. "Did I forget to pick you up?"

"No, but I've got someone you *can* pick up—if you move fast."

"Huh?"

"Your buddy Slide is over by the university selling drugs."

"What!"

"Excuse me, do we have a bad connection or something?" Theodosia said. "I said Slide is over here . . ." She watched as Slide passed a small twist of foil to a guy wearing a starter jacket.

"Yeah, yeah, I got all that. But you say he's there *now*?"

"From the looks of things he's doing a booming business. Maybe even has a BOGO sale going on."

"Quick, give me the details . . . the exact place and I'll send one of my undercover guys over there."

Theodosia gave Riley as much information as she could, then wished him good luck.

"Too bad we couldn't kill two birds with one stone," Drayton said. "Sic the police on Slide and find Jamie."

"I just hope they catch Slide in the middle of a deal," Theodosia said as they walked down the dark alley to her Jeep. Overhead, bare branches rubbed together like clacking bones, and a silver moon emerged from behind a scud of gray clouds.

"Fingers crossed," Drayton said. "And, I'll say it again, that sawmill was beyond disappointing."

Theodosia walked along, nodding, half listening, as Drayton continued to complain about their sawmill experience, but was soon lost in her own thoughts. Of course she hadn't expected to find Jamie at the haunted sawmill. On the other hand, he *could* have been there. Anything was possible, right? Especially since he'd been kidnapped in plain sight and whisked away with no trace. As disparate thoughts rumbled through Theodosia's brain, she was aware of something else. A flapping sound. Footsteps behind her?

Theodosia felt a tickle at the back of her neck, then the tiny hairs seemed to stand on end. She whirled around, certain they were being followed, but there was no one there.

"You okay?" Drayton asked.

"Just feeling jumpy," Theodosia said as they approached her Jeep. "I thought I heard something."

Drayton turned to look. "I don't see anything."

"Good. Let's keep it that way."

They climbed into the Jeep and sat there for a while, both of them lost in thought.

"I didn't think Jamie would be there," Drayton said again.

"No, I guess not."

Drayton slapped his hands against his knees. "Now what?"

"I'm not sure. I have to think about this."

Theodosia drove down the alley, pulled onto Rutledge Avenue, and cruised for several blocks. She drove past the historic Glover-Sottile House and then Colonial Lake Park, its small pond glittering darkly. Just as she turned onto Tradd Street, she realized she'd made a colossal mistake. Because thirty yards ahead of her, two cars had come to a complete stop where a pair of black-and-white sawhorse barriers blocked the street.

"Police barriers up ahead," Theodosia said.

"It's that doggone Halloween parade," Drayton said. "The one Haley warned us about. Is there any way to get through?"

"I don't know. I don't think so."

"You mean we have to sit tight until the parade ends?"

"Or I could back up," Theodosia said. But one glance in her rearview mirror told her that was next to impossible. In the short time they'd been there, four cars had jammed up behind them. So they sat and watched as contingents of ghosts and witches marched past, followed by a couple of floats, then a few marching bands.

"How long does this go on?" Drayton asked. He was antsy, tapping his fingers against the dashboard. "How big a deal *is* this parade?"

"Don't know," Theodosia said. She was still feeling down and a little manipulated. As if the *buzz* clue had been intended to send her scurrying off on a thankless errand.

"Wait, there's a police officer heading this way," Drayton said. "Let's ask him if we can get through."

Theodosia rolled down her window. "Officer?" she called out as he approached their vehicle. "Is there any way to get through this?"

The officer shone his flashlight directly at her, making her blink, then said, "There's a scheduled break in the parade coming up in a few minutes. We'll be letting cars through then."

"Thank you."

29

But ten minutes later there hadn't been a break in the parade, and they hadn't moved an inch.

"This is interminable," Drayton said. "I feel like I'm playing the lead in Samuel Beckett's *Waiting for Godot*."

"You realize only a handful of people would understand your reference?" Theodosia said.

"You did."

"Sure, because I hang around with you. Your erudite musings occasionally rub off on me."

"Is there nothing we can do concerning this parade?" Drayton asked.

Theodosia took a look around again. She couldn't go forward; she couldn't go backward. On the other hand . . .

"I have an idea," Theodosia said. "If I could inch past the car ahead of us, I could hang a left, go down Bedon's Alley, and come out on Elliott."

"Bless you for remembering that charming little alley. But can you do it?"

"It's going to be tight, but . . ."

Theodosia pulled out and started nosing past the car ahead of her. Scraping by with only inches to spare.

"Good thing that fellow's driving a small car," Drayton said. "If it were an SUV . . . no way."

SQUEAL.

"My left tires are rubbing the curb. Let me get all the way up there," Theodosia said as her Jeep tilted noticeably but continued to ease carefully past the car. "Wow. If I get any closer, we'll end up in someone's living room. How am I on your side?"

"The occupants of that car are staring at us as if we're about to rip their car open like it's a tin of sardines. But you're going to make it. Keep going, there's only a couple more feet to go."

Then Theodosia was cranking her steering wheel left as she turned down Bedon's Alley and breathed a sigh of relief. "Thank goodness."

Bedon's Alley was one of Charleston's many hidden lanes and alleyways. It dated back to Revolutionary War times, when it had been a cobblestone alley lined with warehouses and small shops. Now it was a cobblestone alley with those same warehouses and shops restored as private homes.

"Look at this," Drayton crowed as they slipped past the half dozen cozy-looking brick structures, where lights glowed inside. "We've got smooth sailing ahead. Nothing can go wrong now!"

Which was when a *ding* on Theodosia's mobile phone punctuated his words.

Reaching into her jacket pocket, Theodosia fished out her phone, then rolled to a stop under an old-fashioned streetlamp. She looked down, saw the text message that had just arrived, and said . . .

"Whoa!"

"What?" Drayton asked.

Theodosia's answer was to hold up her phone and show Drayton the text message. It said: *R U coming?*

"What's that supposed to mean?" he asked.

But Theodosia's fingers were already working as she texted back: *Who is this?*

Seconds later, a message came back to her: *time 2 find out.* Then the rest of the message appeared: *if u dare.*

Tension starting to creep in, Theodosia texted back: *Who are you? Where are you?*

They both held their breath, waiting for an answer, until a final text message appeared: *buzz buzz.*

"What's that supposed to be?" Drayton asked. "Another dreadful clue?" Then, a moment later, cried, "Oh my stars, this is just like the anonymous phone call you received during the podcast!"

Theodosia nodded as a dark, ominous feeling rolled over her. "It's *exactly* like that. Someone's trying to taunt me with that same *buzz* clue."

"Who do you think sent that text?"

Theodosia was still looking at her phone, but there were no other messages. "If I had to venture a guess, I'd say it's Jamie's kidnapper."

"Why would he text you and not Bettina?"

"Because . . . I'm the one who's been investigating?"

"Is that a question or a statement?"

"Both?"

"Huh," Drayton said.

"You know, Drayton, this might be our only chance."

"What? To get Jamie back alive?"

Theodosia lifted a shoulder. "Not sure. But we do know that this person, whoever they are, has killed once before."

"Celeste," Drayton said slowly.

Theodosia thought for a few moments. "Are you willing to try a long shot?"

"Depends on what you're talking about. And how dangerous it is."

"I have a book I borrowed from Lois that details a couple of old sawmills in the area," Theodosia said.

"Right. Because of the *buzz* reference."

Theodosia reached around and plucked the book from the back seat, cradled it in her hands.

"Please tell me you don't want to go driving around in the dark looking for Jamie, who may or may not be held hostage at an old sawmill," Drayton said. "I mean, it's way too much of a long shot." He was talking rapidly, his voice starting to quaver. "It would be like driving up and down back alleys looking for a lost puppy."

"If your little dog, Honey Bee, were lost, you'd never give up looking for her, would you?" Theodosia asked.

Drayton sat rigid for a few moments, staring straight ahead. Finally, he said, "No, I . . . of course not." He reached over, gently took the book from Theodosia's hands, and ruffled a few pages. "Like you said, Jamie's missing and this might be all we have to go on."

"Bless you," Theodosia breathed.

Drayton sat there for another few moments, holding the book, obviously thinking things over, before he said, "So where to?"

"What's the book say?" Theodosia asked.

Drayton thumbed through the book's index, turned back several pages, studied one page in particular, and said, "There's an old sawmill located near the Wheeler Plantation."

"That's the closest one to Charleston proper?"

He tilted the book to catch a glint of streetlight. "I believe so."

"Then that's where we're going."

Theodosia drove down Spring Street and crossed the Ashley River Bridge onto James Island. "If my recollection is correct, the Wheeler Plantation is just off Highway 61, is that right?"

"That's right," Drayton said. "It's one of the older plantations that's still standing, a rice plantation dating back to the mid-seventeen hundreds."

"But nobody lives there."

"Not for at least fifty or sixty years. Now it's an historical site, a museum."

They drove through a bit of post–World War II urban sprawl, where apartments and smaller homes snugged up with gas stations, fast-food restaurants, big-box stores, insurance agencies, and pizza parlors. Then they hit a nicer neighborhood of several planned communities where plantation-style homes sat like miniature principalities on manicured lawns. Another twenty minutes and they were out in the countryside, passing a few praise houses, shrimp stands, and the occasional house or small farm. It was full-on dark now as Theodosia's headlights cut through the gloom.

Some twenty minutes later, Drayton said, "I believe the turnoff to the Wheeler Plantation is up ahead on our right."

"And then?"

"I don't know."

Moments later, Theodosia saw a sign that said WHEELER PLANTATION, OPEN TO THE PUBLIC TUESDAY–SATURDAY. And underneath, ½ MILE AHEAD. As she slowed and turned in the driveway, the venerable Georgian-style plantation came into view.

"Thank goodness it's closed for the day," Drayton said as he studied the main house. With its massive size and four front columns, the place looked stately and grand, as though hoop-skirted ladies should be lounging on the front veranda and sipping iced tea.

"And the parking lot looks deserted, so hopefully no guides or docents are working late."

"Let's hope there's no snoopy caretaker, either," Drayton said as they rolled into the car park. "Or gardener, since they have an absolutely spectacular azalea garden here."

"But where's the sawmill? Oh wait, I see a sign."

It read WHEELER PLANTATION MUSEUM, with an arrow that pointed straight ahead to the old plantation, and HISTORIC BUCKTHORN SAWMILL, with an arrow that pointed left. But there was no sawmill in sight.

"Fingers crossed," Theodosia said as they bumped down a narrow gravel road, disappearing into a dark grove of trees. The trees grew thicker the deeper into the forest they drove, tires crunching underneath, leaves brushing the windshield and tickling the sides of her Jeep.

"I'm guessing from the denseness of this forest that the sawmill is no longer a working sawmill," Drayton said.

Another five hundred yards and they came to the end of the road, where a gravel lot had room for a half dozen cars.

"Still no sawmill," Theodosia said as they exited her Jeep.

"I'm guessing down that pathway," Drayton said.

They started down the path just as the moon sailed behind a bank of gray clouds.

"Dark out here," Theodosia said.

"And spooky," Drayton said.

A rustle in the nearby bushes made Theodosia swerve to her left just as her phone rang.

Ding.

"Hello?" Theodosia said, not knowing who to expect. But it was Riley. "Did you get him? Slide?" she asked.

"I'm waiting to hear," Riley said. "We sent one of our undercover agents over to make a buy. Bobby Kern."

"The one you guys refer to as Harold Teen? Who looks like he's about nineteen years old?"

"Except he's really twenty-eight."

"Let's hope you get lucky and catch Mr. Slide."

"Say," Riley said, "I wanted to tell you that Martin Hunt checked out. He was in Atlanta on the day of Bettina and Jamie's wedding. Attending a men's sportswear show. We got that confirmed."

"So Hunt's off the hook as a suspect?"

"Completely," Riley said.

"But no word on Jamie yet?" Theodosia asked.

"Nothing." Then, "Where are you, anyway? You sound funny."

"Just hanging out with Drayton."

"Well . . . be careful."

"Sure. You know me."

Riley laughed. "I do. That's why I'm telling you to be careful."

When Theodosia hung up, she turned to Drayton and said, "That's one down."

"How so?"

"Riley got confirmation that Martin Hunt was in Atlanta the day of the wedding. Some kind of buying trip."

"That narrows it down. Somewhat."

"And nothing on Jamie yet." Theodosia hunched her shoulders against the chill that was starting to creep in and wished she'd worn a heavier jacket. "But Jamie could still be here. Held captive by . . . someone."

"A one-in-a-million chance, but we'll still take a look."

They continued down the path as the wind rose, whistled eerily, and blew away a few clouds. Now smaller puffs of clouds flew past the low-hanging moon like witches on broomsticks.

"It definitely feels like Halloween," Drayton said. Even he looked nervous and chilly.

Then, like a gray hovel rising up out of the earth, the old sawmill came into view.

"There it is," Theodosia whispered.

"Looks deserted," Drayton said.

"More like dilapidated."

They tiptoed along a trail that grew narrower and a little damp. Off to their left were a few odd *plips* and *plops* from a nearby swamp that threatened to encroach on them.

"This is awful," Drayton said. "I've probably ruined my church shoes. Obviously, my socks are soaking wet, too."

Walking up to an open-sided building, they could see nothing. No people, no saws, just a gray, weathered shell of a building with a small pile of lumber stacked inside. No Jamie, no kidnapper, no nothing.

Theodosia shook her head. "This isn't working. It was a bad idea from the get-go."

"But what about those texts you got?"

"Like you said before, maybe a prank—that jackhat Adam Lynch. If he can design websites and write code, chances are he's a competent phone hacker as well."

In silent agreement, they turned and walked back to Theodosia's Jeep and climbed inside. Theodosia turned on the engine and cranked up the heat.

"This was always a long shot," Drayton sighed. "Time to call it a night?"

Theodosia hated to give up but didn't know what else to do. With a heavy heart she said, "I think so."

That's when her phone *dinged* again.

30

"No," Theodosia said.

Drayton stared at her in the darkness of her vehicle. "What is it, another text?"

Theodosia answered with a wooden nod.

"What's it say?"

She showed him the text. It said: *im still waiting 4 u.*

"Somebody's really getting their jollies by playing cat and mouse with us," Drayton said. "Do you still think it's Adam Lynch trying to send us down the wrong path?"

"We're already down the wrong path," Theodosia said. She felt completely worn to the bone. They'd been conned, tricked, and practically tormented. Shaking her head, she said, "Drayton, I just don't have a clue."

"That's the problem," Drayton fumed. "We *don't* have a clue!"

Theodosia thought for a few moments, wondering if the texts she'd received were even legitimate. On the other hand, somebody was trying their best to draw her in. So if this was legit, how far could she push this person?

Why don't we give it a shot and see?

Theodosia texted back: *I need a clue.*

They waited, not really expecting any kind of response. But a full minute later another text message appeared. This one said: *see u ursa major.*

"That's a clue? Are they still taunting us?" Drayton wondered.

"I don't know. Does *ursa major* mean anything to you?"

"The only thing that comes to mind is the bear constellation."

"A constellation," Theodosia said. "You mean like we're supposed to gaze skyward and try to locate it? See where it points?"

"Ursa Major is an enormous constellation," Drayton said. "The Big Dipper is only a small component of it."

"Then I'm completely confused."

Drayton frowned. "Unless . . ."

"Unless what?"

"Do you have a map?" Drayton asked. "Not just of Charleston but a state map?"

"Sure, in the glove box."

Drayton handed Theodosia the book, then opened the glove box. While Theodosia flipped on the overhead light, he pawed around inside and found the map, unfurled it, sighed heavily, and turned it right side up. Then he studied it.

"What exactly are you looking for?" Theodosia asked.

"Give me a moment."

Theodosia gave him a moment. Several moments, in fact.

"Okay." Drayton tapped a finger against a spot on the map. "Take a look at this."

Theodosia leaned forward, squinting in the dim light. She

could just make out a few words. "Bear Swamp? You think *ursa major* refers to Bear Swamp?"

"It's possible," Drayton said. "What if there's a sawmill located in or near Bear Swamp?"

"Is there?"

"Let me see that book again."

Theodosia handed Drayton the book.

He paged through it, stopped, then nodded to himself.

"Look at this," Drayton said, turning the book so Theodosia could see what he'd discovered. There was a black-and-white photo of a dilapidated-looking sawmill. A caption below the photo said LOGGING HEART PINE IN BEAR SWAMP.

Theodosia studied the map again. "Doesn't seem like there's much out there, just wilderness and acres of swampland."

"But we're not too far away."

"No, probably not. If I cut back to the Savannah Highway, we could head north on Davidson and hit County Line Road."

"Then what?" Drayton asked.

"Then nothing. We're in Bear Swamp at the mercy of . . . water and muck and trees and . . . various reptiles?" Theodosia eyed the map again. "This Fishburne Creek that flows through the swamp, hopefully it hasn't spilled its banks from all the rain we've had."

"Speaking of which," Drayton said as a few fat, wet drops plopped down on the windshield. Then the drops turned to rivulets as the intensity increased.

"Oh joy," Theodosia said.

They headed for Bear Swamp, driving through the dark night, the windshield wipers keeping up a steady *whap-whap*, the defroster puffing out air to keep everything from fogging up.

Tires hissed off wet pavement as they passed small farms, open fields, wooded areas, and several large swamps that edged right up to the narrow two-lane blacktop road they were following. And once they'd driven through the small village of Red Top and left its few comforting lights behind, they found themselves in the middle of nowhere.

Theodosia slowed down. "Where are we?"

"On the fringes of Bear Swamp, I imagine," Drayton said.

They continued down a winding road that had once been paved in asphalt but was now reduced to bits and crumbles. Then they crossed a narrow wooden bridge, the boards rumbling and cracking precariously beneath their tires. At which point the road basically petered out to a rutted trail of mud and smooshed-down grass.

"Jamie couldn't be out here," Theodosia muttered to herself as she drove on. "This must be somebody's idea of a dirty trick."

"Don't know," Drayton said as they came to a fork in the so-called road. Trees closed in, rain sluiced down harder, and lightning flashed on the horizon like bursts of cannon fire in an old World War II movie.

"That does it, we're lost," Theodosia said as she stopped her Jeep, water ponding all around them. "This has to be the most forlorn spot in the low country. In all of the universe. I don't . . . I'm not sure now what to do." She touched a hand to her chest to try and quiet her thumping heart, then tilted her head back to rest her throbbing neck muscles.

Ding.

"What?" Theodosia said.

"Excuse me," Drayton said. "But I'm fairly sure you just received another text message."

Wearily, Theodosia looked down at the screen, then jerked in shock. Because what she saw horrified her and made her stomach lurch. Someone had sent her a grainy photo of Jamie. But it wasn't like anything she'd seen before. Jamie was laid out flat on some kind of conveyor belt, his body bound with thick ropes. His eyes were half-closed and his face wore a deathly pallor.

"Look at this, Drayton!" Theodosia's voice shook with emotion. In fact, her entire body was starting to shake.

Drayton gazed at the image on the screen. "Jeepers!" he cried, his voice cracking as it rose on an upward trajectory. "That's Jamie?"

Blinking back tears, Theodosia said, "Someone's holding Jamie prisoner and I don't know what to do. Which way to go."

"Take the left path," Drayton said without hesitation.

"Um, right, because now we really do have to find him," Theodosia mumbled, almost buckling under the stress.

"No, left," Drayton said.

Theodosia sniffled, trying to pull herself together. "Left. Okay, got it." She gripped her steering wheel hard, then started rolling ahead. "You have a feeling about this?"

"I have a twinkle."

"Is that anything like an insight?" Theodosia asked.

"No, it's merely a twinkle. My uncle Alfred had the gift and so did my grandnana. Well, maybe not a gift per se, more of a quirk. In any case, they both had strong feelings about what might happen, what *could* happen."

"So what's going to happen to us?" Theodosia asked. The driving was perilous, and she had to focus extra hard on keeping her vehicle in the ruts.

"I don't know. Tune in tomorrow."

"That's a weird thing to say for a guy who detests television." Theodosia knew she was chattering nervously, but she couldn't help it.

"Only ninety-five percent of the programming," Drayton pointed out, which brought a faint smile to Theodosia's face.

They drove another half mile or so, with swampland on both sides of the rutted lane. When lightning flashed, they could see stark outlines of tupelo and black oak trees standing in briny, dark water. Finally, they came to an impasse that jolted them to a stop. A pile of fallen logs.

"There can't possibly be a sawmill out here," Theodosia said. If it hadn't been for that awful photo of Jamie, she would have been ready to turn around.

"An enormous pine forest once stood here, and there's a railway nearby," Drayton said. "So it is entirely possible."

"A forest and a railroad," she murmured. "You're sure about that?"

"Fairly sure."

"So maybe . . ." Theodosia opened the door and leaned out. "At least the rain's starting to let up."

"And there's a path up ahead," Drayton said. "See?"

"Maybe." Theodosia could sort of make it out.

"We're here, we should give it a shot," Drayton said. "Even though my shoes are already half-ruined . . ."

"And we're chilled to the bone," Theodosia said. "So what's a little more suffering?"

They climbed out of the Jeep and started walking. But it was tough going. The path was soggy and the underbrush thick and imposing. It was constant bushwhacking without benefit of a machete. Frogs croaked in a low-country symphony, and Theodosia was sure that, between rumbles of thunder, she could hear the distinctive grunt of an alligator.

But they kept moving, vines tugging relentlessly at their ankles, wet leaves slapping their faces. It was dark, scary, and beyond uncomfortable.

Suddenly, Theodosia hunched her shoulders and came to a dead stop.

"What?" Drayton asked as he peered around, his eyes scouring the dark woods. "Did you see something?"

"No, I thought I . . . smelled something."

"Probably wood rot from all these dead trees."

"For a moment it smelled like someone was baking cookies."

"Out here?" Drayton let loose a sharp laugh. "That's rich." He took a step forward, caught his foot on a gnarled root, and stumbled. Caught himself just before he catapulted into a muddy ditch.

"You okay?" Theodosia asked as she grabbed his arm.

"I think so," Drayton said as an owl hooted overhead.

Then, suddenly, unexpectedly, Theodosia's phone started to ring. The owl immediately stopped hooting as Theodosia, fearful of who this caller might be, swallowed a gulp of air and answered, "Yes?"

"Theodosia? Theodosia Browning?"

"That's right." Theodosia frowned as she pushed a hunk of damp hair off her forehead. She didn't recognize the voice.

"This is Karl Rueff. I got a message to call you."

"Karl Rueff," Theodosia said, excitement and a small amount of relief coloring her voice. "Thank you for returning my call."

"What do you want?" Rueff asked. He sounded both hurried and bored. "Do we know each other?"

"Not exactly," Theodosia said. "But I have a question for you. This is going to sound convoluted and strange, but someone who works at Milne and Kerrison Public Relations told me you had a major story killed last year?"

There was silence for a few moments, then Rueff said, "What?" in a querulous tone.

"I'm talking about your AI program. Supposedly, there were too many bugs in it to launch, so you told your PR firm to put a damper on all press and publicity."

"I don't know who told you this—in fact I'd *like* to know who it was—but your information is completely mixed up."

"How so? I don't understand," Theodosia said.

"That AI program was a solid hit for Bluestone. Before we'd even beta tested it, we got a nibble from Wyndmere in Palo Alto and ended up selling it to them for two hundred million."

"So the AI wasn't a dud?" Theodosia looked at Drayton, surprise and confusion etched on her face. Drayton gave an offhand shrug.

"If you call two hundred million dollars a dud, then sure." Rueff paused long enough for Theodosia to hear background sounds, hollow-sounding PA announcements that told her he must be at an airport. "They're calling my plane," Rueff said. "Gotta go."

"Thank you," Theodosia said, but he'd already hung up.

"That was Karl Rueff?" Drayton asked.

"Yes, and he just told me the strangest thing. A complete and total contradiction from what Babs told me."

Drayton shook his head, looking a little lost. "What do you mean?"

"Babs told me that her PR company engineered a kill story on a software product that Rueff's company developed. Something to do with AI that turned out to be a total flop."

"So?"

"Rueff just told me they sold the software to a firm in Palo Alto for two hundred million dollars."

"Sounds like one of them is lying big-time."

"And somehow I got the feeling it wasn't Karl Rueff,"

Theodosia said. "Especially since his story can be easily fact-checked."

"Why would Babs lie?" Drayton asked.

"I don't . . . ," Theodosia started to say. And that's when she definitely got a whiff of perfume.

31

"Hidden Hearts," Theodosia murmured. "Orange blossoms and top notes of vanilla."

"Hearts?" Drayton said. "Vanilla?"

"It's Babs," Theodosia whispered. "She's out here somewhere."

"Coffee shop Babs?" Drayton cried. He sounded positively gobsmacked. "What are you talking about?"

Theodosia grabbed Drayton by the arm and shook it. "Drayton, Babs Campbell is the one who rigged the greenhouse. She's the one who tasered Bettina and kidnapped Jamie."

Drayton's mouth was practically hanging open. "But she's . . ."

His words were interrupted by the loud *putt-putt-putt* of a motor starting up. It grumbled for a few moments and then caught with a throaty gasoline-powered roar. Which was immediately followed by the high-pitched scream of a saw cutting through a slab of wood.

"The sawmill!" Theodosia cried.

"Huh?" Drayton said, whirling about.

A split second later, a bright white light popped on, hitting them directly in their eyes and spotlighting them like two startled deer.

Blinking at the harsh intensity, inwardly cursing herself for walking into Babs's trap, Theodosia stared into the brilliant light, trying to see if it really was Babs. There, a low, evil chuckle floated toward them as Babs angled the flashlight away and stepped out of the gloom. She was dressed all in black and aiming a flat, gray pistol at them, her hair disheveled and her face pink with pure anticipation. She looked like a needy wraith who'd just crawled out of the pits of hell.

"You kept me waiting long enough," Babs called out in a loud, insolent voice. "I was beginning to think you two would *never* figure this out. And you, Theodosia," she chided, "you're supposed to be the *smart* one. Shame on you for bumbling around like a dolt. Jamie's been wondering if you'd ever come and rescue him."

"Where is Jamie?" Theodosia demanded. She glanced at Babs's feet and saw she was wearing Sorel boots.

I'm dealing with a calculating, dangerous woman. Better take care.

It was also the moment Theodosia decided she had to face Babs like you would a dangerous animal. Show no fear. Push back hard. Fight if you have to.

"Jamie's tied up at the moment," Babs said with a nasty giggle. "Come on." She waved her pistol at them. "March on over here and see for yourself."

Theodosia and Drayton walked, at gunpoint, into a sawmill that was barely standing. It had one rickety back wall and a partial roof made up of bare, denuded wooden ribs that sagged badly. But when Babs flipped on a light switch, the inner mechanisms looked to be in decent working order.

And, of course, there was Jamie. Lying on a kind of leather

conveyor belt, tied securely, his feet a mere twenty inches from a giant circular blade with jagged edges.

"Help me," Jamie cried feebly.

"We will," Theodosia said. "I promise you."

"Oh, probably not," Babs said. "Because you two have become quite a problem for me. That said, there's always room for one more." She waggled her pistol at Drayton. "How about you? Want to lie down and take a ride on the Saw-Go-Round?"

Theodosia gritted her teeth. "Don't you dare threaten him."

"Watch that mouth of yours or I'll shoot you right between the eyes," Babs growled.

"The police are one step behind us," Theodosia said, hoping, praying, that Babs wouldn't call her bluff.

"The police are nowhere!" Babs shouted. She tilted her pistol skyward and fired.

BOOM!

Both Theodosia and Drayton ducked their heads as a bullet zinged off something metallic.

"Why are you *doing* this?" Drayton asked. He was shaking like a leaf but trying to be reasonable because . . . well, because it was his nature.

Babs waved her pistol in Jamie's direction. "That snake completely threw me over for a mealymouthed little blond trick. But I played it smart. I took my time and knew that one day I'd get even."

"That 'one day' being the day of Jamie's wedding?" Theodosia said. "Only that didn't work out as planned, did it?"

"Celeste, the brainless fool, ran into the greenhouse first," Babs spat out. "So I had to devise a backup plan. A game, a treasure hunt, so to speak. And I've so enjoyed pulling the strings and playing games master."

"You're insane," Theodosia said.

Babs shook her head. "More of a garden-variety narcissistic sociopath." She raised her left hand, pinching her forefinger and thumb together. "With a bit of psychopath thrown in for fun."

As Theodosia continued to go back and forth with Babs, arguing, she happened to glance over into the woods. And much to her shock, saw a pair of headlights bouncing toward them way off in the distance.

Help on the way? she wondered. *But who is it?*

Just as hope bloomed in her heart, she noticed that one of the headlights was crooked and canted to the left.

I know that car, it belongs to Bill Glass. Glass to the rescue? Theodosia shook her head. *No way, he'll bumble this for sure. What to do? What to do now?*

Because Theodosia had no other cards to play, because she could only pray that Glass might pull a rabbit out of a hat, she decided to try to de-escalate the conversation.

"I apologize if I've offended you in any way," Theodosia said. "So let's try and work this out. Why not let Jamie go and we'll all drive back to Charleston? We can get warm, get dry, and talk to Bettina. She's reasonable, you're reasonable, I'm sure we can figure something out. I know you really don't want to hurt anyone, and I'm sure you have no desire to go to prison."

"You're more insane than I am if you think I'll fall for that cheap ploy," Babs said with a snort. Then she turned to Drayton and said, "Ready, Freddy?"

"You harm a hair on that man's head and you'll answer to me!" Theodosia shouted. She took a step toward Babs, wondering how fast she could move, how skilled Babs was with that gun.

"Shut up!" Babs ordered. "Back the hell off. Be the genteel Southern tea lady we know, love, and are bored with." She pointed her pistol at Drayton and said, "Do it. Lie down on the conveyor belt."

Theodosia stepped in front of Drayton to shield him. "No way. You'll have to deal with me first."

"Him first, your turn comes later," Babs said. Her grin morphed into an ugly grimace as she raised her pistol and focused her aim on Drayton. "Stop fooling around and lie down. Do it now."

"Never," Drayton said.

Babs switched her aim from Drayton to Theodosia. "What if I killed the tea lady first? Would that change your mind?"

"Don't do it, Drayton!" Theodosia yelled. But Drayton, looking ashen-faced and terrified, climbed awkwardly onto the conveyor belt and lay down.

"You," Babs said to Theodosia. "Pick up that rope over there and tie him up."

"You'll never get away with this," Theodosia said.

"I already have," Babs said. "Pick. Up. The. Rope."

"Do it, Theo," Drayton pleaded. "Or she'll kill us both."

WHAP, WHAP, WHAP! Sudden thunder boomed in the sky overhead. Trees shook and sheets of leaves rained down.

"What?" Babs screeched as she squinted up at the misty night sky through missing boards.

Theodosia looked up, too, wondering what could be happening. Then she saw it. A helicopter, hovering directly above them, its blades causing the treetops around them to thrash and sway. The roar grew louder, the downdraft more severe, as giant blades whirled in the dark sky.

"Helicopter!" Theodosia shouted. It was a shout of joy, a shout that said, *Now we've got a chance!*

Babs watched in pure terror as the large helicopter hovered overhead, then began its descent. "No!" she screamed as she raised her pistol and began firing at it.

At the same time, Theodosia lunged for Drayton, pulling

him off the conveyor belt. Together they hung on for dear life as the helicopter swooped in lower.

Sawdust, dirt, wood chips, and bits of damp leaves swirled around them like an angry tornado. Jamie screamed in terror as the helicopter dipped low, and Babs was literally knocked off her feet by the downdraft. In that single instant she was thrown to the ground, and her pistol flew out of her hand.

Quick as a fox, Theodosia dropped to her knees and began scrabbling in the dirt, searching for the pistol.

And then, just like in the movies, an officer in SWAT tactical gear slid down a rope and landed directly on top of Babs. With his smoked black bubble helmet, he looked like an alien from outer space. Without hesitation, he pulled Babs to her feet, spun her around like a child's top, and snapped a plastic tie around her wrists.

And right on cue Babs started bawling.

32

"I had no part in this!" Babs screamed as a second SWAT officer slid down the rope. "I'm innocent! I've been trying to *rescue* Jamie, to *free* him! These people here"—she gave an accusing nod at Theodosia and Drayton—"kidnapped him! They're ka-pow crazy!"

The more Babs fussed and pleaded, the more she was ignored. Theodosia picked up the gun, handed it to one of the SWAT guys, then ran to Jamie and started undoing his bonds. Once that business was taken care of, she turned to one of the SWAT guys and said, "But how did you know . . . ?"

Like a crazed wildebeest, Bill Glass burst out of the woods and galloped toward them. His hair stood on end as if he'd been plugged into a light socket, his face was smudged with grime, and his jacket hung askew. He looked like a refugee who'd just been spit out of a coal bin.

"I followed you guys!" Glass shouted at Theodosia. "And when I saw you were in trouble, I called your boyfriend."

"You what?" Theodosia said as her phone *dinged* in her jacket pocket. Startled again, she grabbed it and said, "Hello?"

"Are you okay? Tell me you're okay," Riley said, urgency coloring his voice. "SWAT got there in time?"

Theodosia let loose a convulsive shudder. "Riley! Yes! Just in the nick of time. And, thankfully, we're all okay. Well, Jamie's reasonably okay even though Babs did try to kill him."

"And Drayton?"

"Drayton's good." Theodosia looked over at Drayton, who gave her a confident thumbs-up sign.

"You're lucky Glass called me in time."

"But . . . but you deployed an entire SWAT team? Just for us?" She felt overwhelmed with gratitude.

"There was a bit of serendipity involved. SWAT was actually out there already, flying nighttime training maneuvers."

"Wow," Theodosia said. She was still trembling as adrenaline coursed through her veins like a fast-moving stream. "I guess we're going to need to talk about this, huh? Like, tonight? Soon as I get home?"

"You got that right," Riley said.

"Is this . . ." Theodosia tried not to cry. "Is this going to be a problem? For us?"

Riley gave a deep chuckle. "Only for you."

Everything seemed to jump into hyper speed then. Theodosia said goodbye to Riley. Babs was formally arrested and read her rights. Bill Glass was suddenly talking a mile a minute and backslapping everyone. And Jamie was ceremoniously helped to his feet. He staggered a short way, then spun in a circle, looking like he was about to collapse like a cheap card table.

"Whoa, buddy," one of the SWAT officers said to Jamie. "You don't look so good."

"I don't feel so good," Jamie said. He touched a hand to his stomach and let loose a noisy belch.

"We'll take you back in the helo with us, okay?" the SWAT guy said. "It's faster than an ambulance. Meanwhile, you'd better take it easy. Sit down and try to relax."

Jamie fixed the SWAT officer with a one-eyed, vacant stare. "You want me to relax? After a concussion, broken nose, and hand surgery? After which I got tasered, kidnapped, and strapped to a board for the last twenty hours where every mosquito within ten miles dined on me? Seriously?"

"Jamie?" Theodosia said.

Jamie wobbled around to face her like an arthritic old man. Flapping his arms, he said, "What?"

"Just say thank you to the nice officers," Theodosia said.

"And you can thank Theodosia for doggedly searching for you," Drayton added. He pulled himself to his full height, straightened his bow tie, and stared forcefully at Jamie. "She's the only reason we're out here."

"Thank you," Jamie stammered.

"Wait, wait, wait!" Bill Glass shouted. "Hold everything, guys. Before you go all kumbaya on me, I need to snap a picture!"

"Seriously?" Drayton muttered. "A photo?"

"He did kind of save the day," Theodosia whispered to him.

"That's right," Bill Glass said encouragingly as they all milled around. "Everybody crowd in together. SWAT guys, let me see those guns. Theo, edge closer to Drayton, will you? Jamie, you're great, just keep that dazed, wonky look on your face. Oh yeah, this is gonna be perfect to go with my big story."

"Glass," Theodosia called out. "Are we just about done here?" She couldn't wait to get back to Charleston. To hug Earl

Grey, take a long, hot shower, then snuggle in with Riley and explain (leaving out the really bad parts) exactly what had happened.

Bill Glass lifted his camera. "Big smiles!"

Click.

FAVORITE RECIPES FROM

The Indigo Tea Shop

Pumpkin Muffins

3⅓ cups all-purpose flour

3 cups sugar

2 tsp. baking soda

1½ tsp. salt

1 tsp. cinnamon

1 tsp. nutmeg

1 cup oil

4 eggs

⅔ cup water

2 cups pumpkin (canned)

PREHEAT oven to 350 degrees. In large bowl, mix together flour, sugar, baking soda, salt, cinnamon, and nutmeg. Now stir in oil, eggs, water, and pumpkin and mix well. Fill well-greased muffin tins ¾ full. Bake for 25 to 30 minutes or until toothpick inserted in center comes out clean. Yields 12 muffins.

Sun-Dried Tomato Tea Sandwiches

½ cup sun-dried tomatoes, drained of oil
8 oz. cream cheese
8 slices bread

PLACE sun-dried tomatoes in food processor and blend until chopped fine. Add the cream cheese and puree. Spread mixture on 4 slices of bread and top with remaining bread. Slice off all crusts, then cut each sandwich into 4 quarters. Yields 16 tea sandwiches.

Haley's Easy Turkey Meat Loaf

1½ lb. ground turkey, uncooked
½ green pepper, diced
½ red pepper, diced
1 egg
½ cup breadcrumbs

PREHEAT oven to 350 degrees. In a large bowl, gently mix together turkey, green peppers, red peppers, and egg. Add the breadcrumbs and lightly mix. Place turkey mixture in greased loaf pan and bake for approximately 40 minutes. Yields 4 servings. (Note: Before baking, you can also top meat loaf with ketchup and brown sugar to taste.)

Ricotta and Cream Cheese Cannoli Filling

Ricotta cheese, 16 oz. dry and strained
1 cup heavy cream
1 cup powdered sugar
½ cup cream cheese
½ tsp. vanilla extract
Cannoli shells (store-bought)

MAKE sure your ricotta cheese has been strained overnight so it's not too wet. Crumble your ricotta cheese into a mixing bowl, then add cream, powdered sugar, cream cheese, and vanilla extract. Mix on low speed until well combined. Fill 6 cannoli shells with filling. Refrigerate until ready to serve. Yields 6 desserts.

Super Easy Cake Mix Cookies

1 package cake mix (any flavor)
1 egg
¼ cup oil
¼ cup water
1 cup nuts, chopped
1 cup raisins or chocolate chips

PREHEAT oven to 350 degrees. In large bowl, combine cake mix, egg, oil, and water. Beat until well blended. Stir in nuts and your raisins or chocolate chips. Drop by teaspoon onto a greased cookie sheet—about 1 inch apart. Bake for 15 minutes or until golden brown. Yields about 4 dozen cookies.

Drayton's English Crumpets

1 package active dry yeast
1 tsp. sugar
¼ cup warm water
⅓ cup milk, room temperature
1 egg
4 Tbsp. butter, melted
1 cup all-purpose flour
½ tsp. salt

IN large bowl, combine yeast, sugar, and warm water. Let mixture sit for 15 minutes, until bubbly. Blend in milk, egg, and butter. Now add flour and salt and beat until smooth. Cover and let stand in warm place for 45 minutes until dough doubles in size. Using crumpet rings on a buttered, low-heat griddle, pour batter into crumpet rings. Let cook about 7 minutes until holes appear and tops are dry. Remove rings and flip crumpets to other side and brown lightly. Yields 8 to 10 crumpets. (Note: Serve crumpets warm with butter and jam.)

Baked Mozzarella Bites

½ cup fine breadcrumbs
¼ tsp. ground cumin
¼ tsp. ground red pepper
¼ tsp. salt
1 package mozzarella cheese, 8 oz.
1 egg, beaten

MIX together breadcrumbs, cumin, red pepper, and salt in bowl. Cut mozzarella into ½-inch cubes. Dip cubes into beaten egg mixture, then into breadcrumb mixture. Chill in refrigerator for 2 to 3 hours. Preheat oven to 350 degrees and place mozzarella bites on cookie sheet. Bake 5 to 7 minutes or until cheese begins to melt. Yields 3 dozen. (Note: These are delicious dipped in warm tomato sauce.)

Cinnamon Scones

2 cups all-purpose flour
3 Tbsp. sugar
1 Tbsp. baking powder
1 tsp. ground cinnamon
⅓ tsp. salt
6 Tbsp. butter, cold
½ cup cream
1 egg
1 tsp. vanilla extract
1 cup cinnamon chips

PREHEAT oven to 375 degrees. In a large bowl, add flour, sugar, baking powder, cinnamon, and salt. Stir to combine. Add butter to mixture, cutting into the dry ingredients until there are only coarse crumbs of butter. Add cream, egg, and vanilla and stir again. Now add cinnamon chips and stir until well incorporated. Place dough on well-floured surface and form into a round circle about 10 inches in diameter. Cut dough into 8 equal-sized scones. Place scones on well-greased baking sheet and bake for 16 to 20 minutes or until scones look well-set. Yields 8 scones. (Note: Best served warm topped with butter, Devonshire cream, or jam—or use all three!)

Haley's Heartwarming Tomato Bisque

1 Tbsp. butter
1 Tbsp. olive oil
1 onion, medium size, diced
1 carrot, diced small
2 cloves garlic, smashed and peeled
Can of whole tomatoes, 28 oz.
1 cup water
1 tsp. salt
⅛ tsp. black pepper
1 tsp. dried basil
¼ cup cream

HEAT butter and olive oil in large saucepan over medium heat. Add onion, carrot, and garlic. Sizzle and stir for 5 minutes. Add tomatoes, water, salt, pepper, and basil. Bring to a boil while stirring, then reduce heat and simmer for 15 minutes. To finish soup, remove from heat and stir in cream until well blended. Reheat to simmer and serve. Yields 4 servings. (Note: Top bisque with shredded cheese or croutons to make it extra special.)

TEA TIME TIPS FROM

Laura Childs

Shanghai Tea

All the grand hotels in Shanghai serve marvelous afternoon teas—and you can, too. Decorate your tea table in red and black and score a few Chinese fans from your local party store. Begin with a tall glass of iced black tea, spiced and mixed with sweetened condensed milk. Crab salad and cucumber slices make wonderful tea sandwiches, and everyone loves shrimp rolls or warm Chinese pork buns. If you want a hot tea, your guests will love oolong or even chrysanthemum tea. For dessert visit your local Chinese bakery for egg custard buns and mochi balls with sesame filling. Or you can offer dainty servings of petits fours and French macarons. After all, Shanghai is an international city!

Brontë Sisters Tea

Capture the moodiness and slightly Gothic aura of an English manor home with a purple tablecloth, stoneware, dark red flowers, and half-melted candles. Pile stacks of Emily and Charlotte

Brontë's books on your table. Serve raisin scones with clotted cream for your first course, then tea sandwiches of cucumber and dill for your second course. Your main course could be a ploughman's platter—a delightful array of dark bread, ham, Scotch eggs, potato salad, and dollops of hearty mustard. The perfect tea for your luncheon would be Simpson & Vail's Brontë Sisters Black Blend. For dessert serve a decadent brownie-rosemary cake.

Spring Fever Tea

Spring is in the air with bountiful bouquets of flowers and floral china on your tea table. Give each guest a packet of flower seeds as a favor. Kick your celebration off with white chocolate chip scones and Devonshire cream, then serve egg salad and watercress tea sandwiches. For an entrée consider shrimp salad in lettuce cups. Enhance your food with an Assam tea, and for dessert serve balsamic strawberries with Brie cheese.

Tropical Tiki Tea

Create your own little tea time tiki hut by arranging your tea table with tropical fruits, ferns, fresh pineapples, and sunglasses from the party store. If you're holding your tropical tea outdoors, add tiki torches or colored lights. For your first course, serve coconut scones with honey butter. Tea sandwiches can be chicken salad with chopped pineapple, or you can opt for chicken shish kebabs with chicken, pineapple, onion, and red pepper. Serve a banana compote for dessert and delight your guests with ginger- or orange-flavored black tea.

Long Live the King Tea

Rule Britannia is the watchword here. Start with a creamy damask tablecloth, then add your finest plates, teacups and saucers, glassware, and silverware. Then it's time to get creative by decorating your table with flowers, British flags from the party store, tins of English biscuits, or boxes of shortbread. Got a ceramic bulldog? Add him to the mix. Now go British with your menu. Start with cream scones served with Devonshire cream and lemon curd. Cream cheese and cucumber tea sandwiches are always delightful as a second course, and your third course could be Scotch eggs or Coronation Chicken (this is basically chicken salad served in a buttered, toasted brioche bun). For your tea consider Earl Grey, always a British favorite, and serve a Victoria sponge cake for dessert.

TEA RESOURCES

TEA MAGAZINES AND PUBLICATIONS

TeaTime—A luscious magazine profiling tea and tea lore. Filled with glossy photos and wonderful recipes. (teatimemagazine.com)

Southern Lady—From the publishers of *TeaTime* with a focus on people and places in the South as well as wonderful tea time recipes. (southernladymagazine.com)

The Tea House Times—Magazine with tea etiquette, recipes, tea reviews, and so much more. Go to www.theteahousetimes.com for subscription information and dozens of links to tea shops, purveyors of tea, gift shops, and tea events.

Victoria—Articles and pictorials on homes, home design, gardens, and tea. (victoriamag.com)

Fresh Cup Magazine—For tea and coffee professionals. (freshcup.com)

Tea & Coffee—Trade journal for the tea and coffee industry. (teaand coffee.net)

TEA: Ceylon Tea: Barefoot in Sri Lanka—Gail Gastelu's enchanting pictorial of "tea island."

TeaTime Scones—The definitive book on scones from Lorna Reeves, editor of *TeaTime* magazine.

New Tea Lover's Treasury—The history and romance of tea by James Norwood Pratt.

The Tea Book—By Linda Gaylard, perfect for beginners.

The Story of Tea—By Mary L. Heiss and Robert J. Heiss, nominated for a prestigious James Beard Book Award.

A Tea Reader—By Katrina Avila Munichiello, an anthology of tea stories and reflections.

Tea Poetry—Traditional and new tea poetry compiled by Pearl Dexter.

AMERICAN TEA PLANTATIONS

Charleston Tea Garden—The oldest and largest tea plantation in the United States. Order their fine black tea or schedule a visit at bigelowtea.com.

Table Rock Tea Company—This Pickens, South Carolina, plantation is growing premium whole leaf tea. (tablerocktea.com)

The Great Mississippi Tea Company—Up-and-coming Mississippi tea farm now in production. (greatmsteacompany.com)

Big Island Tea—Organic artisan tea from Hawaii. (bigislandtea.com)

Mauna Kea Tea—Organic green and oolong tea from Hawaii's Big Island. (maunakeatea.com)

Ono Tea—Nine-acre tea estate near Hilo, Hawaii. (onotea.com)

Minto Island Tea Growers—Handpicked, small-batch crafted teas grown in Oregon. (mintoislandgrowers.com)

Virginia First Tea Farm—Matcha tea and natural tea soaps and cleansers. (virginiafirstteafarm.com)

Blue Dreams USA—Located near Frederick, Maryland, this farm grows tea, roses, and lavender. (bluedreamsusa.com)

Finger Lakes Tea Company—Tea producer located in Waterloo, New York. (fingerlakestea.com)

Camellia Forest Tea Gardens—This North Carolina company collects, grows, and sells tea plants. Also produces their own tea. (teaflower gardens.com)

TEA WEBSITES AND INTERESTING BLOGS

Destinationtea.com—State-by-state directory of afternoon tea venues.

Teamap.com—Directory of hundreds of tea shops in the US and Canada.

Afternoontea.co.uk—Guide to tea rooms in the UK.

Seedrack.com—Order *Camellia sinensis* seeds and grow your own tea!

Thedailytea.com—Formerly *Tea Magazine*, this online publication is filled with tea news, recipes, inspiration, and tea travel.

Allteapots.com—Teapots from around the world.

Teacups & Cupcakes Facebook Group—All things tea and vintage.

Teasquared.blogspot.com—Fun, well-written blog about tea, tea shops, and tea musings.

Relevanttealeaf.blogspot.com—Musings of tea's integral role in everyday life.

Teawithfriends.blogspot.com—Lovely blog on tea, friendship, and tea accoutrements.

Tea.Bellaonline.com—Features and forums on tea.

Napkinfoldingguide.com—Photo illustrations of twenty-seven different (and sometimes elaborate) napkin folds.

Worldteaexpo.com—This premier business-to-business trade show features more than three hundred tea suppliers, vendors, and tea innovators.

Fatcatscones.com—Frozen ready-to-bake scones.

Kingarthurflour.com—One of the best flours for baking. This is what many professional pastry chefs use.

Californiateahouse.com—Order Machu's Blend, a special herbal tea for dogs that promotes healthy skin, lowers stress, and aids digestion.

Vintageteaworks.com—This company offers six unique wine-flavored tea blends that celebrate wine and respect the tea.

Downtonabbeycooks.com—A *Downton Abbey* blog with news and recipes.

Auntannie.com—Crafting site that will teach you how to make your own petal envelopes, pillow boxes, gift bags, etc.

Victorianhousescones.com—Scone, biscuit, and cookie mixes for both retail and wholesale orders. Plus baking and scone-making tips.

Englishteastore.com—Buy a jar of English Double Devon Cream here as well as British foods and candies.

Stickyfingersbakeries.com—Delicious just-add-water scone mixes.

TeaSippersSociety.com—Join this international tea community of tea sippers, growers, and educators. A terrific newsletter!

Melhadtea.com—Adventures of a traveling tea sommelier.

Bullsbaysaltworks.com—Local South Carolina sea salt crafted by hand.

PURVEYORS OF FINE TEA

Plumdeluxe.com
Adagio.com
Elmwoodinn.com
Capitalteas.com
Newbyteas.com/us
Harney.com
Stashtea.com
Serendipitea.com
Marktwendell.com
Republicoftea.com
Teazaanti.com

Bigelowtea.com
Celestialseasonings.com
Goldenmoontea.com
Uptontea.com
Svtea.com (Simpson & Vail)
Gracetea.com
Davidstea.com

VISITING CHARLESTON

Charleston.com—Travel and hotel guide.

Charlestoncvb.com—The official Charleston convention and visitor bureau.

Charlestontour.wordpress.com—Private tours of homes and gardens, some including lunch or tea.

Charlestonplace.com—Charleston Place Hotel serves an excellent afternoon tea, Thursday through Saturday, 1:00 P.M.–3:00 P.M.

Pooganspor ch.com—This restored Victorian house serves traditional low-country cuisine. Be sure to ask about Poogan!

Preservationsociety.org—Hosts Charleston's annual Fall Candlelight Tour.

Palmettocarriage.com—Horse-drawn carriage rides.

Charlestonharbortours.com—Boat tours and harbor cruises.

Ghostwalk.net—Stroll into Charleston's haunted history. Ask them about the "original" Theodosia!

Charlestontours.net—Ghost tours plus tours of plantations and historic homes.

Follybeach.com—Official guide to Folly Beach activities, hotels, rentals, restaurants, and events.

Gibbesmuseum.org—Art exhibits, programs, and events.

Boonehallplantation.com—Visit one of America's oldest working plantations.

Charlestonlibrarysociety.org—A rich collection of books, historic manuscripts, maps, and correspondence. Music and guest speaker events.

Earlybirddiner.com—Visit this local gem at 1644 Savannah Highway for zesty fried chicken, corn cakes, waffles, and more.

Highcottoncharleston.com—Low-country cuisine that includes she-crab soup, buttermilk fried oysters, Marsh Hen Mill grits, and much more.

ACKNOWLEDGMENTS

An abundance of thank-yous to Sam, Tom, Dru Ann, Elisha, Kaila, Lori, MJ, Bob, Pearl, Pumpkin, Jennie, Dan, and all the wonderful people at Berkley Prime Crime and Penguin Random House who handle editing, design (so many fabulous covers!), publicity (amazing!), copywriting, social media, bookstore sales, gift sales, production, and shipping. Heartfelt thanks as well to all the tea lovers, tea shop owners, book clubs, booksellers, librarians, reviewers, magazine editors and writers, websites, broadcasters, and bloggers who have enjoyed the Tea Shop Mysteries and helped spread the word. You are all so kind to help make this possible!

And I am overwhelmed with gratitude for all my special readers and tea lovers who've so thoroughly embraced Theodosia, Drayton, Haley, Earl Grey, and the rest of the tea shop gang. Thank you so much and I promise more Tea Shop Mysteries to come!

Keep reading for an excerpt from Laura Childs's next Tea Shop Mystery . . .

Death at a Firefly Tea

Firefly Night in Japan is celebrated amid groves of cherry trees and on sacred temple grounds. Watchers arrive by the thousands, awestruck by fireflies that flicker like tiny glowing lanterns against a tapestry of darkness, heralding the approach of warmer weather.

Here in Charleston, South Carolina, on the darkened patio of the Tangled Rose B and B, tea shop maven Theodosia Browning was celebrating the little bugs' arrival with a Firefly Tea. And under the lush cover of darkness, the fireflies' command performance was pure magic.

"You see that grove of azaleas? There are literally hundreds of fireflies buzzing around in there," one guest cried.

"And look how the hedge lights up," said another. "Absolutely amazing."

"Just stupendous."

"I thought a Firefly Tea sounded weird, but this is delightful."

Theodosia smiled to herself as she slipped around the

tables, feeling her way in the dark as she refilled teacups with a special blend of Japanese Sencha tea. The weatherman on W-BAM had predicted rain for this evening; instead they'd been gifted with warmth and an industrial-strength dose of humidity. Which had thankfully prompted the little fireflies to launch their brilliant light show.

Once her teapot was empty, Theodosia stepped into the B and B's cozy kitchen, where Drayton Conneley, her tea sommelier extraordinaire, and Haley Parker, her chef and baker at the Indigo Tea Shop, were staging this evening's dinner.

"They're loving your tea," Theodosia told Drayton. "As well as your orange and pecan scones, Haley. And, just as we'd hoped, the fireflies appeared right on schedule. The little buggers are hanging out in the arborvitae hedge, flitting among the magnolias, and hovering over that small reflecting pool, giving a laser light show worthy of Pink Floyd."

"Right on," Haley said.

"And aren't we lucky Neela Carter cultivated such a gorgeous, semitropical garden?" Drayton said. "One that actually attracts fireflies." Neela Carter was the proprietor of the Tangled Rose B and B and one of Drayton's dear friends.

"More like you were lucky to book it," Haley said. She was checking her oven, making sure each squab was turning a rich golden brown.

"*Smart* to book it on this precise date," Drayton said. "It would appear the *Farmers' Almanac* was spot-on when it predicted a bumper crop of fireflies for South Carolina." He cocked an eye at Haley. "Say, how much butter did you use on that squab?"

"You don't want to know," Haley said.

Theodosia gazed at the citrus salads sitting on the counter and decided it was probably time to kick dinner into high gear.

"Maybe I should start clearing tables so we can serve our second course?"

"Do that," Drayton agreed. "While I drizzle on the strawberry vinaigrette."

Theodosia cleared while Drayton drizzled. Then, once the salads were served, eaten, and dispatched with, Haley pulled her squab from the oven, plated them, and added sides of Charleston gold rice and crispy brussels sprouts with smoked paprika aioli.

"Heavenly," Drayton declared. "Time to surprise our guests with the main entrée?"

"Let's do it," Theodosia said. Balancing several plates on large silver trays, they each carried the entrées out to the patio, where they were met with a round of applause.

"Thank you," Theodosia murmured as she began serving the squab. She was thrilled with her guests' reactions as well as the turnout they'd gotten this evening. Her friends Delaine Dish and Brooke Carter Crockett were there, along with a contingent from Drayton's beloved Heritage Society. There was also a table of Historic District socialites, members from the Broad Street Garden Club, and several more tables filled with neighbors and guests from the inn. So thank goodness everything was clicking along like clockwork.

When Theodosia raced back into the kitchen to grab a few more entrées, she said, "Drayton, this may be our best nighttime event ever."

"I agree," Drayton said. "A velvety warm evening, a delicious menu, and a guest list that includes a few society doyennes."

"I'm guessing you're referring to Mrs. Van Courtland and her friends?"

"I am indeed. If Mrs. V takes a shine to our tea service and food, we'll have it made." He gave Theodosia a knowing look. "She serves on the boards of the Charleston Ballet Society, Westmore Foundation, Architectural Preservation Guild, and Children's Art Association."

"She's also sitting at the same table as my aunt Libby."

"Ah, they know each other?"

"I'm fairly sure they do," Theodosia said.

"Nice that your aunt was able to travel all the way from Cane Ridge Plantation to join us."

"One of her friends drove her in, and then she'll stay over with me."

"Perfect," Drayton said.

Theodosia helped serve the rest of the entrées, then paused on the patio to take it all in. Hidden in the darkness as she was, the venue fairly sparkled. Flaming tiki torches reflected in the tiny pool like a thousand points of light. Her tables gleamed with Herend Printemps china, Baccarat stemware, and Buttercup by Gorham silverware. Centerpieces of pink Juliet roses were flanked by flickering white tapers that cast a warm glow.

Oh dear me, I hope I'm not starting to glow as well.

Theodosia hurried into the kitchen and peeked in a small mirror that hung by the door.

No, her peaches-and-cream complexion looked just fine even after all the running around. But her hair—eek! The humidity might be beneficial to fireflies, but it was murder on her hair. Already full to begin with, it swirled around her lovely face, giving the impression of a woman in a Pre-Raphaelite painting. Thankfully, Theodosia didn't wear a lot of makeup, so there wasn't much to smudge. She'd only used a swoosh of mascara to highlight her ice chip blue eyes and give her lashes some extra oomph.

"Our guests are loving their dinners," Drayton said as he

pushed his way into the kitchen. Sixty-something and dapper, with just a touch of gray hair, Drayton looked the role of the perfect Southern gent. He was gallant to a fault and always impeccably dressed, favoring tweed jackets and his beloved Drake's bow ties.

Theodosia, on the other hand, stuck to silk T-shirts and comfortable khakis for her workdays at the Indigo Tea Shop. Although tonight she wore a long black skirt with a black off-the-shoulder blouse.

They made quite a team, the two of them, and over a half dozen years had turned the Indigo Tea Shop on Charleston's famed Church Street into a must-stop for tea.

"You've matched your dessert tea to our Alaska bombes?" Theodosia asked.

"Naturally. Of course I was torn between crème brûlée and caramel black tea," Drayton said. "But I finally decided on the crème brûlée." He wiggled his fingertips. "A blend guaranteed to dance across our guests' palates."

As her resident "tea guy," Theodosia trusted Drayton implicitly. He'd learned his trade at the tea auctions in Amsterdam, could differentiate between a tippy Yunnan and a Formosa oolong, and always knew when to toss a tea if it had lost its flavor or become a touch bakey.

"Hey, guys," Haley said as she slammed her way into the kitchen. "I'd say we've got a hit on our hands." Upbeat, bordering on exuberant, Haley Parker was mid-twenties and a sheer delight to be around. Besides being a skilled baker, she could cook like Gordon Ramsay. Could swear like him, too.

"We were just saying this ranks as one of our best evening events ever," Theodosia said.

Haley held up a finger. "But there's one more course to go. My pièce de résistance Alaska bombe."

"Ice cream, sponge cake, and baked meringue," Theodosia said. "Yum."

"Which we shall coat with hot high-proof rum and flambé tableside," Haley said. "Did you remember to bring the butane torches?"

"We've got the torches and we're ready to fire them up. Just say the word," Drayton said.

Twenty minutes later, once the tables were cleared and the dessert tea was poured, Haley said the word: "Okay, I'll serve the Alaska bombes and you guys follow me around, pouring on the rum and doing the flambé part, okay? Just take care with those torches."

"Please," Drayton said. "This isn't our first rodeo."

Haley served the first two tables as Theodosia and Drayton followed, stopping at each place setting to pour the rum and use their butane torches to set the Alaska bombes ablaze. And what a sight it was. Between the dancing blue flames from the desserts, and the candlelight and fireflies, the atmosphere seemed to shimmer exotically.

When Theodosia approached Delaine and Brooke's table, Delaine gave a delighted clap and cried, "A fiery end to an evening of fireflies!" Her high-pitched voice rang out loudly, as it so often did.

Theodosia gave her friend a tolerant smile. "Just be careful to let the flame burn out before you—" She stopped abruptly. Because two tables over, a strange commotion had erupted. Someone—one of their female guests—was suddenly in distress. There were sharp, hacking coughs from the guest and cooing sounds from the people sitting around her as they administered gentle pats on her back. But nothing seemed to assuage the poor woman's choking fit. Thirty seconds later, the woman—oh my goodness, it was Mrs. Van Courtland!—broke into labored, panic-stricken gasps. Then she bellowed out a series of convulsive, painful-sounding whoops as her shaking hand sought to grab a glass of water but succeeded only in tipping it over.

Theodosia dropped what she was doing and raced toward that table. Catching her foot on a chair leg, she stumbled but somehow caught herself and managed to get back on her feet. But that short delay meant that Mrs. Van Courtland's face had already turned a peculiar shade of blue even as her hands beat desperately on the table and her eyes began to roll back in her head. Then her entire body began to shake violently as white froth formed at the corners of her mouth and flecks spattered down the front of her pink Dior jacket.

"Someone call 911!" Theodosia cried, instantly regretting that she'd left her phone in the kitchen.

Aunt Libby and another woman pulled out their phones and began dialing while another tablemate screamed, "I think she's stopped breathing!" Which caused every guest at the dinner, all thirty-six of them, to push back their chairs in unison—SCREECH—and clamber to their feet. Some watched in horrified fascination, others shouted suggestions (creating an unhelpful cacophony), while a few shrank from what looked like a hellish situation.

Theodosia grasped a desperate, nearly asphyxiated Mrs. Van Courtland under the arms and, with the aid of another woman, laid her down on the cobblestones. As she prepared to do the Heimlich maneuver, hoping she remembered how, she was interrupted by a soft yet authoritative voice.

"Let me," a woman said. "I'm a nurse."

"Thank you," Theodosia said as the woman knelt down and, instead of doing the Heimlich, pinched Mrs. Van Courtland's nose closed, breathed gently into her mouth, and began a series of chest compressions.

"Did she choke on something?" Theodosia asked as she stood up and hastily moved out of the way.

"I think it was her Alaska bombe," one of the women at the table offered. "The waiter sprinkled extra sugar on hers."

"Sugar?" Theodosia said. Nobody was supposed to put sugar on the desserts.

"And the flambéed crust was awfully crisp," Aunt Libby added.

"I'm sorry, but nobody's flambéed your Alaska bombes yet," Theodosia said. Then she looked around and saw that all the Alaska bombes had indeed been flambéed.

What?

"A waiter came by with his butane torch," another woman at the table pitched in.

Flustered, Theodosia's eyes searched the patio. She knew Drayton hadn't been at this table. So who would have done it? Certainly not Haley. Glancing around, she kept one eye on Mrs. Van Courtland, who didn't seem to be responding particularly well, and another on the suddenly emptied patio, where glowing candles, torches, and fireflies suddenly made everything feel like a dimly lit, strangely tilting fun house. And that's when she noticed what she thought was a dark figure standing near the back hedge.

Wait one minute, were her eyes playing tricks on her? Was someone really there? Was she seeing actual fireflies blink on and off, or was that some weird reflection? Like light bouncing off the buttons of a man's jacket?

Then, like an apparition out of a film noir horror movie, the shadowy figure turned and slowly slipped through the back hedge. And oh, what a strange illusion it was! First he'd been standing there, subtly blending in, then there'd been a soft, almost imperceptible ruffle of leaves, after which he'd disappeared completely. Like Alice tumbling down the rabbit hole.

Since two dozen people were now shouting into their phones, presumably calling 911 or alerting the media, Theodosia knew she'd better do something fast. Because her hunch that this man was an unwelcome visitor had suddenly turned into a terrible feeling of dread. And if this stranger *had* snuck in and put something in poor Mrs. Van Courtland's dessert, she'd better try and apprehend him!

Theodosia was across the patio in a heartbeat, pushing her way into the hedge. But it was no easy task. Tiny branches prickled and pinched her hair unmercifully and sliced at her cheeks. She pummeled the branches with her hands, fighting her way through what felt like brambles and thorns, dispersing any number of fireflies. Then, halfway through the hedge, Theodosia got stuck. Taking a deep breath, forcing herself to move forward, she kicked her feet, grasped at flimsy stalks, and fought her way through. Seconds later, she plunged through the hedge and landed on Legare Street. Naturally it was pitch-black with just a string of old-fashioned globe streetlamps to light the way.

So where did this stranger run off to?

Theodosia spun left, then right, as shadows danced and played tricks on her eyes. Then there was sudden movement up ahead, maybe half a block away, as someone skulked away.

That's him, it has to be him!

A lifelong jogger, Theodosia took off like Usain Bolt launching from the starting block.

"Stop!" she shouted as she tore down the street. "Stop!"

When Theodosia pulled to within fifteen feet of the stranger, she slowed her pace.

"You there!" she called.

The man stopped dead in his tracks and stood motionless for a few moments. Then he turned slowly and stared at her with an attitude that felt both unafraid and strangely menacing.

Theodosia blinked as she stared back at the man. He wore a long, dark jacket, some sort of hat—maybe a French beret?—pulled low over his brow, and a black mask that covered his nose and mouth. It occurred to her then that she was totally defenseless in this standoff. Yes, she could run him down, maybe even harass him, but she couldn't *take* him down. For that she needed the police.

Theodosia figured she had but one thing in her bag of tricks—a big bluff.

"I've already called the police," she said. Her words rang out strong and pure in the night air, sounding (fingers crossed) almost authoritative.

There was no answer from the man for several moments. Then he let loose a low chuckle that morphed into an unholy rumble of laughter. A bright light suddenly flicked on, and the butane torch he was holding sparked to life, hissing like an angry cobra. But his torch was much larger than the ones Theodosia and Drayton had used—and *theirs* could reach temperatures upward of two thousand degrees Fahrenheit. Now the flames from the man's butane torch swirled and crackled in a feverish, demonic dance, growing ever larger until they took on the appearance of a World War II flamethrower. Holding his torch at arm's length, the man pointed it directly at Theodosia.

Mesmerized, she watched blue and gold flames twitch and quiver.

This man is crazy-dangerous. Now what?

Now nothing. She truly was defenseless. Only one option left . . .

Theodosia spun around and sprinted back toward the Tangled Rose B and B. Glancing back over her shoulder every few minutes, she worried that she was being followed, torn between hoping that she was and hoping that she wasn't.

When Theodosia arrived back at the Tangled Rose, the patio was an open-air calamity. Two EMTs were bent over Mrs. Van Courtland's body, working frantically. Detective Burt Tidwell and two uniformed officers were nervously standing by. And a half dozen other officers were trying desperately to corral and interview the shell-shocked guests.

Detective Tidwell's head shot up when he saw Theodosia rush in. "You," he said. It was obvious they'd had any number of run-ins before.

"There was a man," Theodosia said. She sounded shaky and more than a little breathless. "He was right here on the patio, and then he slipped through the hedge. I think he put something in Mrs. Van Courtland's dessert." She stopped and leaned forward, hands on knees, gasping, trying to pull in a cleansing lungful of air. Then she pointed toward the hedge. "I followed him—right through that hedge, trying to chase him down." She was talking louder now, caught in the throes of anger and regret. "I almost had him until he turned a butane torch on me!"

"We figured that's where you went," Tidwell said. "Drayton said he saw you run after him. There should be patrol cars flooding this entire neighborhood within three minutes."

"They'll be too late," Theodosia said. Then she glanced down at Mrs. Van Courtland and saw that the EMTs had wound down their lifesaving maneuvers. "Oh dear Lord, is she dead?"

One of the EMTs, a woman in a blue jumpsuit with a name

tag that said E. JAMES, pulled off her vinyl gloves and nodded. "I'm afraid we weren't able to save her."

Tidwell spun about, moving quickly for such a large man, to bark orders at his two officers. "When Crime Scene arrives, we need every fiber, hair, twitch, and twig bagged and tagged. We also need to bag those desserts and transport them to the lab for analysis."

"The Alaska bombes," Theodosia murmured as her hand fluttered to her chest. "Please tell me she wasn't poisoned."

"More like drugged," Tidwell said, looking pointedly at Theodosia. He was a big bear of a man—large head, rounded shoulders, stomach the size of a weather balloon. Tonight, he wore a shabby green jacket that clashed horribly with his brown slacks, as well as heavy steel-toe, kick-in-the-door cop shoes.

"The man I saw, the one I chased," Theodosia said. "He must have done it."

The second EMT, who was still kneeling alongside Mrs. Van Courtland's lifeless body and holding a syringe, glanced up at Tidwell and said, "Almost sure it's Captain Cody."

"Wait, you already know who did this?" Theodosia cried.

Tidwell turned and gazed at Theodosia with sorrowful dark eyes. "No."

"Then what?" Theodosia flapped her arms in frustration.

"Captain Cody is the street name for fentanyl."

Find out more about the author
and read excerpts from her mysteries
at laurachilds.com,
or become a Facebook friend
at Laura Childs Author.